To my dear Alpha Kappa sister, Anne Wilson, with love and appreciation for her friendship,
Emily Cary

The Loudoun Legacy

The Loudoun Legacy

A Novel

Emily Cary

iUniverse, Inc.
New York Lincoln Shanghai

The Loudoun Legacy

Copyright © 2007 by Emily Cary

All rights reserved. No part of this book may be used or reproduced by any means, graphic, electronic, or mechanical, including photocopying, recording, taping or by any information storage retrieval system without the written permission of the publisher except in the case of brief quotations embodied in critical articles and reviews.

iUniverse books may be ordered through booksellers or by contacting:

iUniverse
2021 Pine Lake Road, Suite 100
Lincoln, NE 68512
www.iuniverse.com
1-800-Authors (1-800-288-4677)

Because of the dynamic nature of the Internet, any Web addresses or links contained in this book may have changed since publication and may no longer be valid.

This is a work of fiction. All of the characters, names, incidents, organizations, and dialogue in this novel are either the products of the author's imagination or are used fictitiously.

ISBN: 978-0-595-46808-9 (pbk)
ISBN: 978-0-595-70537-5 (cloth)
ISBN: 978-0-595-91098-4 (ebk)

Printed in the United States of America

This book is dedicated to Reverend Daffyd H. Edwards, Enid Edwards, Beryl George, Annie James, Tom James, and Ray Williams for their roles in illuminating the legacy John Davis carried from Pembrokeshire, Wales to Loudoun County, Virginia, and to the incomparable British author Mary Stewart for her guidance and love of Welsh history.

CHAPTER ONE

She slammed on the brakes. First the Beltway traffic, then construction on the Interstate, and now gridlock. A rain-induced fender-bender blocked the highway.

A voice deep inside taunted her, *Amanda Prescott, you'll never escape from Washington.*

In all directions there was not an inch for maneuvering, and just when she *had* to get away.

With a hailstorm pummeling the car and the pungent odor of exhaust fumes seeping through the vent, she switched on the car radio to the good music station. At that worst moment possible, the strains of Sibelius's *Valse triste* disinterred sad memories. Her chin trembled and the tears begin to fall, slowly at first, then steadier until her face was awash. She might as well have turned off the windshield wipers; she saw only the blur of taillights as cars ahead gingerly skirted the shattered glass and metal.

The faster the salty tears flowed, the harder she sobbed, wrapped in self pity, until the cruel smack of her car against the one ahead unleashed a plume of steam. The engine coughed to a halt. Now the joke was on her.

She shuddered, unable to fathom why the fates ruled against her once more by aborting her anticipated vacation in Florida. What good was it to give up her apartment and store its contents for the summer to conserve money? Now she was on her own with even greater expenses looming through the downpour.

The folly of her rash move flashed before her eyes. A week earlier, she was a secure and relatively content legislative aide to Aaron Shellenberger, the senior Senator from Florida; today she was no better off than the eager interns who scamper through the halls bearing documents from one office to another, overdose on the heady Washingtonian atmosphere, and socialize with their fellow wide-eyed peers for no remuneration other than a letter of recommendation should they aspire to a real job.

Amanda was but a rung above them in seniority and skill. Her conservatory training did not qualify her for a political career. She, in fact, had never contemplated moving in that direction, but when the offer came out of the blue, she gratefully accepted it without question. Certainly her earnings were woefully small compared to the salaries of others on the senator's staff, most of them career government workers with years of service under their belts. Still, her colleagues welcomed her uncanny talent for cryptanalysis, an ability in great demand and scant supply.

From the time she could read, her father coached her in the art of solving codes, beginning with the simplest puzzles until she mastered intricate examples in both written and numeric languages. Had she not displayed extraordinary musical talent, she might have pursued mathematics in college, but by that time her father's work kept him overseas most of the year and he had minimal input on her career choice. Besides, the Peabody Conservatory scholarship was too good to refuse.

During her father's lengthy assignments away from home, Amanda and her mother huddled together awaiting news from him. The limited communications arrived sometimes by letter, other times through his office, rarely by telephone. Often it was a relief to hear nothing, trusting the adage that "no news is good news." At an early age, Amanda was forbidden to mention her father's work to friends or neighbors. Behind the necessary secrecy, his reputation was admired by Washington's innermost circles. For that very reason, Senator Shellenberger had confidence in Jim Prescott's daughter. By the time she had served his office for two years, he was so impressed by her abilities that he promised a promotion contingent on advanced security clearance.

As the rain and hail pelted her car, Amanda's last exchange with the senator came back with a rush. He had stopped by her desk in the outer office to pick up several documents dropped off earlier by a page. Impeccably dressed in the dark suit favored by politicians, he looked from a distance like a humorless businessman, but the kindly twinkle in his eye dominated as he neared.

Leaning over her desk, he spoke in a low, confidential voice. "Amanda, why don't you take a leave of absence for a few months of R and R? Goodness knows, you can use it."

"You must be joking."

"Actually, I'm not. Thanks to the quirks of government funding, we've just had word that my classified project has been delayed. The accounting office says the funds are on hold until the fourth quarter. That's par for the course."

"Then my security upgrade …?"

"That, too."

Amanda's swallowed. "I was so hoping it would work out."

"It will, it will, have no doubt about that. The minute the okay comes through, we'll get you right back on board."

Her head swirled. "You're implying that I don't have a job for now?"

He waved his hand, visibly brushing aside her concern. "It's a temporary thing. You know all about these kinds of glitches. I'll hold your security badge in the office. There's no need to turn it in."

"The security badge is the least of it. What will I do in the interim?"

His smile was fatherly. "They way I look at it, this is an opportunity for you to visit Meg and see how she's adapted to my home state."

Amanda brightened. "She'd like that. So would I." Then the awful truth resurfaced and reality gripped harder. "If I didn't have to worry about the apartment rent and the upkeep of my car, I'd jump at the chance to loll on the beach."

"Those are excuses, not reasons," the senator said. "This is a time to let responsibility take a holiday. Give up your apartment, put everything in storage, and hit the road. Since you'll be at a higher salary level, you can shop around when you get back for a place that suits you better."

"Don't I wish." Amanda and Meg had been close friends since graduating from Peabody Conservatory. For several seasons, they performed as a duo—Amanda on piano and Meg on harp—at embassy parties and classical music society gatherings. Separately, they played with various chamber groups throughout the Philadelphia to Washington corridor.

Amanda was the first to be picked up by a management group. With increasing frequency, she was booked as soloist with regional orchestras. Then came major breaks leading to recitals in respectable halls. While Amanda's career thrived, Meg plodded along playing whenever and wherever she could and auditioning each time a symphony orchestra posted a harp vacancy.

Amanda felt a sharp pang through her heart at the senator's next words. "How's Meg doing? My wife and I are still talking about her concert at the French Embassy … and of course the memorial program that none of us will forget."

Suppressing her sorrow, she spoke evenly. "The last time we chatted, she was very upbeat. She struggled for quite a time, but now she has a steady gig playing the harp at one of those elegant hotels on Palm Beach and she's teaching on the side. It's not the National Symphony Orchestra, but I gather it pays her bills and she loves her surroundings."

"All the more reason why you should take a break while you can." He waited expectantly for her response.

At last, she admitted. "You tempt me."

The senator grinned. "Maybe I'm getting through. The Select Committee on Intelligence needs you, but the government moves like a turtle crawling backwards. Take a break while you can."

"You have a way with words. No wonder you've been elected for four consecutive terms."

"If it weren't for my superb staff, I'd be a poor excuse of a government servant. Look, I can't discuss any details now, but once the funds are released and the project gets underway, our office will be working around the clock. Take advantage of the lull." As he walked away, he called over his shoulder, "Please think about it, Amanda. You might want to talk it over with Kathy. I know you trust her judgment."

Kathy Owens, the senator's private secretary, ranked among Amanda's favorite people. From Amanda's first day on the Hill, Kathy had been her mother hen. A conscientious, competent woman and the power behind the senator's office, Kathy had been left with two children to support after her husband's fatal heart attack some years earlier.

A mutual friend, knowing that the young widow needed a job in a hurry, recommended her to the senator, whose reputation for compassion sprang from the many good deeds he quietly accomplished. He and his wife quickly took Kathy and her children under their wing, moved them into a pleasant Silver Spring neighborhood, and paid for the youngsters' education. After college, both girls found responsible positions, giving their mother—and the Shellenbergers alike—reason to be proud.

The moment the senator left, Amanda slipped into Kathy's office to discuss her options. Once the decision became obvious to both women, there was no turning back.

"You go, girl," Kathy said, laughing. "Our boss makes good sense, as he always does. If I were a few years younger, I'd join you. Even though I haven't lived there for years, I can still feel the Florida sand between my toes."

Back in her office, Amanda rang up Meg.

"We'll have a spectacular time, Amanda," her friend promised. "The gorgeous beach and lots of gentlemen about town will take your mind off the past."

Amanda stiffened. "I'm coming to see you, Meg, not to become entangled with a man. It would be hard to date again so soon."

"Soon? It's been over a year, long past a respectable period of mourning. You owe it to yourself to get out."

"That's just the problem," Amanda spoke softly to avoid being overheard. "You're the only one who knows how guilty I feel because I wasn't in love with Craig and didn't have the courage to break off with him. Dating at this point would make me feel even worse."

"You handled the situation beautifully, Amanda. He died believing you cared. That was the greatest gift you could have given him."

"There was so much going on in my life, I couldn't think straight. Dad was officially listed as missing right after we met, so I had nobody to consult. It was the first time in my life I was truly alone. I clung to Craig for moral support."

"We all need somebody. When he proposed, you probably felt that you had no other option."

"Craig was an outgoing person who made me feel wanted. It was my fault for encouraging him. Then everything came crashing down with that medical diagnosis."

"You went through a terrible time, I know. With both of your parents gone, you only had each other. Still, considering how he talked you out of your career, you owe him nothing more."

"That's unkind, Meg."

"It's not unkind; it's the truth. I'm speaking as your close friend. If your boss is giving you a reprieve for a few months, you should take him up on it."

A fine bit of advice that had been. Now Amanda was trapped on Route One, the old Richmond Highway, going nowhere. She blinked back a tear. From the initial confirmation that Craig's headaches were caused by an advanced tumor, she had suppressed her emotions. At this moment, the windshield wiper was her disciplinarian, chiding her for trying to speed away from the unhappy memories of his illness.

The entire scenario had been short, as fatal illnesses go, lasting less than a year from the date of the first medical opinion. Even before they became engaged, Craig complained about the headaches, blaming them on the tension before his bar exams, but neither he nor Amanda moved to postpone wedding plans until the tumor went on the warpath like an army tank mowing down everything in its wake. During those hideous final days, he became a vegetable, unable to perform the simplest tasks. Even worse, he did not recognize her.

Before Craig entered the picture, her life revolved around music. From her first public performance, she amassed high praise from knowledgeable critics and monetary prizes as a finalist in several prestigious competitions. But the storied triumph a concert pianist craves began to seem insignificant the night of her recital at Strathmore Hall in Bethesda.

When the buzzer sounded in her dressing room, Amanda took a final glance of approval in the mirror. The rented gown in a bedazzling shade of emerald green complemented her eyes. The upswept hairdo, she had to admit, was a dramatic success, right down to the dark, wispy curls the hairdresser had positioned across her brow and against her cheeks. She smiled back at the young woman in the mirror one last time before leaving.

As she reached the end of the corridor to wait in the wings, the stage manager whispered, "It's a full house. Here, take a peek." He directed her to the curtain peephole.

Pleased, Amanda scanned the house and confirmed there was not an empty seat. She was about to back away when she noticed a young couple who appeared to have little in common. The woman might have been any Washington career woman in any government office. Her lips moved rapidly as she addressed the man by her side. Seated on the aisle, he nodded politely as she chatted nonstop, but his eyes never glanced toward his companion. They were focused on the grand piano at center stage.

Amanda found him impossible to ignore. Frowning, she wondered if she knew him from school; perhaps they had met on the Hill. Not even the dim theater lights blurring his features could diminish the impact of his presence. The air he projected was one Amanda knew well: the confidence and honesty of a humble man who has suffered deeply while accomplishing feats beyond his wildest dreams. She had studied about great figures of history who carried themselves with similar grace, but until now she had not observed it in any living man other than her father. Even as she fought to take her eyes off the stranger, she saw her father in him, so distant in reality and yet so near and dear to her heart.

Throughout the evening, Amanda had the gnawing sensation that her future was taking a curious detour. Each time she peered into the darkened audience, she and the man exchanged glances. The bedimmed setting blurred his face, yet she was positive that his eyes were fixed on hers. At times, they seemed to blaze with such intensity Amanda nearly lost her composure. A romance novelist might have attributed the attraction to destiny, a psychic connection across time and space.

The notes rolled off her fingers automatically. To her astonishment, the planned encore gave way to a medley of romantic songs that expressed her innermost longings. Afterward, when Craig stepped forward from the sea of smiling faces to introduce himself and praise her interpretation of a Debussy piece, she could not readily identify him as the catalyst, but he spoke with such conviction that she linked him to the man on the aisle and accepted his presence without question.

During the following weeks, Craig pursued Amanda so aggressively that she succumbed to his proposal without evaluating how marriage to a young lawyer would redesign her life. Always practical, he pointed out the many ways their marriage could suffer from the lengthy absences her concert career would entail, but he eagerly encouraged her to accept the clerical position on the Hill offered by a family acquaintance. She had never considered such a thing, but when it came out of the blue, she decided it warranted consideration, especially since the salary—modest though it was—surpassed her infrequent performance fees.

Like most young musicians, she needed that day job. Blinded by Craig's attention and common sense advice, Amanda cast aside her ambition and bowed to his wishes. Succumbing to his arguments, she convinced herself that the most practical way to utilize her music ability was through its adjuncts, math and cryptography. In the weeks to come, Senator Shellenberger offered her many such opportunities in projects assigned by his CIA affiliates.

As Craig's condition worsened, her salary was essential; dreams of conquering international audiences evaporated for good when she sold her piano to help cover some of his enormous medical expenses. Once the funeral was past, Amanda was jolted into restringing her life for the second time in as many years. Resigned to losing both Craig and music, she knuckled down to her job on the Hill, hoping it would help shed invisible chains.

Now, less than twenty miles south of Washington, she was still shackled in their grip. Only yesterday she had boasted to the office staff that nothing could keep her in town except an invitation to perform at the White House. She failed to count on Washington's snarled roadways. Visions of the benevolent Florida sunshine warming and strengthening her body and soul were demolished by the cold, dreary rain, the impenetrable line of cars, and her own carelessness.

Amanda knew the terms of her automobile insurance policy well enough to recognize that she was at fault. Even as a teenager giddy with a driver's license, she drove cautiously, aware that the driver causing a rear-end collision is always in the wrong, no matter the weather. Swiping the back of her hand across the errant tears, she snatched her keys from the ignition and stumbled out of the car, anticipating a tongue-lashing.

The approaching figure was barely discernable in the mist. "I'm terribly sorry," Amanda began.

"Don't worry, dear." A cheerful, motherly cheerful voice eased Amanda's apprehension at once. Belying the silver strands escaping from beneath her pink rain hood, the oncoming matron moved with agility that bespoke years as a tennis aficionado or a horsewoman. "It was bound to happen."

"I saw the storm warning in the paper. I should have waited."

The lady chuckled. "Maybe the weather was a factor, but the traffic didn't help. In a backup like this, it's just a matter of time until one car runs into another." Even as she spoke, the crunch of metal and tinkle of glass chards confirmed that two more cars were wedded unceremoniously. "Lucky we're near Pohick," she added.

"Pohick Church? That's one of the few historic sites in this area I've never visited."

"Then you're in for a treat. It's just ahead. I'm on the Altar Guild. We'll call a wrecker from there."

A stream of water and anti-freeze gushed into the roadside ditch from Amanda's inert car. Helpless, she switched on the flashers and followed obediently.

The lady smiled and held out her hand as the younger woman climbed in beside her. "I almost forgot my manners, dear. I'm Sheila Cameron."

Several hundred yards later, introductions accomplished, Sheila turned off the highway and into a parking lot alongside a quaint place of worship. She gestured toward a smaller, adjacent building. "We'll telephone from the office. Come along."

Slipping from the driver's seat, she motioned Amanda to follow.

As Amanda shut the solid car door, she readily understood why the accident had not disturbed Sheila; the Mercedes, a veritable tank, was built to deflect flimsy cars like hers.

The heady scent of boxwood enveloped the churchyard as they hurried across a path lined with magnolia trees, their creamy blooms emitting an intoxicating aroma heightened by the rain. They mounted stone steps flanked by pink azaleas and entered the office. While Amanda shook the water from her raincoat, Sheila rang up a nearby garage and spoke with the familiarity of a steady customer who warrants prompt service.

Then she indicated a comfortable leather chair and offered Amanda a book. "Here's something to read while you wait. Meantime, I'll be in the church setting up the communion silver for Sunday. Martin is very dependable. He'll be here in no time."

With that, she was gone, leaving Amanda to fret about the time being lost and the contribution her disabled car was making to commuter rage. To settle her nerves, she opened the book and began leafing through its pages.

"That's the story of Pohick Church. Are you interested in history?"

Amanda fairly flew from her seat at the sound of a deep male voice from across the room. As her eyes became adjusted to the light, she saw the clergyman lounging on a window seat, his face shaded by a cowl. "I never saw you. Please forgive me for taking your chair."

He waved her back into the chair. "Please stay seated. I'm cheating by indulging in a short rest." The smile in his warm voice contrasted with the severity of his cassock.

Amanda eased back into the chair, soothed by his presence. "To answer your question, I love tradition, whether it's history, music, or art. I've lived near Washington most of my life, but this is my first visit to Pohick Church. The architecture is lovely."

"We can thank George Washington for that. He and the other vestry members supervised its construction."

"They had an eye for classic lines," Amanda said. "My mother taught American history. My fondest memories of her are the weekend trips we took together to see the historic buildings she loved throughout Virginia, places like Monticello, the Governor's Palace in Williamsburg, and Stratford Hall plantation on the Northern Neck. She taught me that architecture styles come and go, but colonial design is always pleasing."

"That explains why nobody has tried to change or modernize this structure."

"If only the walls could talk."

He chuckled. "They already have. During the Civil war, the Union soldiers stabled their horses here and left mementos of their stay in graffiti."

"In one sense, that's a pity, and in another it adds to the building's history. Has the graffiti been preserved?"

"Only in photographs taken before the walls were plastered over. It's rumored that the soldiers also left coins, stolen goods, and other souvenirs in the walls and ceiling." "Secret hiding places, you say? I love mysteries. Have you ever poked around here, Reverend ...?"

"Conyers ... Henry Conyers. I'm not Pohick's rector, just a visitor. And you are ...?"

"Amanda Prescott."

"Amanda is a beautiful name that goes back to colonial times," he said. Amanda felt her cheeks redden as he continued. "Like you, I love mysteries. Northern Virginia is a hotbed of intriguing accounts of secret rooms and hidden fortunes. Given the opportunity, I'd be tempted to explore those rumors."

"You'd fit right into a detective agency, or the FBI, maybe even the CIA," Amanda gushed without thinking how such a worldly suggestion would sound to a man of the cloth.

He swallowed whatever he was about to say. Taking the silence as disapproval, she sought to undo her boner. "Forgive me. I didn't mean to imply that you're a misfit in your profession."

His sunny laugh held no malice. "No apologies necessary, Amanda. You're a pretty good detective yourself to read that into me. My profession demands that I keep on top of everything."

"I'm sure a clergyman is constantly learning. It must be challenging to help people deal with the problems they face today."

"Life's a challenge, that's true. Fortunately, we're given strength to overcome tragedy."

"Even traffic mishaps?" She gestured toward the highway. "My car's part of that snarl. Thanks to the rain and my inattention, I smashed into Mrs. Cameron's car. Hers survived, but mine succumbed."

"I heard her phone the garage. They'll solve your problems."

Amanda sensed that cars were a world apart from Henry Conyers's domain. His specialty was saving lives instead of Detroit's disasters. Tall, well built, with shoulders that strained beneath the robe, he conveyed strength of body and character. She liked him instantly without reservation.

"I'd like to help, but my knowledge of cars is very basic," he apologized. "I hope the accident hasn't ruined your plans."

Since Craig's death, she had lacked the courage to open her heart to strangers, but buoyed by Henry's compelling presence and the wealth of human understanding his position signified, she said, "Truthfully, I was trying to escape from my own unhappiness."

He nodded, understanding without saying a word. Slowly, she began to unburden her heart. She spilled secrets to the clergyman that she never believed she could share with a stranger. Looking back on that moment, she wondered whatever possessed her to babble on about how she had given up her career for Craig, how his illness had taken him away, and why she was headed for Florida to seek solace in pleasant surroundings and await her security upgrade. She explained it all away with the pat phrase she repeated to folks in the office who wondered why she was taking a leave, "I'm looking for a fresh environment to give me a new lease on life."

"Sometimes we don't need a change of location so much as a change in outlook," Reverend Conyers said.

"In your profession, you've probably seen hundreds of people whose lives have turned upside down, but I wasn't prepared. If I were middle-aged, I might understand. Even if giving up the piano was unwise, I thought it was for a valid reason. Now it's too late to go back that route, but at least I have a job I enjoy, or will when the clearance comes through. I never planned on a silly thing like a fender bender."

"Don't worry, Amanda. Everything will work out better than you could ever imagine. God never gives us burdens we can't handle." His voice was gentle.

She sighed. "I think He overestimates my limit."

"A few months from now, you'll wonder why you ever doubted the future."

"I'd give anything to share your faith and optimism."

At that precise moment, Henry rose and beckoned her to the window. "Here's proof that faith pays off."

A whirling amber beacon glancing off the wet pavement marked the presence of a tow truck near her stalled car.

"Thank goodness." She snatched up her belongings and dashed headlong out the door, ignoring Henry, her manners, and the teeming rain.

Lechryd, Pembrokeshire, Wales, 1725

He stood to survey his work. Satisfied, he smiled to himself. His eagle glance confirmed success in reverting the stream from the baptismal pool to its normal path. The casual observer never would suspect its existence, drawn instead to the water tumbling over rocks, intent on completing the journey to Cenarth Falls.

Since childhood, he had paddled his coracle in the River Teify below the mighty falls, fishing for salmon about to leap its rocks in search of salva-

tion. Today, he was preparing to sail deeper waters in another kind of vessel. Like the salmon, he, too, sought salvation.

One last glance from the farmyard confirmed that the baptistery was shielded from view. Its location between hawthorn hedgerows surrounded by vigorous clumps of elder had been planned by his father years ago. Now entrusted with the secret ministry, he must ensure that worshipers remaining on Welsh soil were protected.

To that end, he had planted rowan trees, used since ancient time to repel evil from churchyards and homes alike. Some people believed the danger came from witches and spirits of the dead. He knew it came at the hands of the Kings men.

CHAPTER TWO

Amanda nearly collided with a sturdy man in a rain slicker. "I hope you're Martin."

"One and the same. You own this car?"

"Yes. Is it …?

"Worth saving?" He stroked his chin. "That's a tough question, ma'am. In any case, repairs will take at least a week."

"Surely you're not serious."

"I'm a very serious guy. I'll know better once it's in the shop. In addition to a new radiator, you need a new front end. And the frame looks bent. Nothing we can't handle, but I hope your insurance is current. It'll cost a heap."

Amanda's legs felt weak. She had cleaned out most of her bank account to pay outstanding bills and cover her expenses in Florida until funding for the position was approved. Martin had just delivered a financial bombshell.

He grabbed Amanda's elbow as she began to sway. "Hey, don't worry. I'll give you a loaner while this one's in the shop."

"You don't understand. I was leaving town. I gave up my apartment and don't have a home here anymore." She fought to stem the tears.

"That's a pretty wrinkle. Still, things could be worse." He handed her a tissue.

"I can't imagine how."

"For one, you could have been injured. Come on now, admit there's a bright side to your problem."

His folksy voice and the support of his strong arm were comforting. She managed a weak smile. "You make my troubles sound so insignificant, I'm embarrassed. Things wouldn't look quite this bleak if I had a place to stay while the car's being repaired."

Martin beamed. "Lucky you. You ran into the right person. Sheila Cameron's family made a fortune in Northern Virginia real estate. When the last of the company's founders died, she inherited one of the most successful and respected agencies around. She has apartment buildings, condominiums, town houses, single homes, you name it. She'll find you a place to stay."

"You really think so?"

"I know so. And it won't cost a cent. She's a great lady. Can't say the same for her son, though." Martin frowned. "Some kind of prodigal, away for years, it seems. Nobody knew he existed until he showed up recently and she gave him a plush position. Caused some talk, believe me. I lease my garage from the Cameron company, and not a week goes by that he isn't after me to move my business. Wants to erect a multi-million dollar office complex on the land, like the ones at Tysons Corner and Fair Oaks."

"Can he force you out?"

"Probably could, but his mother's still the head of the company and she knows that my business is essential to the locals. They rely on me. Office buildings would just add more traffic jams."

Amanda surveyed the scene dominated by her hulking, immobile car. "Nobody can move because of me."

"That's why the sooner I tow your car to the garage, the better." Martin held out his hand. "Let me have your keys. I'll help you unload your things before I take it away. Explain your situation to Mrs. Cameron and she'll take care of you until your car's ready."

It sounded too easy to be true. Amanda let Martin carry her suitcase back to the church office. She could hardly wait to apologize to Henry Conyers for her curt departure. To her dismay, he was gone.

She went in search of Mrs. Cameron.

Inside the sanctuary, enclosed pews marched down both sides of the aisle. Cheerful whitewashed walls and high arching windows defied the gloomy weather pressing against the panes. She was inspired to climb the stairway to the choir loft for a close inspection of the organ when a metallic sound from behind startled her.

"I'm sorry if I frightened you." Sheila Cameron was placing silver chalices on the altar as she spoke. "Did Martin ever come?"

"Yes, he did."

"Splendid. Then he'll have you on the road in no time." Sheila stood back to admire the classic simplicity of her arrangement.

"I don't think so."

Sheila wheeled around. "Then it's a big job?"

"A very big job."

"Oh, dear. That's a shame. Can I give you a lift home?"

"Yes ... and no. You can give me a lift, but there's no home to go to. I gave up my apartment in the district. Most of my friends live on the Maryland side of the Beltway and none of them have room to put me up for any length of time, so I certainly can't impose on their good nature." Unable to control her emotions, Amanda burst into tears.

Wordlessly, Sheila scurried down the aisle and guided her to the nearest pew. Cloistered within, Amanda unburdened herself to a stranger for the second time that hour.

As Amanda neared the end of her lament, Sheila donned a serene, determined expression and began patting the younger woman's knee in a rhythmic, understanding motion, never missing a beat. "How lucky you are. I can solve all your problems at once. You need a place to stay and I have the perfect spot. It's a beautiful furnished apartment in one of my buildings near Tysons Corner. I keep it available for visiting friends, relatives, and occasions such as this."

Exactly as Martin prophesied, she added, "You're welcome to stay there as long as you like—at absolutely no cost. And since that's settled, it occurs to me that I might tempt you with a temporary position in my McLean office."

"Thanks, but I don't...."

"Nonsense. I size up people quickly and I can tell that you'll fit right in with my staff. Those I hire must be intelligent, well spoken, and striking in appearance. You fill the bill perfectly. In addition to your attractive outfit, I'm impressed by your nails. They aren't long and distracting like so many I see today."

Amanda laughed. "That's by default. A pianist must have short nails at all times. I learned the hard way when I caught one between piano keys during a fast cadenza and it ripped off. Remembrance of the pain is sufficient reminder to keep them short."

Sheila smiled. "Well, whatever the reason, you look very smart and put together. I'll be honored to have you on my staff." Before Amanda could protest, she continued. "Now you needn't commit yourself until you've tried it for a few days. I'm certain you'll discover that it's a dream career."

"Really, I know absolutely nothing about ..."

Sheila waved off Amanda's protest. "It's *perfect* for you and *you're* perfect for it."

"I doubt that. Real estate agents need special training, and ..."

"We'll give you all the training you need for the present. If you stay on, you'll have to pass a state exam eventually, but credentials aren't important right now. We're successful because I run the business on the premise that a charming, considerate woman is far more persuasive than a fast-talking wheeler-dealer."

"I don't follow you."

"You've had a traumatic experience, so I won't fill your head with a lot of trivia. Everything will become clear once you get started." She shook a finger at Amanda. "There's a purpose behind everything in this life. Something prevented you from leaving town and brought you directly to Pohick."

Sheila seemed to be saying exactly what Reverend Conyers had implied. Amanda resisted the temptation to back away.

Sheila's enthusiasm was overpowering. "You don't want to believe me, but it all fits together. How else could you meet someone like me who is looking for someone like you?"

Helpless to protest, Amanda let Sheila guide her to the parking lot, well aware that she was being manipulated. Still, common sense told her that the proposed arrangement offered temporary salvation. A free apartment and a stimulating job opportunity were not easily had, if only briefly. One slight problem remained: Martin's promised loaner had not yet materialized.

Sheila must have read her mind. "You'll have a company car, of course."

It seemed too perfect, too pat, but Amanda's ability to reason was exhausted. She knew only that she had been transported physically and mentally from despair to a yen for adventure.

During the drive to Tysons Corner, the rain subsided and the fog lifted to offer a dramatic view of Cameron Terrace. Inside the sleek apartment building, a birdcage elevator rose jauntily from the lobby.

Sheila giggled as they soared to the ninth floor. "Isn't this fun? This building was designed by an architect better known for his posh hotels. I convinced him to create something sensational for us. Ah, here we are."

She ushered Amanda off the elevator and toward a door flanked by palms stretching toward a skylight. They entered a living room elegantly arrayed in Italian damasks. Plush carpeting extended down a short hallway to a bedroom. Beyond the formal dining area, a kitchen gleamed with stainless steel. Sheila drew open the draperies to reveal a balcony high above a street bustling with cars and pedestrians, all reflected in the amber glass façade of the building opposite. The ambiance reminded Amanda of the stage set for a sophisticated comedy she had attended at the Kennedy Center.

Sheila studied her face. "Do you like it? Is it comfortable enough for you?"

"It's lovely. I'll be more than comfortable here."

"I hoped it would please you. Now don't fret about supper. I'll have it sent in, breakfast too. And tomorrow morning, someone from the office will pick you up. Please feel free to phone your friend in Florida so she'll not expect you as planned."

Amanda's smile was genuine. "Thank you for everything. Will I see you tomorrow?"

Sheila shrugged. "Probably not. I'll be at our main office most of the day, but you'll be in capable hands. My son Burke is office manager of the McLean branch. He'll indoctrinate you."

Even before Sheila left, the misgivings returned. Was Burke Cameron the son Martin had mentioned so derisively? If there was a catch to all of the good fortune being forced upon her due to her own negligence, perhaps the prospect of encountering Burke Cameron was ample argument for refusing Sheila's offer.

Amanda said as much to Meg when she rang her later that evening. "Here I am lounging in a gorgeous apartment and filled to the brim after indulging in a scrumptious dinner delivered to the door by a chef. It's all too orchestrated to be legitimate."

"It sounds fabulous, and if I were you I'd be sitting on a cloud," Meg said.

"It's also a bit spooky. Cameron Terrace sits on Gallows Road ... at the highest point."

"So?"

"This is where the early settlers hanged criminals. They built the gallows at the most visible place around for all to see. I can't help wondering if the displaced ghosts of those falsely accused of crime are hovering nearby."

"Shame on you, Amanda. That's what comes from being exposed to all those CIA and FBI folks who creep around the Senator's office. By the way, one came around last week."

"One what?"

"A spook. One of those anonymous men in black working on security clearances."

"That's because I'm scheduled for an upgrade when my promotion is approved. They must be contacting everyone I gave as a reference. What did he ask?"

"The usual. He wanted to make sure you're a gung-ho patriot. I liked him a lot better than the others who've been around in the past."

"Why so?"

"His voice reminded me of Robert Goulet singing Sir Lancelot's numbers in the original 'Camelot' recording."

Amanda laughed aloud. "You and your Broadway idols. Did he resemble a knight on a charger eager to rescue a damsel in distress?"

"It was hard to tell beneath those shades, but he oozed muscle."

"Don't they all."

"He was different, Amanda, not the least bit conceited and aloof like most of them, and he was very sympathetic with your situation."

Amanda stiffened. "My situation? What do you mean?"

"He asked about Craig, and how his death affected you."

"That's curious. I wasn't aware they get that personal."

"I assured him you aren't pining away and are capable of throwing yourself into any task you're handed. He was impressed by your decision to stay to the end because you didn't want to hurt Craig, even after realizing what you felt for him wasn't love."

"I wish you hadn't gone into that, Meg. You're the only one I've told. It's nobody else's business."

"It was all right, Amanda. He said he understood perfectly and even seemed relieved. I suppose he felt you can do a more serious job now that no strings hold you down. When he asked about your career plans, I told him I'll try to convince you to start performing again."

Amanda spoke sharply. "You know that's not practical."

"Maybe not, but when you come down we can revive our duets on the spectacular concert grand in the hotel lobby. There's nothing like romantic tunes to lure some of the great looking, eligible bachelors staying here."

"You won't give up, will you, Meg? I wish I knew an eligible bachelor right now. The way my finances are today, I won't get to Florida until I pay for the car repairs."

"In the meantime, though, you might meet some fantastic prospects."

"I seriously doubt that," Amanda said, as her mind drifted once more to the unpleasant prospect of meeting Burke Cameron.

Cilfowyr, Pembrokeshire, Wales, 1725

Twelve more baptisms were accomplished. Twelve more brave men had defied the King. Today they were departing to spread the word, three to the north, three to the east, three to the south, and three to the west. The nine remaining on land must beware of the soldiers pounding the dusty highways and byways in search of religious traitors.

The three turning west were bound for a Welsh settlement in the colonies where the King's agents could not pursue them. But theirs was a heavier burden, for they had been entrusted with treasures from Cilfowyr, the white farmhouse, where believers had gathered to worship in secret for thirty years. Now as the Crown sought to stifle them, the appointed time had come to disperse and spread the word across the sea.

CHAPTER THREE

Melodic chimes awakened Amanda. Propelled from bed by their urgency, she snatched her robe and hobbled into her slippers with all the glamour of a drowsy puppy. The miniaturized view through the security peephole focused on a beaming delivery boy balancing a tray of croissants, exactly what she needed. The moment she flung open the door, a warm, yeasty aroma filled the room.

"Compliments of Carol's Kitchen. The card's on the tray." He thrust the whole affair into her hands and boarded the elevator before she could set the tray on a table and rummage through her purse for a tip.

Enlisting some fancy footwork, she kicked the door shut and headed for the kitchen. A cursory foray through the well-stocked cabinets revealed an array of staples guaranteed to help one survive a blizzard. She selected a tin of coffee and set a pot to brew on the stove while examining the card. Sheila's breezy, authoritative manner registered on paper exactly as it did in person.

> Good morning, Amanda. Enjoy. Janel Bates, one of our agents, will pick you up about ten. Wait in the lobby and watch the driveway for a burgundy car with our gold Cameron logo. We're all thrilled that you're joining us. Sheila C.

Who, Amanda wondered abstractly, is thrilled? And why? She tore off a flaky layer of croissant and popped it into her mouth. As the rest of the remarkable pastry disappeared, her silent questions floated away to the bottomless pit of unsolved mysteries. The croissants, a tall glass of freshly squeezed orange juice, and two satisfying cups of hot coffee elevated her spirits. She showered quickly and slipped into her most respectable "dress for success" suit in banker's gray and a silk turquoise blouse that accented her eyes.

Descending to the lobby, she smiled to herself. Why, she felt almost at home in the ridiculous birdcage elevator. Outside the revolving door, the regal Cameron colors on the car parked at the entry commanded attention. She extended her hand to the driver. "You must be Janel. I'm Amanda Prescott."

Janel returned her smile. "I picked you out right away. You definitely have the Cameron stable look."

"Stable?" As Amanda slipped in beside Janel, she marked that the young woman in the black designer suit was not unlike a prancing filly, her severe blonde bob softened by a perky velvet bow.

Janel suppressed a giggle. "Just a figure of speech ... with a fragment of truth. We win the sales race through fair means rather than foul, although we might have to take our clients for a ride to win the prize, if you understand what I mean."

"To be truthful, I don't. You're talking about the agents?"

"That's right. Super Agents, we call ourselves. We make sales in situations that would stymie others."

"How are you different?"

"Sheila didn't tell you?" Janel smiled knowingly. "I'll let our honorable honcho explain."

"You're talking about Burke Cameron?"

Janel's eyebrows arched. "You've heard about him?"

Amanda became defensive. "What should I have heard?"

"Nothing in particular, just that he recently appeared out of the blue and right away was appointed lord of all that the Cameron Agency surveys."

"Is he ... *difficult* to work with?"

"Burke's the devil personified, so I'm told. I wasn't around when he blew up at a new hire and threw her out. Just a day or so after he arrived, he called her into his office and a short while later, he started yelling at the top of his lungs, calling her stupid and incompetent and demanding that she leave. Everyone who overheard was shocked beyond belief. They were helpless to do or say anything when she ran out the door crying. Nothing like that ever happened before at Cameron Agency. Fortunately, I began working here long before he came and haven't had much contact with him. I'm out of the office most of the time, except when I have extra assignments, like picking you up, for instance, or delivering a contract."

Janel's description of Burke Cameron disturbed Amanda, but the serenity on her face suggested that she did not fear for her own job. Clearly, she was a go-getter, all the more reason for Amanda to feel guilty about keeping her from the work she obviously enjoyed and had great success doing. Embarrassed by the position Janel was placed in on her account, Amanda blurted, "I'm sorry to be intruding on your time."

Janel's response confirmed that she did not regard her role of chauffeur as a burden. "No intrusion at all. I don't have much chance to touch base with our colleagues because I'm so busy. This is a very pleasant change of routine."

"What about the other agents? Are they friendly, or is there a lot of rivalry among them?"

"That's the great thing about this job. We deal with top-of-the-line properties and we're each assigned clients exclusively, so it makes no difference who sells which house. It's merely a matter of matching a client to one that suits his life style. Money is no object to most of them."

"What determines your assignment?"

"Sheila likes to match our personality with that of the client," Janel said. "Also, some prefer blondes, while others like redheads."

Amanda snorted. "Not exactly an intellectual decision."

"Hardly, but it works. Of course everything's very much above board. That's understood. Sheila hires 'class' agents. Looks count for only about ten percent of our sales."

Amanda was stunned. "You're saying that the agents actually make sales because of their looks?"

"Did I say that?" Janel shot her a grin. "We transfer properties from one distinguished owner to another. If an agent's appearance helps to cement a deal in a hurry, that's a plus nobody's crude enough to mention."

"And there's no jealousy among the agents?"

"Jealousy is never a problem. There's enough business for everyone. We love our jobs. Where else can you dress nicely each day, meet stimulating people, help them find a place to live if they're new in town, or improve their life style if they're locals, and earn a generous salary? We're more like sisters than competitors. Knowing Sheila, I'm certain she took a fancy to you because this job requires a very special person and you fit the need. Someone who looks like Miss America but talks like a Valley Girl need not apply. We're proud that the Cameron Agency has an international reputation for first class service with a high society atmosphere."

"High society?" Amanda knew for a fact that she did not fit that description.

"A well-rounded education is probably a better term. Since many of our clients come from overseas to important positions in this country, we have to be able to converse on subjects from politics and great literature to horse breeding and opera."

Amanda sighed audibly. "You make Cameron agents sound like a cross between United Nations ambassadors and proper Bostonians. I'm afraid your company requires someone with more self assurance than I have."

"Nonsense. Modesty is the key. You don't recognize your own greatest asset."

Amanda softened slightly under Janel's kindness, but she could not shake her serious reservations about being cast in an unexpected role ... and meeting Burke Cameron. Momentarily, Janel swung into a parking lot amidst a fleet of cars bearing the Cameron logo. Before them was a sleek building of tinted glass and black marble. Once through the revolving door, they entered a reception room furnished in antiques, original oil paintings, and exotic plants. The young woman at the front desk smiled warmly. "Amanda, this is Robin, our indispensable receptionist," Janel said.

Robin extended her hand. "And you must be our new agent. You'll love working with our great team. By now, you probably have met the Camerons."

"She knows Sheila, but not 'his nibs,'" Janel said. "He's next on the agenda."

"Good luck." Robin's tinkling laughter heightened Amanda's apprehension. "Don't let him change your mind. The rest of us here are really quite normal."

Amanda returned Robin's earnest smile with a guarded one. "I'm looking forward to this experience, even though it's not like anything I've ever done."

"If you like variety, you'll get it with the Cameron Agency," Robin promised. "Every day you meet new people and see homes that are absolutely gorgeous, the kind you'd give anything to own yourself. I always wish I were the one moving in instead of the wife left behind."

Janel caught Amanda's puzzled expression. "What Robin means is that most of our clients leave their families at home while they come to investigate Washington's housing situation. With all the money they have to spend, they're bound to find a place to please their better halves. It's the less affluent men who bring their wives along to help work out a financial compromise. After all, real estate in the Washington area is among the most expensive in the country. A family living in a spacious brick colonial home near Atlanta may have to settle here for a Cape Cod cottage with a carport."

"Quite a come-down," Amanda said.

"That's never our problem," Janel assured her. "Our clients rarely ask the cost of a house before deciding to buy it because we deal only in 'point' houses."

"'Point' houses? I'm not familiar with the term."

Janel smiled. "Real estate jargon. Two million point eight, four million point five and on up—strictly the upper brackets."

At that moment, Robin responded to a persistent buzz from the intercom.

"Yes? ... Right here ... Janel brought her ... Yes, sir." She turned to Amanda. "Mr. Cameron will see you now."

Robin's knowing glance evoked a titter from Janel. "You're on your own now, Amanda. I've done my duty. If I'm still in the lounge after your indoctrination lecture, please stop in. I'd love to hear your reaction."

"Thanks, Janel. I may need your moral support."

Robin pointed the way. "Through the door on your left and down the hall to the last office. Knock to let him know you've arrived."

As the door closed behind her, Amanda found herself in a long, carpeted hallway, its walls adorned with paintings of stately mansions set upon sumptuous grounds. She proceeded cautiously to the far end, her sensible side reticent, even afraid, locked in battle with her natural curiosity. She rapped firmly to announce her arrival.

"Come in." The voice was gruff.

Amada took a deep breath before entering a large, airy office. A window ran the length of the opposite wall. It offered a dizzying view of Tyson's Corner traffic. A skein of vehicles snaking through the local streets and those racing along the parallel elevated highway pulsated in perpetual motion. The office, in contrast, was serene. Austerely furnished with a wall of bookshelves, leather lounge chairs and a large desk of warmly rubbed cherry, it was enveloped by the soothing strains of Stravinsky's Dumbarton Oaks Concerto.

The lone occupant, bent over a sheaf of papers on the desk, acknowledged Amanda's arrival by raising his hand to direct her into a chair. She expected him to speak when she sat down, but he continued working deliberately, peering so intently at the papers before him that she could not discern his features for the sake of a shock of dark hair tumbling across his forehead.

At length he looked up. Bloodshot eyes of steel grey surveyed her from behind horn-rimmed glasses. In his mid-thirties, the man possessed a forceful jaw and agreeable features that begged partnership with a friendly smile, but his lips, firm and mirthless, suggested sharpness in both dealings and disposition. They formed a natural scowl as he spoke.

"Ms. Prescott, I presume?" The sarcasm was unmistakable.

"Yes, I ... I'm Amanda Prescott."

"What causes a concert pianist to sell her soul?"

"Excuse me?"

"My mother informs me that you play the piano with great artistry. You were embarking on a promising career. Whatever possessed you to stop?"

Amanda gasped at his insolence. "That was a personal decision."

"What was the logic behind it?"

She sat forward. "Mr. Cameron, that has no place in this interview. In fact, I don't recall giving your mother the details. But since you ask, I became engaged to a man who wanted me to stay at home when we married and I agreed to abide by his wish."

"Foolish, *very* foolish. You forfeited a future you'd been planning and working for all your life. And in the end you didn't marry him."

Unable to believe what she was hearing, Amanda matched his level gaze. "I didn't marry him because he died."

"I'm obliged to offer my condolences. But surely you regret giving up your career to satisfy his selfish wishes."

She stared in disbelief. His crude remark transported her back to the evening she met Craig. The persistent force that had filled her with euphoria as she stood in the Strathmore receiving line now dug once again into her heart. The ironic presence of music she loved playing in the background compelled her to relive all the doubt that had overwhelmed her as she wrestled with Craig's request.

Did I make a mistake abiding by his wishes? Probably. Dare I admit that to this man? Never.

"Well?" Amanda's long silence was trying his patience.

Steadily, she said, "That's a two-part question, Mr. Cameron. I'm sorry I gave up my career because I'd much prefer playing a piano than discussing my private affairs with you, but I sold mine and can't afford to replace it. For the past few years, I've supported myself working on the Hill in Senator Shellenberger's office. Right now I'm awaiting a security clearance upgrade and was on my way to visit a friend in Florida when I ran into your mother. Literally. With my car out of commission, I fell under her spell, and here I am, against my better judgment.

"Am I sorry about anything else? Absolutely. I'm sorry I've wasted my time going through this absurd farce of the past twenty-four hours. No matter how tempting your mother's proposal sounded to me yesterday, it's not worth undergoing the kind of verbal assault you dish out. Frankly, sir, I find you rude beyond belief. I can't imagine how you maintain a business if you treat prospective employees in this manner."

She stood abruptly, intent on stalking out. Inexplicably, his expression softened. When he spoke, his voice was pleasant to the ear, gruff no longer. "You passed the test, Ms. Prescott. With flying colors."

"What test?" Amanda fairly shouted.

The corners of his eyes crinkled. "My test. I had to be sure you can handle others who might ask the same kinds of impertinent questions. I know about your situation and I deeply regret that you deny the public the pleasure of your talent. As you may surmise, I'm fond of music myself, and if I had your ability I wouldn't be sitting in this office. I'm humbled to have you on this staff and I promise that you never again will have to submit to a conversation of this nature." He rose and held out his hand. "Please, Ms. Prescott. Please forgive me ... and stay."

His stance was imposing, his handshake firm. Had she not been alerted by others to his mean streak, she might have judged him to be warm and sincere. Amanda astonished herself by slipping back into the chair, her fury somewhat diminished. Still, words would not come. She listened as he continued.

"Your clients deserve no details about your private life. Neither do I. Here's the bottom line: this job requires both guts and social graces. You have them. In spades. We deal with people who may have questionable backgrounds, but that's not your concern. If they have financial problems, others will handle that end of the contract. Your job is to please those assigned to you without crossing formal boundaries and becoming more chummy than offering a handshake, if you grasp what I mean."

"I certainly do."

Amanda's indignant response unleashed a half-smile. "I know you'll uphold our standards. Once you've mastered the system, we'll place you with a client." When she failed to respond, he paused. "Is there something wrong with my face?"

"I'm sorry if I stare, but you don't look anything like your mother."

He suppressed a grin. "You're very observant. Please utilize that talent in your job. I'm told that I look like my father did at this age, which may explain the discrepancy on my maternal side, but that has nothing to do with your job at hand."

Amanda reddened. "I didn't mean to be flip."

"I know you didn't. I have the same habit. Others call it being forthright. Right now, though, we need to forget our personal frailties and concentrate on the specifics of your job and the Cameron training process."

At least he didn't mince words. She settled back and tried to absorb the information he imparted in terse, technical phrases. He spoke quickly, unemotionally, pausing at intervals to allow her input, but by the time she could lasso her thoughts and formulate an intelligent question, he had bounded on to a new topic. As the orientation drew to a close, he placed a CD-Rom before her and tapped it with his forefinger. "Everything you need to learn, Ms. Prescott, is on this disk."

"That's it?"

He removed his glasses and riveted his eyes on hers. "Do you know a better way?"

"I assumed I'd shadow another agent."

"That would be an imposition. This way, you learn at your leisure. If you have any questions, someone's always in the office. This method is far more efficient for our purposes. It would take years of work in real estate to run into all the potential problems covered on the CD-Rom. By studying it, you'll see them all in a matter of hours—or days, whichever you need."

"Exactly how long do I have?"

"Take as long as necessary. The material allows you to work at your own pace." A brief smirk slid across Burke Cameron's face. "Of course, I've pegged you as being very intelligent. In which case, I suggest you aim for the end of the week."

"And if I disappoint?"

"You won't." He rose and directed her to the door.

Once it closed behind her, Amanda clenched her fists. She was being manipulated by both Burke and his mother. Why had she agreed to this ridiculous arrangement? She had no background in real estate. How could she gracefully disentangle herself from a situation with all the trappings of a murky scheme? Before she could argue herself into escaping out a side exit, a door directly ahead opened and Sheila emerged.

Cilfowyr, Pembrokeshire, Wales, 1725

"Hurry, wife. The ship awaits in Cardigan Bay."

"Please, husband. Let me search our home one more time. Perhaps we have forgotten something."

"We have forgotten nothing. Everything of value is on Brother Picton's cart. He wishes to leave. Even the children cower there, knowing we are

in danger. Come. There is no time to lose. The echo of hoof beats confirms they know of our ship."

CHAPTER FOUR

"I was about to send a search party after you," Sheila said. "Judging by the length of time you were with Burke, you two must have gotten along very well. I suspect he found you fascinating."

Amanda could only stare at such a suggestion. Ignoring the young woman's reaction, Sheila clasped her wrist and changed the subject. "Come along, Amanda. I'll get you started on the CD-Rom before I rush out to an appointment."

"There's no need to trouble yourself," Amanda protested.

"No trouble involved. The sooner you begin, the sooner you'll be prepared to serve our clients. I know you'll be an asset to the agency."

Sheila's forceful kindness prevailed. Amanda soon was luxuriating on a sofa piled with downy pillows. Before her was a giant screen pulsating with colorful graphics. An actor masquerading as a realty specialist promised a thorough explanation of Cameron sales techniques, potential stumbling blocks to a successful closing, and ways to overcome them. His dazzling teeth telegraphed a pricey history of weeks spent studying the office ceiling of a specialist in cosmetic dentistry.

The tasteful room stinted on nothing. Tinned delicacies filling an ebony breakfront were matched by the contents of a refrigerator disguised as a Chinese chest. An Oriental screen hid a stove and microwave. A bunch of grapes and a crisp apple later, Amanda was well into the basic sales methods.

By late afternoon, she almost felt ready to begin selling homes, if only to escape the actor's annoying mannerisms. Especially his incessant smile.

In the middle of her reverie, Robin's voice came through the speaker, jolting her back to reality. "Amanda, can you take a break?"

"Actually, I was about to call it a day."

"Perfect. Your car's ready. Thought you'd like to get acquainted with it."

"My car? Do I really get one?"

The smile in Robin's voice breezed through the speaker. "You're not going to travel by horse and buggy, Amanda. The car goes with the territory."

After making note of where she should begin the next day, Amanda headed to the front office with a jaunty step in anticipation of a car similar to the one Janel drove.

She was not disappointed. The top-of-the-line model had every option imaginable, including a navigation screen on the instrument panel and a television for passengers in the rear seat. She slipped behind the wheel, eager to test every button and switch. The contrast with her dilapidated crate, now resting in Martin's garage, was enough to turn Amanda into a believer. She smiled to herself, appreciating life's sudden upturn; a moment later, she frowned, unable to shake the notion that everything was working out too smoothly for her to have fallen under the Cameron spell by accident.

By the end of the week, despite her aversion to the actor, she had mastered the entire CD-Rom, made copious notes, and learned the locations and specifications of listings on the print-outs Burke left in her box. Boldly, she approached Sheila and announced, "I'm ready for a client."

"That's one of the fastest reads I remember," Sheila said.

"Reading is not the same as selling," Amanda reminded her. "Maybe I won't have the right technique."

"We don't use techniques," Sheila said. "Courtesy, honesty, and deference to the client are our primary requisites. You'll be perfect for Mr. Elmont. He'll be in the Ritz-Carlton lobby tomorrow at nine."

"What should I know about him?" Now that a flesh and blood client was about to become a reality, Amanda's self-confidence began to sag. What if she forgot everything crammed into her brain over the past few days?

Sheila shuffled through papers on her desk. "Pretty much the usual. Money's no object, but the house must be colonial style, preferably something with a history. Evidently his wife requires a traditional setting for her antiques. I gather that he has some kind of business in Chicago and plans to open an office here, most likely to handle government contracts. The usual. As soon as he finds a place, his family will join him."

"There are lots of colonials in these computer listings," Amanda said. "I'll go through them, pick out the best prospects, and make appointments with the owners to avoid wasting time tomorrow."

Sheila smiled. "Good, good. I'm impressed by the way you retained those details. You might fit in one house before lunch. Then take him to a nice restaurant. The Cameron Agency picks up the tab, of course," she added, sliding a company credit card across the desk. "It's a business expense that pays off many times over. Saves you time, impresses the client, and gives him some flavor of the community."

"Where do you suggest?"

"Use your best instincts. There's a restaurant for every client. Sometimes you have to opt for convenience, but the general rule is to match the ambiance with the individual. For instance, Clyde's at Tyson's Corner appeals to gregarious people who like crowds and a high noise level. Sophisticates and wine connoisseurs prefer the continental atmosphere of L'Auberge Chez Français in Great Falls. Folks who like a quiet, informal atmosphere will enjoy The Depot in Warrenton.

"On the other hand, social climbers go for the Red Fox Inn in Middleburg, even though the food's dreadful. And there's always a fair number who go gaga over gum shoes. The CIA hangs out at the Vienna Inn and the Serbian Crown in Great Falls. Be sure you don't take potential spies or spy novelists there."

"Is that to protect the spies or the CIA?"

Shelia's laugh matched hers. "A bit of both, but you'd be the one to suffer. Your clients would be so engrossed with eavesdropping that you'd never get around to the business of selling houses. Don't worry, Amanda. You'll catch on quickly."

So it was that Amanda was seated with her first client in the cozy candlelit dining room of Tuscarora Mill Restaurant in Leesburg perusing the luncheon menu.

"Herb soups sounds interesting," observed Justin Elmont, the bald, bespectacled man across the table. Reserved in mien, he nevertheless studied the menu with overt signs of a generous appetite.

"I've never been here, Mr. Elmont, but I'm told that everything on the menu is prepared from authentic colonial recipes that originated here in Leesburg. I'm going to try the baked potato with shrimp, cheese and wine sauce."

"I'll have the deviled eggs with ham and asparagus," he said, rummaging through the basket of hot dinner rolls until one caught his fancy.

Amanda led the conversation throughout the meal, mindful that the sales lessons had cautioned the agent to learn as much as possible about the client. But by the time the waitress in a flowered colonial gown whisked away their empty platters, everything about Mr. Elmont, his business, and his family remained a mystery—other than his rejection of the house they had viewed earlier and his culinary preferences, which were considerable.

"My wife would frown, but I'm going to have the walnut rum pie," he said. "What would you like for dessert?"

"Just a cup of coffee," Amanda decided, reluctantly. The sweets described in the menu exuded calories on paper alone.

"Please. Something more substantial. It's my treat."

"Thank you, but no," she said, exercising her authority. "This is on the Cameron Agency. You are our guest."

He protested weakly. "That's not necessary. I had to eat, after all."

"True, but meals are part of the package deal. As long as you're house-hunting, the Camerons want to smooth the process. Besides, it's helpful to sample the restaurants in the various communities and learn where to have a nice meal after you're settled."

"The Camerons think of everything, it seems," Mr. Elmont said.

"That's why we're the top agency in town." Amanda surprised herself by already exhibiting pride for her new employer.

By the time she and her client returned to the car bearing the Cameron logo, Amanda knew exactly where to go next on their tour of prospective homes. Leesburg, the county seat of Loudoun County, Virginia, is a haven for Washington-weary bureaucrats who value pastoral weekends and miniature estates. Horses are a requisite. The architectural styles range from faithfully restored Eighteenth Century farmhouses to sterile glass domes.

Even though she knew that Mr. Elmont was not in the market for anything so starkly natural, she suggested pausing on their way to the next appointment to explore an underground dwelling. The builder's effort to conserve energy received raves in the recent issue of a popular house and garden magazine. Amanda took its prominent position on her computer print-out—flagged by a fluorescent yellow slash—as ample reason for a detour, if only to boost her knowledge of the area.

"Why not?" Mr. Elmont seemed amiable enough. "Always like to know the latest trends."

The house was several miles west of Leesburg off a narrow gravel road winding up to the Short Hill, a low mountain range so named by early settlers. Amanda would have missed it altogether had she not spotted a newly excavated driveway.

"That red clay looks forbidding," she said. "Do you mind if I park on the shoulder? It's just a short walk to the house."

"You'd think the builder would have finished details, like paving the driveway," Elmont grumbled.

"Out here, the focus is on keeping everything natural." Amanda picked her way carefully along the dusty expanse to the building that flowed into the hilly terrain. After opening the lock box to retrieve the front door key, she stepped ahead of her client to survey the interior.

She found it surprisingly bright for a house topped by an earthen mound. Welcome sunlight slanted down from skylights in the timbered ceiling. The stone walls of the large central room and the informal circle of couches around an ornamental tree conveyed an atmosphere as cool and fragrant as a Colorado forest.

Just as she began wondering why Mr. Elmont had not followed her into the house, his head poked through the doorway. "Catching a glimpse of the countryside. Must be some old churches around here." He could not disguise the excitement in his voice.

"I'm not the one to ask, although there certainly must be some, considering the area's colonial history. I imagine you could learn a lot at the local library. After you move here, you can explore to your heart's content."

"You're right. We'd better concentrate on finding a house." He surveyed the place with disinterest. "I'm afraid this doesn't suit me. If you don't mind, I'd like to move on."

"The homes we'll see next are much more traditional," Amanda assured him. "This is a fascinating concept, though, for the right person. The literature says that no matter how warm it is outside, the house remains comfortably cool in summer and retains heat in the winter, not at all like the traditional above-ground house."

"That may be so, but its disadvantages are clear."

"Such as …?" She was eager to learn what objections a prospective client might have to the unique design.

"It's confining. The only windows are in the front of the house, so you never see what's behind you."

"Out here, there won't be much to see except deer, raccoons, and foxes. You could always step outside to satisfy your curiosity," she offered.

Without warning, Mr. Elmont stamped his foot. "You're not trying to hand me the typical realtor's line, are you?"

His reaction startled her. "Of course not. I'm simply thinking out loud. Someone's bound to fall in love with this house and setting, even though it's not what you have in mind. I need to make a note of every plus and liability so I can match it with the right person."

Mr. Elmont became immediately solicitous. "I didn't mean to offend you. Some agents try to sell their clients the first house they show. I want to see every possible option for me that's on the market."

"You're right to adopt a conservative approach," Amanda assured him. "I'm afraid I'm not always so wise. If I were the buyer, I'd probably take the first house that struck my fancy instead of weighing all the pros and cons, but the decision in this case isn't mine."

"Then let's be on with it." Mr. Elmont consulted his watch. "I'd like to see a fair number of homes before evening."

"What we don't see today, we can visit tomorrow."

"Yes, maybe. It all depends." He became vague.

"Mrs. Cameron said that you're on my schedule for tomorrow, and for as long as it takes to find you a house," Amanda reminded him.

Concern swept across his face. "I'm surprised that she'd tie you up like that. I have to spend some time on my business affairs. Can't devote every minute to house-hunting."

"You aren't tying me up," she assured him. "I'm here to help you find the right place. If you aren't available, I can go on my own to investigate the various options and eliminate the ones that won't suit you for one reason or another."

Mr. Elmont's expression softened. "If you've no objection to a sporadic arrangement, I won't worry about monopolizing your time."

He started down the driveway while she returned the key to the lock box. By the time she caught up with him, a truck blocked their exit.

The driver leaned from the window. "Can I help you folks?"

"We've been looking at the house," Amanda said. "Are you the builder?"

As the man swung down from the cab, she marked a thick neck suggesting years of intensive body-building. Short-cropped hair topped a ruddy complexion. His attire was neat, yet rumpled, to be expected on a warm day. "You might say so. What do you think?"

"I'm intrigued, but it's not what my client has in mind," Amanda said.

The man extended his hand to Elmont. "Tom Grigsby's the name. Too bad I can't sell you on what's bound to be the wave of the future. This is the model, but the plan should sell quickly. Lots of energy-saving features."

"My client is looking for something he can occupy right away." Smoothing over her quick, curt response, she added, "I'm Amanda Prescott from the Cameron Agency."

Grigsby grinned. "I saw your car and figured as much. Your organization has a great reputation ... and not just for real estate. Maybe you have another client who'd be interested. If so, come around. Anytime."

Did she detect a leer? Taking an instant dislike to Tom Grigsby, she said, "With all the wonderful homes available in the area, I doubt that I'll get back soon."

"If you don't have a client in mind, you might want to consider this house for yourself. It has lots of advantages. I'll be glad to give you a personal inspection of the property. You could do worse."

The caveman type, Amanda thought to herself, discarding any fondness she felt initially for the unique house. "I'm not in the market," she snapped. "When I am, I'll settle for something with a bit more character."

Grigsby brightened. "An older home, you mean? It just so happens I live in one a couple of miles from here. Goes back to 1742. With stone walls two feet thick, it was the energy-saving style of its day, but I can't add solar heating until I replace the roof. If I can sell it, I may move into this one."

Justin Elmont's eyes widened. "1742, you say? Is it on a large lot?"

"Depends on what you mean by large," Tom Grigsby said. "It sits on about eighteen acres."

"Then it's secluded?"

"It's on an unimproved road like this one, if you like privacy."

Elmont beamed. "Very much. I—uh, my wife also likes something with history. It sounds worth seeing. By the way, do you know of any other buildings about that age in the vicinity?"

"Sure do. There are several churches, and even some old taverns. They say George Washington patronized all of them." Grigsby laughed heartily.

"What can you tell me about them?"

Grigsby scratched his head. "Not a thing, except they all need fixing up. I'm a builder, not an antique collector or a millionaire. Most of the really old places around here are falling apart, but if someone had the money and took the pains to modernize them while keeping their charm, they'd sell well."

"Mr. Elmont doesn't want a handyman's special," Amanda said. The client profile she had studied suggested that he was not the type to spend his weekends refurbishing a dilapidated house. Besides, she was committed to finding him a home that would earn her a commission worthy of the Cameron Agency.

Hurriedly, Elmont said, "Ms. Prescott's right. I'll leave that job to someone else. But I'd really like to see what you're talking about to get an idea of life here two centuries ago."

"You'll have plenty of time for that after you're settled," Amanda said. "For now, we'd better move along. Several owners are awaiting us." She walked on ahead, expecting him to follow, but before going many yards, she realized that he was still chatting in earnest with Grigsby and scribbling in a notebook.

At length, Elmont looked up and caught Amanda's annoyance. After shaking hands with Grigsby, he joined her, waiving the notebook. "It sounds worth seeing. I told him we'd stop by tomorrow afternoon."

Inwardly, Amanda fumed. Elmont had just shown his hand and proved that he was available the next day after all. She was doubly angry because Tom Grigsby's house was not one of Cameron's listings. If Elmont bought it, the agency would have to split a commission. She was annoyed at herself, too. Were she not such a novice, she would have been more astute and steered Elmont clear of Tom Grigsby.

The longer Amanda pondered the encounter, the clearer it became to her that it was planned, that Grigsby's underground house was highlighted on her sheet by someone in the office for a reason. He could not have known they were coming, could he? Studiously ignoring his wave, she gunned the motor and headed toward the main road.

Cardigan Bay, Wales, 1725

"Brother Davis, you come at the final moment. The captain was about to sail without you."

"Forgive us, Brother Phillips. We heard the King's men passing along Newcastle Road. We could not travel the direct route over the Roman bridge. Instead, we followed the low road through St. Dogmaels and crossed the mud flats."

"You are safe. That is all that matters. See, even in the dark our friends have gathered to wish us farewell."

"And Brother James …?"

"No fear. He and his family are below. Come, let us stow the treasures.

CHAPTER FIVE

It was after seven when Amanda delivered Justin Elmont to his hotel and promised to pick him up by noon the next day. All the houses they had viewed that afternoon were colonial in design, but far too modern for his taste, even though some had watched several generations live and die within their walls. Amanda thought them all charming and would have welcomed living in any of them. Why, she wondered, had he rejected one grand country home after another in anticipation of seeing Tom Grigsby's pre-Revolutionary dwelling?

Since it was past dinner time, she did not expect to find many lingering at the Cameron Agency. Robin was not at her desk, so she went directly to Sheila's office to leave a brief report on the day's events. The sunset filtering through the shaded windows cast light on the desk. The computer's illuminated screen saver emphasized the emptiness of an office minus a human occupant.

Locating a pen from the depths of her purse, Amanda was about to jot her message on Sheila's notepad when a door across the hall opened softly and a passage from Howard Hanson's "Romantic" Symphony escaped from within. Momentarily, she sensed another presence.

"Ms. Prescott?"

The speaker's identity was a given. Burke Cameron monopolized the doorway, a quizzical expression on his face. He seemed reluctant to enter the room. "If you're looking for Sheila ... uh, my mother, you should be advised that she keeps bankers' hours, very short bankers' hours."

"It's not urgent. I was about to leave her a note."

"Can I help?"

"Probably not. I got myself into a situation that can't be resolved until my client decides on a house. Just so it's not Tom Grigsby's."

Burke's eyebrows shot up. He took a step forward. "Grigsby? You've met him already?"

"Why … yes, at his underground model." Amanda sensed that she had struck a chord. "I didn't like him one bit, especially when he managed to interest Mr. Elmont in his other house."

"Hold it!" Burke moved closer. "Elmont actually is considering the house Tom lives in?"

"So it appears. When he learned that it dates back to 1742, he became ecstatic. From that point on, he turned up his nose at everything I showed him. If he likes it as well as he thinks he will and decides to buy from Grigsby, that means I'll …"

"Lose a commission?" Burke read her thoughts before she finished. "Don't worry. If I know Tom, he'll be a gentleman and give you a hefty percentage, even though it's not our listing. After all, you did supply the buyer."

"That's a helpful way of looking at it," Amanda said. "So you know Grigsby and think it's not a problem?"

"None. Trust me. Anything else bothering you?"

"No. You've answered my question. Thanks anyway."

Amanda zipped her purse shut and was about to move toward the door when Burke plunged his hand into his jacket pocket and pulled out a slip of paper.

"I nearly forgot. You had a call earlier. I took the liberty of jotting down the message."

The sheet he handed Amanda bore a telephone number and a name she recognized instantly: Reverend Henry Conyers.

Burke studied her face. "Anything wrong?"

"Wrong? Not at all, but rather a surprise."

"A surprise?"

She had no intention of divulging more than he needed to know. "The caller is someone I met recently and didn't expect to see again. This gives me the opportunity to thank him."

"For a favor?"

She was aware of her eyes narrowing as she sought to put Burke Cameron in his place. "For a kindness that gave me the courage I lacked at the moment." The words tumbled out before she could evaluate how they might be received.

"That's very commendable."

"Yes. Yes, it is. Meeting him proved to me that there are still a few people in the world interested in helping others, kind people who surely were put on earth to heal broken hearts …" She bit off the sentence within a whisker of baring her soul before Burke.

There was no need to worry that he would take advantage of her vulnerability and toss off a stinging barb, for he was staring out the window and nodding, almost unaware of her presence. A long, awkward silence passed before he turned to face Amanda and said, "You're exactly right. No matter what hardships a person faces, the outlook can shift dramatically with a smile or a kind word." He must have read her mind because a moment later he grinned apologetically and added, "And you're thinking that I'm the antithesis of your hero."

She turned scarlet. "I never … besides, he's not my hero, merely an acquaintance."

Burke's lips curved into an enigmatic grin. "You don't have to explain. He's a casual friend for now, but there's no telling what the future has in store."

That stiffened her backbone in a hurry. "Mr. Cameron, you delved into my personal life once before and promised never to repeat that transgression. While you're far from the mark in this instance, you're overstepping your bounds."

She detected a twinkle in his eye. Had she misjudged him? "Ms. Prescott, you make a very strong point. I have indeed overstepped my bounds and beg your apology." His smile deepened. "Still, I'm betting on Henry."

Frustrated, unable to conjure up a clever response, she turned on her heels and quit the office.

As she marched down the hall, he called after her, "Please don't forget. He's expecting to hear from you."

Back at the apartment, Amanda sliced some plump tomatoes and grated a few carrots onto lettuce for a modest lunch to counteract the heavy noontime dinner, all the while contemplating the slip of paper with Reverend Conyer's telephone number. He had contacted her first, so it would not be out of order to return his call. Still, not wishing to appear pushy, she showered, completed her bedtime ritual, and climbed under the covers before gathering the courage to dial him. He must have been seated alongside the phone because he answered at the first ring. His deep, unmistakable voice gave her goose bumps.

"Reverend Conyers, this is Amanda Prescott. My employer took your message. I hope it's not too late to call."

"Not at all, Amanda. Sheila Cameron filled me in on what transpired after we met. The events of that day were so upsetting for you that I've been wanting to get in touch. How are things going for you?"

"They're going in every conceivable direction. My car's still in the shop, but I have the use of a much fancier one. I'm essentially homeless except for the fact that Mrs. Cameron moved me into a beautiful apartment that sits on the site of the colonial gallows. I work for a man who flares hot and cold, so I have no idea how to behave in his presence. And I'm obliged to appease strangers who say they want one thing then go after the complete opposite."

A gentle laugh, and then, "Amanda, I'm confident that you have the grace and wisdom to handle both the man who vexes you and the strangers who expect you to turn cartwheels for them."

"You flatter me. In truth, I start each day feeling as if I've been shot out of a cannon. Sheila talked me into this temporary situation against my better judgment. Even though much of it fascinates me, nothing can ever be the same as …"

"As sitting at a piano and making beautiful music?"

Amanda sighed. "You can't imagine how I miss my piano. You must have sensed that when we met. Still, I thoroughly enjoy my job on the Hill and the people I work with, and just as soon as my clearance arrives, I'll be back on the payroll. My only loss is that the accident kept me from visiting my friend in Florida, but there'll be other opportunities. In the meantime, the Cameron Agency allows me to explore the Virginia countryside. For someone steeped in history from childhood and intrigued by relics from the past, that's a huge bonus."

"I admire your positive attitude. That's what impressed me at our brief meeting. I was especially touched by your personal sacrifice, giving up your music to benefit another, and I was about to make you an offer when you ran out to see about your car."

She shifted uneasily against the pillows. "An offer?"

"You sound suspicious. No need. Let's say that I know a practical way to get you back into the world of music and take some of the stiffness out of the piano I bought as a wedding gift for my wife."

Amanda nearly dropped the phone. "Your … wife?"

"My wife-to-be, that is. I'm still single, but when I saw a fine piano at a price I couldn't refuse, I bought her wedding present. It seemed like the perfect gift because she loves to play. It was delivered earlier this week, so I'd really appreciate your opinion about the action, tone, and other qualities."

"I'll be happy to evaluate it for you."

"Then that's settled. It's not just a matter of evaluation, though."

"No?"

"What I'd really like is for you to regard it as your practice piano. You're welcome to come by any time and play for as long as your heart desires."

Amanda struggled to regain her composure. "What about your fiancée? She should be the one to decide if a stranger has access to it."

"That's not a problem. I bought it as a surprise without discussing it with her. You can do both of us a favor by breaking it in. It would give me great pleasure to see you return to your former skill level."

Amanda's heart beat faster. "There's nothing I'd like better than to turn back the clock."

"Do you really want that, Amanda? Wouldn't it be even more exciting to move into the future?"

She thought a moment. "You've called my bluff. The desire is there. All I need is someone to urge me on."

"Then consider me your task master. I recently bought a house. There's very little in it except the piano and the recessed lighting that allows you to see the keyboard no matter the time of day you come. Since it's not occupied, you're welcome to visit any time. You'll find a house key under the front door mat. Hang onto it."

"I simply don't know what to say, or how to thank you, Reverend Conyers."

"To begin with, call me Henry. The thanks are all mine for putting the piano to its proper use. After you've tried it out, will you give me your evaluation?"

"By all means." She jotted down the address he dictated. Its location in a lovely suburban neighborhood astonished her. Clergymen, she knew, traditionally have few living options other than houses belonging to the church; only those with inheritances or working wives purchase their own homes. Henry, she concluded, must be among the prosperous minority.

"Then that's settled, Amanda. Please try the piano soon. I'll look forward to your appraisal."

"No more than I look forward to playing once again, Henry. Thank you, thank you, from the bottom of my heart."

"My pleasure, Amanda. Goodnight, now."

"Goodnight, Henry."

Long afterward, Amanda clutched the address to her heart. While the promise of a temporary practice piano was a dream come true, there was more baggage to Henry's offer than she dared admit. His presence, even across the telephone wires, was overwhelming, and his kindness shone through every word with all the grace and empathy one expects from a man of the cloth, but he was nothing like the celestial and distant clergymen she had known growing up.

The cowl obscuring his face at Pohick prevented her from studying his face. No matter, the cassock could not disguise the virility and sensual appeal of the man whose voice sent shivers cascading up and down her spine at their initial meeting. Even then, she was aware that a woman could fall for him at first encounter. She fell asleep wondering about the one he had chosen to marry.

Cardigan Bay, Wales, 1725

Wisps of light filtered from behind the Presili Mountains. As the blackness gave way to dawn, he could see dark shapes along the quay, members of the congregation who dared to stand shoulder to shoulder as the ship set sail. He slipped his arm around his tiny wife. She was shivering more from fright than the salty spray.

She glanced up. "Do you hear it?"

He smiled down at her. "Our friends are singing 'Hen Wlad Fy Nhadau,' Land of our Fathers. It's their gift to us, the song that wishes travelers good fortune on their journey."

Her eyes shone expectantly. "Do you believe its promise that we will return to Wales one day?"

"I cannot see into the future, but I must believe that the strife will end, though perhaps not in our time. If we are no longer on earth when that comes to pass, we must believe that those who follow us will realize the promise."

CHAPTER SIX

Dewdrops shimmered along the hedges lining Snicker's Gap Road the next morning, conquering the devil within Amanda that teetered between irritability sparked by Burke Cameron and high spirits when thoughts of Henry Conyers surfaced. In the passenger seat, Justin Elmont beamed expectantly.

Just outside Hillsboro, they turned onto Short Hill Mountain Road. Elmont drank in the rolling fields to one side, the sun-dappled peach orchard on the other. "It really is isolated," he said, a bit too cheerfully, Amanda thought.

Aloud, she said, "For someone who doesn't have a nine-to-five job, it's perfect."

Several dusty miles later, she drew to a stop and consulted the map she had printed from one she googled on the office computer. Once she was certain of the correct turn leading to Tom Grigsby's house, she proceeded forward for nearly a mile before veering onto a lane that a less astute driver would miss. By the time they reached their destination, the lane had dwindled to little more than a rutted footpath.

The stone house rose from a hillock crowned by towering oak trees. Twin chimneys announced fireplaces at either end of the dwelling. Though adequately attended, the building and grounds were not nearly so grand as those they had seen the previous day, but Elmont smiled broadly. Amanda sensed that he was prepared to make this purchase without further discussion.

Tom Grigsby lolled on the front stoop, awaiting them. As he stood to acknowledge their arrival, Amanda caught a clear view of the stone threshold. She could not contain her delight. "What fascinating markings! Are they Indian petroglyphs?"

"Could be," Tom said, affably. "Don't know much about those things."

He shook their hands firmly, then ushered them into a short hallway. A staircase directly ahead climbed to the second floor. To the right, a framed archway separated the hallway from a large kitchen—or great room—that was built around an open hearth. A parlor with a formal fireplace was directly opposite.

Amanda studied the wide-plank flooring and the hand-hewn railings. "This is obviously one of the oldest homes in Loudoun County. Quite a treasure."

"No doubt about it," Tom agreed. "The master bedroom was originally at the rear of the kitchen, but I've turned that into a workroom. The kitchen is so large it can be used as a family room. As you can see, even though the house is old, it has ample space and features that can accommodate a modern family very nicely."

"What's upstairs?" Before Tom could respond, Justin Elmont bounded up the steps to see for himself.

"Four bedrooms and two baths," Tom called after him. "Watch your head. The ceiling slants down to the eaves in the rear."

"Bathrooms in colonial days?" Amanda asked.

Tom laughed. "The early settlers had no indoor plumbing, I'm sure you know. These bathrooms were originally a sewing room and a nursery."

"You really want to sell the house?" She hoped to discover a hidden agenda.

"Yes and no," he said. "I'm fond of this place, but the new one intrigues me. I'd like to experience firsthand the advantages and disadvantages of an underground structure. If it proves to be the great design I think it is, I'll build others on speculation."

"If this house were mine, I'd not sell in haste. Because of its antiquity, it's probably worth far more than you think."

Tom Grigsby rubbed the stubble on his chin. "You may be right. It has some unusual features. The original weather boarding on the front of the house, for instance. When I began researching, I learned that it's is called 'ship-lap.' It's wider and thicker than your standard clapboard with a flat finish nobody's reproduced since the Eighteenth Century."

"Interesting," Amanda mused, trying to avoid his eyes, but that proved impossible.

They burned into hers, signaling that he was about to share a confidence. Once he earned her full attention, he lowered his voice. "The wing at the rear of the parlor is even more interesting. It's downright curious."

"Curious? What do you mean?"

"There's a secret hiding place. You can't reach the second story of that wing from the upstairs The only way up is a staircase behind the bookcase."

Smiling broadly at her expression, he crooked his finger. She followed without hesitation across the parlor to the wing. It was an informal sitting room, the inside wall occupied by a floor-to-ceiling bookcase. Tom grasped hold of one panel and eased it away from the wall to reveal a narrow archway. Behind the entry was the promised staircase.

Amanda's jaw dropped. In that instant, she shelved her reservations about Grigsby. "Can we go up?"

"There's no time." He place a forefinger across his lips. "And please don't say *anything* to Elmont. The joy is in the pleasure of the hunt. Until I stood outside the house one day and sized it up, I hadn't realized that a section of the second floor was unaccounted for from within. When I began searching for a way up, I tried every board in the house thinking that one surely would give way, but I overlooked the bookcase that appeared to be built right into the wall."

"You'd actually sell him this house without explaining how to reach the upstairs wing?"

"In a heartbeat. I bought it blind. Now it's someone else's turn. Besides, this wing is odd for other reasons." Even though Elmont was shuffling about upstairs beyond hearing range, Grigsby modulated his voice to a hoarse whisper. "Now I'm a very realistic guy, but I've lived here for nearly five years, and every time I go up there, I get a strange feeling. Really spooky."

"The house is haunted?" Amanda's voice squeaked.

"Not so loud." Grigsby shot her a warning frown. "Tradition is that the Davis family who built it brought a large fortune from Wales and hid it nearby. It's never been found, and some folks believe that the family ghosts will lead some lucky person to it."

"A family of ghosts? A lost fortune? That's incredible."

"I thought so too, until I checked the courthouse records. The immigrant's will gives each child some land and 'a key to the family treasure.' If the key to that fortune turns up, what a story."

Amanda laughed. "You're selling the house because you don't like living with active ghosts?"

Tom grinned. "That's as good a reason as any. I trust you won't tip my hand. Especially when I say I'll be happy to pass along to the Cameron Agency a good deal more than the standard fee."

Her thoughts flashed back to Burke's lack of concern about writing up a deal with Grigsby. "Does Burke Cameron know about this house?"

Grigsby merely smiled. "Your employer knows many things, and he knows me well. Just promise that the staircase will remain our little secret."

Amanda was stunned. Grigsby was asking her to conceal knowledge about the secret passageway. She was sorely tempted to tell Elmont. Still, she could not shake the gnawing feeling that Grigsby was right and the staircase was better left a secret.

No sooner had Grigsby sealed the staircase from sight than Elmont reappeared in the archway. To divert his attention, Amanda pointed toward the window. "We've been admiring the view. See how the mountain range reflects the sky. No wonder the early settlers named it the Blue Ridge."

Elmont beamed. "Grigsby, this is exactly what I'm looking for. I know we haven't discussed price, but I'm willing to meet your terms. How soon can I move in?"

Tom Grigsby demolished Elmont's concern with a wave of his hand. "By the time you're ready, I'll be in the underground house. I anticipate no problem."

"Well, that's a quick decision, one that seems to please everyone," Amanda said. "Since you're both eager to come to terms, we'll go back to the office and write up the sale." Now she knew what Sheila meant by easy transactions.

During the drive back to Tysons Corner, Amanda was aglow with satisfaction. Within twenty-four hours, her first client had decided upon a house, not one she had located for him, but a sale, nevertheless, that would be credited to the Cameron Agency.

After completing the initial paper work and notifying the title company to undertake the search, her pride was restored. She was about to relax for the first time in days when it suddenly occurred to her that Senator Shellenberger thought she was in Florida. Realizing he had no way of notifying her when her clearance was approved, she grabbed the phone and dialed his office straightaway.

An intern put her through to Kathy Owens, the friend she regarded as her rock. Kathy had been there throughout the siege with Craig. Like Meg, she encouraged Amanda to resume social activities after a decent interval, assuring her that she would do likewise given the same circumstances. When Kathy's oldest daughter was married, Amanda and Meg played at the wedding, one more reason to be embarrassed for not contacting her sooner.

Kathy's cheerful scolding drowned out Amanda's mumbled apologies. "What will I do with you, Amanda? We expected you to get in touch sooner, especially since you're still in town, and …"

"You knew I never left?"

Kathy's guard flew up. "We heard something to that effect."

"You did? Who passed along that information?"

Kathy's lighthearted laughter cleared the air, but not the questions whirling around in Amanda's head. "I'm not at liberty to say, Sweetie, simply an unnamed source. The Senator's down on the floor. I'll tell him you called the moment he comes back. Right now, though, I'm all ears to learn what you've been up to. Tell me everything."

Amanda did not have to be prompted. She told Kathy about the dreadful storm, the accident, the free apartment, the Cameron Agency, and the company car. The more she rambled, the more absurd it all sounded.

Kathy was impressed. "Now that's what I call an adventure. The best part is that you're learning a new skill. I've often thought that real estate may be the way for me to go when and if the Senator decides it's time to retire. You'll have plenty of tips and experiences to share when you come back to the office." Amanda heard Kathy catch her breath before adding, "Most importantly, I'm betting you'll find that special person."

Thunderstruck, Amanda tried to laugh that off. "No you don't, Kathy. You and Meg are my Greek chorus of matchmakers. The right man will make himself known."

"Be sure you're prepared to recognize him. Don't be taken in by someone with the wrong credentials."

"Meaning …?"

"Meaning that the one you're destined to marry would gladly go to the ends of the earth for you. Anything less would be a compromise."

"That's a tall order, Kathy. They don't make many men like that nowadays."

"One is all you need."

"You'll be the first to know when I spot him. That's a promise."

"Amanda, your voice is so cheerful I feel better already. It sounds as if you've tackled those demons and haven't a care in the world. By the way, now that you're driving a snazzy company car, what are you doing about yours?"

"Oh, m'gosh!" Amanda's spirits plummeted back to earth with a thud. "I'd better try to call Martin again."

"Martin?"

"The mechanic who towed my car. His answering machine always says he's out and will get right back to me. I'm beginning to think he doesn't exist."

Kathy's optimistic smile bounded across the telephone wires. "Don't worry about a thing, Amanda. Enjoy this experience for what it is, and remember that the end is in sight just as soon as the good old government accounting office, 'the company,' and the unseen powers that be get their heads on straight. In the meantime, think of your experience as a life bonus."

Amanda remembered Kathy's words when she sat in on the settlement and received her first substantial check for a job well done. Even Burke Cameron expressed appreciation of her accomplishment, yet something about his demeanor and of others around the table gave her the feeling all was not as it appeared on paper. She decided to stop worrying when the teller at the local bank accepted her endorsed check.

Armed with the confidence that a healthy bank account inspires, Amanda returned to the office and dialed Martin for the umpteenth time. As usual, his optimistic voice—courtesy of the answering machine—assured her he would call back shortly. After leaving the message that she was finally in a position to cover the bill for his services and would pick up her car just as soon as he made it available, she hung up and turned her attention to uncovering more secrets with the help of the computer.

Right after Tom Grigsby presented her with the bombshell of the secret room, she had scoured the Loudoun County and Fairfax County courthouse records and the Internet to ascertain his honesty. Along with a photocopy of the deed for the property transferred to him by the Davis Family Trust, she found mortgage papers confirming his purchase of the land for the underground house. Those public documents and everything else she tracked down indicated that he was a solid citizen employed by a development company with headquarters in nearby Vienna.

Justin Elmont was another matter. No matter where she searched, his name never popped up, not in Chicago, not in Virginia. Not anywhere. Sheila had given Amanda the impression that Elmont ran a company seeking government contracts, yet he might as well have come from Mars. She found nothing. He attended the settlement accompanied by a lawyer the Cameron Agency supplied, so Amanda trusted that Sheila—or her representatives—had dug into his background sufficiently to ascertain his financial qualifications. She would have prodded Sheila for more details had not Burke repeatedly assured her that the agency thoroughly investigated Cameron clients. Now Amanda's antenna was up and the doubts were multiplying.

Deep down, she was relieved that her involvement in that sale was over. Secrets, under any circumstance, are not easy to keep, and the one Tom Grigsby had revealed was too arcane to ponder for long without letting it slip to the wrong person. Perhaps, she thought, it was time to seek a logical explanation on her own.

The Welsh Tract, Pennsylvania, 1740

He hurried from the meetinghouse filled with news of richer lands. Within fifteen years, the three men charged with spreading the word westward had accomplished far more than they ever dreamed possible. Brother James, it was true, had not lived long enough to complete his pledge. He took ill during the voyage and died before the new land was sighted. Once his body was offered to the waves, his sorrowful wife and children found a home with his cousin, Brother Phillips. Upon landing, they made their way to Merion and carried out Brother James's assignment by establishing the Baptist meetinghouse.

Brother Davis and his family had settled at the southernmost part of the Welsh Tract near Chester. Every month, ships arrived in Philadelphia harbor bearing Welshmen seeking freedom of worship. What good fortune, he thought, that he had accidentally met an itinerant preacher bringing world of fertile acres of land in the Virginia colony. His wife had become content with their new life in Pennsylvania and rarely yearned for Wales. Now their grown children helped work their small farm. Although it served the family well, as had their farm in Wales, it could not support an entire community.

But a plantation? His steps quickened as he dreamed of establishing a Baptist meetinghouse adjacent to a plantation that could serve the entire membership in times of want.

CHAPTER SEVEN

Two evenings after accepting Henry's generous offer, Amanda drove to the address he had given her. The red brick colonial, located on a tree-lined cul-de-sac in Fairfax Station, was so new that its lot was freshly landscaped. For a few moments, she sat transfixed, admiring the architecture and the setting. Modest in size, not even pretending to approach the grand estates the Cameron Agency featured, it was exactly what she would have chosen for herself. She blotted out the mental picture of Henry carrying his faceless bride across the threshold.

Although dusk had not yet descended, the coachlights flanking the front door glowed, as if awaiting her arrival. The key stashed under the mat, as Henry promised, slipped easily into the lock. The door fell open onto a center hallway of inlaid flagstones leading to a broad ascending staircase. Her cursory glance to the right took in a room carpeted in a soft blue. It was barren but for the colonial pewter chandelier positioned in the center of the ceiling. One day, she envisioned, the space beneath would be occupied by a Sheraton dining table and chairs.

But there was no time to waste wondering what décor Henry's wife favored. The object of her heart's desire was awaiting across the hall. At the far end of the living room, the piano was framed by a bay window overlooking a patio and a deep yard bounded by woods. Rushing to the keyboard, she tested the action. Her heart bounded heavenward as an exquisite tone filled the room.

Long after the sun sank behind the trees and the ceiling lights flicked on automatically, she played. To her amazement, she had no trouble remembering each note of the repertoire she tearfully abandoned when the buyer came to haul away her own piano. A flood of music poured forth from the storage bins in her brain until she glanced at her watch and was shocked to see that it was nearly bedtime. Reluctantly, she ended her impromptu concert, buoyed by the knowledge that she could return whenever she liked, if not tomorrow, then soon.

She arrived at the apartment energized, eager to call Henry and report on her success. Reluctantly, she rejected that idea, mindful of the late hour. It would not do to intrude on a man who needed to arise each morning with vigor to attend both ecclesiastical and humane duties. But no sooner did she crawl into bed than the telephone rang. Breathless, she bolted upright and answered.

"Amanda? I tried to reach you earlier."

"You must have guessed that I was playing your piano, Henry. It's absolutely magnificent."

He sounded pleased. "You like it?"

"*Like* it? I *love* it. It has the sound and touch similar to one I played at Strathmore Hall, my hands-down favorite. How did you select one so perfect?"

There was a moment of silence before he said, "As a matter of fact, it was originally owned by Strathmore. They sold it to make way for a replacement. A friend in the business knew I was in the market for one and thought this would fill the bill."

"What an amazing coincidence. You couldn't have found a better one. As for your house, the setting and style are everything a woman craves. You do your fiancée proud."

"I value your opinion, Amanda. Everything you say convinces me that I made the right decision in both cases. Now that you feel at home with the piano, please take advantage of it as often as you can."

Amanda laughed out loud. "If I didn't have to show up at the Cameron Agency, I'd be back first thing tomorrow. Those few hours reliving my past have made a new woman of me. Right now I'm prepared for whatever comes my way. Even Burke Cameron."

He chuckled softly. "You take him too seriously, Amanda. No matter what he says or does, don't let him get under your skin. Between you and me, I suspect that his bark is worse than his bite. You should call his bluff."

"I've done that twice. The third time, he'll throw me to the dogs. Until my car is repaired, I need to stay in his good graces. He doesn't seem to have many, except a taste for good music."

"There you are. Every villain has one redeeming feature. Serenade him on the piano and you'll have him eating out of your hands."

"That will be the day."

They parted, laughing, after Amanda promised to report regularly. She was still thinking about their conversation the very next morning as she scrolled through the latest listings on the computer. After some minutes, she glanced away from the screen to rest her eyes and was startled to see Burke Cameron leaning against the door jamb. His eyes, as usual, looked red and strained.

"Oh, I didn't know you were there," she said.

"Sorry. I didn't want to disturb you while you were working."

"I've stopped working for the moment. How can I help you?"

Nothing in his manner suggested the short-tempered ogre the office staff knew. A half-grin conveyed congeniality, and his voice was devoid of bite. In fact, she admitted to herself that he was downright pleasant. "No urgency. I was just wondering if you feel better acclimated to the job now that you've made a sale."

"Satisfaction goes with success. In that sense I'm happier."

"That's what struck me when you came in this morning. You were humming such an upbeat passage from Elgar's 'London Suite' that I half expected you to ring up British Airways and book a flight to Heathrow."

"You're a mind reader. I performed in London two years ago and it all came back last evening when …" She stopped cold. This was something Burke did not need to know.

He caught her slip and pursued it. "What were you doing last evening?"

Remembering Henry's advice, Amanda went for the jugular. "Is there any reason for you to be concerned about how I spend my evenings?"

He seemed taken aback, just as Henry had promised. "Of course not. I simply wondered what put you in such a good mood and what there is about Elgar's music that appeals to you."

Her pit bull attack collapsed into embarrassment. "I'm sorry. I didn't mean to be snippy. Last evening I had the opportunity to play a wonderful piano. It reminded me of my concert in London. When the audience kept clapping and begging for another encore, I chose a piece from Elgar's 'London Again Suite.' It seemed an appropriate way to end the evening."

"Are you rehearsing for an upcoming performance? If you're giving a concert in this area any time in the near future, you can sign me up for a row of tickets."

Amanda shook her head. "That won't happen any time soon. The piano is strictly for practice on a temporary basis. It was made available through the kindness of a friend."

"I see." She expected him to end the conversation there, but he seemed reluctant to leave. "I don't suppose it's anyone I know."

"Probably not."

"Well, then." He took several steps forward. "If you've been practicing, you probably haven't had time to contact your ... er, the clergyman."

She took the bait. "Henry, you mean? He's not my anything. In fact, he's getting married and he purchased the piano for his fiancée. Out of the goodness of his heart, he's allowing me to practice on it."

"Hmmm." Devils surfaced from the depths of Burke's eyes. "That could cause a rift between Henry and his fiancée."

Amanda's hands flew to her hips and the words came so rapidly that she stumbled over them. "Mr. Cameron, it's none of your business what goes on between Henry and me any more than how I spend my evenings."

The corners of his eyes crinkled in amusement. "I was thinking more about the fact that you've been tossed into the pot with the two of them. Sounds like a crowd to me."

Amanda's long, silent stare accomplished little. Instead, Burke's smile evolved into a wide grin, finally erupting in a guffaw. "Do I nettle you, Ms. Prescott?"

"Very much, Mr. Cameron, and I'll thank you to leave."

"Your wish is my command." Pivoting on his heels, he executed a snappy salute and was gone.

Amanda returned to the computer, a smile on her lips.

Now that she was again solvent, she could handle the car repair expenses, but when further calls to Martin's garage continued to be one-way conversations with an answering machine, she took the problem once more to Sheila. Like the voice on Martin's machine, Sheila's rote promises of the past to contact him seemed little more than bluster.

Deftly sidestepping Amanda's mission once again, Sheila commandeered her arm and drew her further into the office. "I'm so proud of the way you completed that very prestigious transaction."

"Prestigious? I don't know about that, but it was a start."

"Rather a speedy decision, didn't it strike you?"

"It did seem hasty, but the minute Tom Grigsby described his house, Mr. Elmont was determined to see it."

"I've known Tom for years. He's been a community activist for as long as I can remember. Always helping good causes when the opportunity arises. We were sorry to see him leave Fairfax County for Loudoun, but he was drawn to the house because of its history. I must say, considering how eager he was to purchase it, I'm surprised he'd want to give it up so soon."

"From the outset, he seemed glad to have it taken off his hands," Amanda said. "He's eager to move into the underground house he designed. You have to admit it's an interesting concept."

Sheila smiled. "To each his own. For myself, I crave sunlight, but then I always did prefer being on a mountain top to an underground cave. But enough of the realty business, Amanda. I want you to meet my dear friend, Sybil Clyde. We've worked together on the Pohick Church altar guild for years. You can imagine how much she's taught me."

So saying, Sheila angled Amanda around to face one of the most striking women she had ever seen. The epitome of elegance, the stranger had silver hair, piercing blue eyes softened by a genuinely warm smile, and a formidable frame that lent an inescapable aura of royalty. Amanda greeted her politely, somewhat puzzled by Sheila's expectant expression.

Sybil nodded graciously.

Sheila gave a half laugh and squeezed Amanda's elbow. "Surely you recognize Sybil, don't you?"

"I'm afraid I ..."

Sheila threw up her hands in mock astonishment. "Amanda, you've been living in a cocoon. Thank goodness we're getting you out into the world. Sybil is the famous researcher of walk-ins and author of the best-seller, *The Revolving Grave*. You must have read it or heard Sybil chat with Oprah, Jon Stewart, and other television talk show hosts."

Amanda reddened. "Of course. I confess that I haven't yet read your book, Ms. Clyde, but I've seen some very favorable reviews in *The New York Times* and *The Washington Post*. I gather that it's about reincarnation."

Sybil smiled warmly. "That's simplifying the premise. The parapsychology department at the state university is examining the theory that remarkable souls assume new bodies to help mankind. We have documented evidence of dramatic shifts in the personality of famous people whose souls have been taken over by restless spirits."

"You're talking about ghosts?"

"Theoretically, walk-ins are ghosts until they settle in new bodies," Sybil explained. "As ghosts, they're merely the same ordinary souls they were before they died, except for the fact that they are disembodied. They reappear in their usual habitats until they find someone who can benefit from their intrusion."

Amanda pondered what she was hearing. "I'm rather confused about how a walk-in can enter another body without giving away clues of its presence. That would be no different than a stranger passing himself off as someone he's not."

"From what we've learned, it appears that the walk-in absorbs all of the host's knowledge and habits," Sybil said. "The main difference is that he can't recall and reproduce the host's emotions. Those he expresses are his very own acquired over the centuries it took to perfect his soul."

"Then a walk-in is always a good person?"

Sybil shook her head. "Not necessarily. A walk-in can be either good or evil. Good souls have courage to refuse takeover by an evil spirit. The average person, who is neither terribly good nor terribly bad, makes the best host. When a good walk-in takes over, the changes are so subtle that deviations in habit are rarely questioned.

"The opposite case is very dramatic. We're certain that an evil walk-in has occurred when we see enormous change in a person, such as when a highly reputable man performs a hideous deed, like murder, and fails to repent. However, we know of many more cases of wicked people who have a complete reversal in character by undertaking a series of good deeds. In general, a walk-in replaces a soul to achieve the desired ends without arousing suspicion or controversy."

"It's all very intriguing," Amanda said. "How did you first become interested in walk-ins?"

With Sybil's approving nod, Sheila began to speak. "It all started at Pohick Church. Sybil and I met when she was investigating events leading to George Washington's take-over by a walk-in."

"Washington?" Amanda was incredulous.

Sheila never wavered. "Absolutely. It's all documented. During his youth, Washington never considered establishing a new nation. Remember, he was an officer for the King of England during the French and Indian War, so his allegiance was with Britain. He may never have become involved in a revolution were it not for a young clergyman at Pohick Church who urged the congregation to seek freedom from oppression. The clergyman died quite suddenly. Within a few months, Washington adopted all of the arguments the clergyman had espoused and began formulating plans for ending the British rule." She paused, allowing Amanda to prepare for the inevitable bombshell. "Washington had become someone else."

Shivers coursed up Amanda's back just before her brain slid into its disbelief mode. "The fact that Washington promoted a revolution doesn't prove that he was taken over by another spirit," she argued. "We're all capable of changing our minds."

Sybil's smile was confident. "There's ample proof in Washington's case."

"What kind of proof?"

"Letters written by people close to him. Most are stored in the National Archives and the library at Mount Vernon."

"You've seen them?"

"Goodness, yes. My book is based on years of research. In one letter to a friend, Martha Washington wrote of a distinct change in her husband, saying, 'If I didn't know he was the same man I married, I would say that he has become in thought, word, and deed his good friend, our recently deceased vicar.'"

"There are others?"

"Many. Some were written by friends and neighbors, others by his military associates. In those days, people had no concept of a walk-in. They merely pointed out the coincidence of Washington's great personality change and his adoption of the clergyman's unique set of values."

"Still, it would be hard to verify such a change today, let alone one that happened two centuries ago."

Sybil smiled again. "You're right to be skeptical, Amanda, but I can convince you. Visit me in Leesburg sometime and we'll go through my notes."

"In the meantime, come back to Pohick Church," Sheila urged. Her voice sank to a whisper. "I've seen the clergyman myself, right by the altar. One minute he's there, and the next he's gone. He looks real enough, but one clue gives definite proof."

"And that is …?"

"He makes no sound when he walks."

Amanda expelled a deep breath. "On the surface, everything you've said seems too absurd to be plausible, but I'd like to learn more."

Sybil handed Amanda her card. "You may be certain that I'll have much more to tell you when you drop by my place. One reason I feel at home in Leesburg is the presence of the Revolutionary spirits who haunt every building and by-way. My heart beats faster when one brushes past me at the old court house, or in the shops along Market and King Streets. They are the heroes and heroines who plotted ways to outwit the Redcoats. You realize, of course, that the British army was encamped right outside the town for several years. Its officers occupied local homes and drank nightly in the Laurel Brigade Inn."

Visions of a ghostly clergyman whirled through Amanda's mind. She knew it was absurd to think that Henry Conyers had any connection with an Eighteenth Century phantom, yet there he was, nudging her practical side. She smiled back at Sybil. "You whet my appetite for mystery. I promise to be in touch soon."

As she left the room, she heard Sheila say to Sybil, "I knew you two would hit it off."

The Short Hill, Virginia 1742

Thomas Davis surveyed the rich soil, rejoicing in dreams that surpassed those he remembered from Wales. Aided by his eldest son, John, and their Baptist and Quaker neighbors newly arrived from Pennsylvania, he had constructed the largest house west of Leesburg. Its dimensions and amenities pleased his wife, none more than the secret staircase leading to a second-story hideaway. Although the possibility of the King's men following dissenters to the colonies was remote after so many years, he thought it best to prepare a hiding place for the treasures in the event of trouble.

The most distant fields were already sprouting wheat, barley, and corn. Close by the house, potatoes, beans, and tomatoes grew in abundance, while the aromatic herb garden vied with the perfume from a riot of wildflowers. Thankful for the strength that enabled him to settle his family in a finer situation than they had ever known, his thoughts turned to the meetinghouse. Just as he, his sons, and their neighbors had traveled down Little River Turnpike to help erect Broad Run Chapel, its minister and all able-bodied members would soon return the favor.

CHAPTER EIGHT

More than a week passed without a second assignment and Amanda began to sense that other members of the sales team were being awarded clients that were due her in turn. While she had never aspired to learn the fine points of the realty business, now that this job had been thrown into her lap, she resented being overlooked on purpose, if that were the case. Still, if her self esteem was lowered by days of boredom, her personal joy soared. A paucity of clients allowed her to scurry from the office at the regular closing hour and drive to Henry's house. There she immersed herself in music, reproducing the composers' visions on the keyboard as quickly as the familiar notes flashed across the screen in her mind. By the time she returned to the apartment each evening, her heart brimmed with echoes of the exquisite passages that came easier with each effort.

Despite the late hour, she looked forward to hearing from Henry. In the beginning, he called several times a week to inquire about her practice session, but their chats soon developed into a nightly affair. They talked animatedly, moving easily from music to literature, to history, to politics, and back to music. Amanda was astounded by Henry's vast store of knowledge, in particular his grasp of music ranging from medieval chants to the Great American Songbook. She eagerly anticipated each evening's delicious adventure in their very proper pillow talk that excluded all intruders, even his fiancée. Especially his fiancée.

Amanda soon began relying on Henry for the moral support she missed from her colleagues on the Hill. The vibration in her ear of his deep, soothing voice coming across the wires debunked notions she had entertained briefly that he was more ethereal than real, notions fueled by Sybil's revelations. When she confided to Henry that she suspected Burke Cameron was trying to drum her out of the agency, his advice came straight from a keen observer of modern mankind, not a time-traveling walk-in.

"You are the most competent woman I know, Amanda," he said. "I'm not very knowledgeable about how real estate offices are run, but I'm certain that your nemesis, Burke Cameron, is aware of your potential. I wouldn't be surprised to learn that he's saving you for sticky situations that require someone with unusual tact and insight. People who can afford expensive property, the kind the Cameron Agency handles, often have questionable backgrounds. Dealing with them requires caution and it takes a special person to cut through to the truth. Something will come your way."

"Just talking with you gives me the courage I need, Henry. Still, I can wait only so long before I lose my patience."

He laughed. "At some point, if you must push the issue, there's nothing wrong with confronting Burke Cameron. He'll either tell you to leave or explain his intentions. He owes you that much."

On the very morning Amanda made up her mind to march into Burke's office and demand to know her status, Robin signaled her over the intercom.

"A new client, Amanda. In the waiting room."

"You caught me by surprise," Amanda said.

"Be prepared for a bigger one," Robin said softly. "This one's a dreamboat."

The moment Amanda entered the waiting room, she understood exactly what Robin meant. The man springing from his seat to greet her could have stepped out of Sigmund Romberg's "A Desert Song." His snappy black eyes, sun-bronzed complexion, and white, even teeth were framed by dark ringlets across his brow. It occurred to Amanda that he would have been attired more appropriately in a sheik's aba, rather than the tropical suit he wore. A carefully sculpted moustache completed the picture.

Robin, visibly mesmerized, managed, "Ms. Prescott, this is Mr. Ali Ahmed."

Ali Ahmed's smile bedazzled. He lunged forward, grasped Amanda's hand and kissed it in a smooth, continental style. "Ms," he pouted. "Does it stand for Miss or Mrs.?"

"I am unmarried."

"How fortunate for the many gentlemen who must delight in your company."

His riveting stare cautioned Amanda to step back discreetly and respond with formality. "It's a pleasure to meet you Mr. Ahmed. The Cameron Agency will do its best to find a home suited to your needs."

"So I am told," he said. "I thrust myself at your feet in the hope that you will help me locate a suitable estate where I can train my race horses."

"A horse farm, is it? Northern Virginia is popular for horse lovers because of its mild climate. Would you like to begin the search today?"

"By all means. At your convenience, of course, Ms. Prescott." He executed a suave bow.

"Very well. If you'll make yourself comfortable in the waiting room, I'll do a quick computer search of some possibilities and plot out an itinerary for this afternoon."

Within a few minutes, several strong possibilities popped up. A few properties on the list were located in adjacent Fauquier County where, Amanda judged, Ali would be compatible with the jet set sophistication of Middleburg's celebrity residents.

After making several telephone calls to arrange appointments, she led Ali to her car. Now that she had a new client to serve, events of the past few weeks—even questions about the mysterious stairway—were filed away in her mind's recesses. Exuding confidence, she navigated the ramp from the Beltway to the Interstate.

"Beautiful," Ali murmured as Fauquier's County's emerald hills rose from the horizon. "But where are the trees?"

Amanda smiled, thinking back to her childhood and the lessons her mother had taught unwittingly during their frequent drives into the country. "This area is called The Plains. The early settlers were just as surprised as you are to find a prairie in the middle of a land thick with forests. The Indians who were here long before the settlers arrived hunted the buffalo herds by burning off the grasses and trees. That gave them a clear view of the grazing buffalo and made hunting easy."

"Buffalo? I've seen them in your cowboy movies, but I had no idea Virginia was so primitive."

"Buffalo ranged throughout the colonies for many years. When the settlers discovered how the Indians kept this area in grassland to encourage the buffalo to return, they decided to continue the tradition of maintaining the plans. The name stuck. The system also helped the farmers who settled here. Since they didn't have to clear it, they had a head start on their crops."

Ali shook his head. "It's hard to imagine buffalo here in such a civilized place."

"The settlers didn't eliminate the buffalo intentionally, but by shooting them for meat and hides, they became responsible for killing them off in Virginia. The pioneers who settled mid-America later outnumbered by far the Indians who hunted buffalo. They managed to repeat the mistakes that happened here. That's why most of the buffalo in this country are confined to the western plains states. Today, the horse is the favorite four-legged creature of the local residents."

Ali drank in the sweep of undulating farmland and one prosperous horse farm after another, all distinguished by white board fencing and immaculate buildings. "That's more to my liking," he said, gazing longingly at the impressive manor they were passing. "Is it for sale?"

"I'm afraid not. Very few go on the market. Most are passed down to family members. We're fortunate to have several choices available for your consideration."

At the next exit, Amanda nosed off the freeway into the small community of The Plains. The first turn took them onto a narrow country road and away from the quaint stores and clapboard houses stitched together alongside the village's main street.

"Do we have far to go?" Ali shifted in his seat, eager to reach their destination.

"Only a few more miles. See, the trees are returning already." Amanda gestured toward a grove of maples bordering a stream. "That's the Little River, so the road we want should be right around the next bend. It's called Boo Hoo Church Road, one of the oddest names I've ever heard. I understand the church got its name from an unhappy event that occurred to one of the families in its congregation."

Chuckling, Ali pointed to the next road sign. "Bust Head Road seems even odder. Do you know the story behind it?"

"No, but it's clear the person who named it had a sense of humor. I hope these signposts aren't telling us something about the farm we've come to inspect."

Ali studied her face. "You enjoy a laugh, I see, like most Americans. Instead of being serious, you look for amusement and humor, even when naming your roads."

"It must have something to do with our heritage," Amanda said. "We have so many conflicting backgrounds and points of view that we'd be furious with each other at times without humor to moderate our daily problems."

"You are a very perceptive lady. The man who wins your heart will be most fortunate."

Pretending she had not heard, Amanda directed his attention to their destination, an expanse of rolling meadows directly ahead. It was outlined by the ubiquitous board fence common to thoroughbred horse farms. The view was not in the least compatible with the absurd name, Boo Hoo Farm, posted at the entry gate.

As far as the eye could see, the driveway was lined with Colorado spruce and Bradford pear trees for the Technicolor drama that nature choreographs annually. Against the bluish fir, the pear leaves—now painted a coach green—offered subtle contrast destined to evolve into a shimmer of reddish-gold come autumn. At the onset of spring, the fir would discard its snowy winter mantle to serve as a regal backdrop for cool white pear blossoms.

The tree-lined corridor soon gave way to a gentle stream meandering past paddocks, automatic waterers, run-in sheds, and a twenty-stall stable that more closely resembled a mansion. Farther along, a stand of willows overhung a pond. Swans glided serenely, generating faint ripples in their wake.

"Beautiful grounds," Ali conceded. "What's the acreage?"

Amanda glanced at the listing. "About three hundred and fifty. That should meet your requirements."

Ali nodded absently. "The stable looks adequate for a start. We can always expand."

Amanda cast him a sidelong glance, astounded that anyone could be so casual about such a magnificent estate. When the mansion finally came into view, she could not refrain from gasping. "Oh, it's lovely."

Ali nodded in agreement.

To Amanda's eye, it was every Southern mansion fantasy rolled into one. It lazed across a broad green knoll, the brick exterior painted a vivid yellow to contrast with shutters that matched the waxy leaves of ancient magnolias standing sentinel at either wing. White columns marched across its face toward the casual ambiance of a side verandah.

She parked on the circular drive before a formal garden freshly planted with early summer annuals. Ali leaped from the passenger seat and hastened around to her door. Grasping her hand, he drew her onto the gravel trace as carefully as if she were crafted from bone china. Eagerly, he asked, "How do you like it?"

"It's breathtaking, but you're the one making the decision. The inside could be a shambles." Despite her outward caution, Amanda was certain the interior was every bit as deliciously perfect.

Mrs. Wardle, the housekeeper, met them at the door. "The owners are at their other home in Bermuda," she said. "Mrs. Cameron is a close friend of the family, so this is her exclusive listing. Feel free to look around."

"Thank you so much," Amanda said. "This is my client, Mr. Ahmed. He needs a place to raise horses."

"The facilities here would be perfect for him." Mrs. Wardle stretched her thin lips into a pinched smile. "And he couldn't find a more livable house. Why don't you begin in the parlor?"

She directed them through a doorway outlined with *trompe l'oiel* pilasters and moldings. The parlor beyond was spacious enough to accommodate antiques softened by deep upholstered pieces, needlepoint accents, and filmy curtains that swayed at the whim of the gentle breezes. The French county motif flowed through the formal dining room and out the wide glass doors opening onto the terrace beyond. Amanda thought it an inspired setting for a hunt breakfast or an elegant, yet informal, dinner party.

Ali's sharp, dark eyes examined the marbleized wallpaper and the walk-in fireplace. "I suppose I could have it redone to my liking," he mused.

Without thinking, Amanda blurted, "Don't you like it? I think it's perfect."

"Nothing is so perfect it can't be improved. Do you really like all this fussiness?" Ali's disdain of the chintz slipcovers on a pair of sofas was evident.

"I probably wouldn't choose that exact print."

"There. You prove my theory that all women like change. After I decide on my house, I'll consult you about my decorating problems."

"That's not part of my job." Amanda wondered exactly how far he believed the Cameron service extended to the clients. "I'm sure you'll find decorators to fulfill your needs."

Ali surveyed Amanda's face, a curious smile on his lips. "I've known you only a few hours, but I value your opinion as an expert … and as a lovely lady." He bowed graciously.

Amanda accepted the pleasantries with a manufactured smile; inwardly, alarms went off. Few things about this man added up to a wealthy horse-breeder except his glib conversation and surface knowledge of horsemanship. Despite her lack of bigotry and natural tendency to trust everyone until their motives became suspect, the attacks of September 11th on the World Trade Center and the Pentagon, the troubling situation in Iraq, and increasing threats by al-Qaeda worldwide had heightened her concern about everyone she met in Washington with a Mid-Eastern background and an odd agenda.

Her apprehension mounted as they climbed the curving staircase to the second floor and he caught her wrist, ostensibly to draw her attention to the carved cherubs cavorting across the ceiling. His grip was strong; she sensed that it would become painful should she attempt to break away. Submitting to his grasp, she allowed him to lead her around the hallway from room to room. The exterior wall of each was dominated by a large sliding window that opened onto a balcony. Deliberately, Ali paused at one, drawing Amanda close to drink in the view.

"Would this scene content you for the rest of your life?"

"I don't know anyone who wouldn't be inspired, but you're the customer who has to be satisfied."

"Ah, so it would appear," Ali said. "Nevertheless, I'll not make a final decision until I have the lady's opinion."

"I'm sure your wife will be pleased with anything you choose," Amanda said, secretly hoping he would let slip the number of wives he left behind, perhaps a harem.

Seemingly taken aback, Ali flashed a brilliant smile and loosened his grip. "My wife? Of course. By all means, she'll be pleased."

Amanda grabbed that opportunity to twist adroitly and break away on the pretext of examining the intricate knob on a heavy door.

On cue, Ali's interest shifted to the door. "Where does that go?"

"Probably to a cedar closet." Amanda cracked it ajar. "Why, here's a staircase. Must lead to an attic." Instinctively, she began to climb. A narrow shaft of light filtered down from a tiny window in the room above. Halfway up, she paused, startled by the sound of creaking floor boards.

"Mice?" Ali, at her heels, spoke in jest, but his voice conveyed tension.

Amanda reached the top first. As her eyes adjusted to the scene, she sucked in her breath. Directly before her was an ancient woman in a rocking chair, eyes closed and mumbling to herself mindlessly.

At that precise moment, Mrs. Wardle called shrilly from the doorway below, "Ms. Prescott! You must not be up there! Please come down immediately!"

Leesburg, Virginia, 1755

"Have you heard, Brother Davis, that the British troops will be quartered in town?"

"Aye, a sad day indeed, even if it is said they will be stationed only until General Braddock moves toward Fort Duquesne to deter the French. This is fair warning that we must keep our symbols hidden except when we assemble."

Moving closer to his friend, he lowered his voice. "We plan a joint meeting with the Alexandria chapter of Freemasons Friday next. Please find out how many of our brothers can travel there."

CHAPTER NINE

At the sound of Mrs. Wardle's voice, Amanda wheeled around and bumped into Ali, who had bounded up beside her. They exchanged puzzled glances before politely obeying their hostess and retracing their steps.

"I didn't realize that someone was up there." Amanda said.

"Is the lady a family member?" Ali blurted the question she was too polite to ask.

Mrs. Wardle pursed her lips as if not quite sure how to respond. Slowly, she said, "She is the mother of the owner. She is quite feeble and prefers to remain in solitude."

"I see," Amanda said, not understanding at all. She was convinced that Mrs. Wardle was withholding vital facts. Surely the elderly woman was too weak to climb the steep staircase of her own accord. If so, someone had to assist her up and down for meals as there were no facilities in the empty attic for dining, or for any other activity. There was another, less palatable option: the woman was being held prisoner. Amanda read the same suspicion in Ali's face. To smooth over the situation, she added, "We certainly have enjoyed seeing this lovely house. Mr. Ahmed has several others to consider, but this has been most interesting. We'll get back to you as soon as he makes up his mind."

"Just one thought," Ali put in. "I wonder how soon the premises can be vacated. Once I decide on a place, I'd like to move in at the earliest possible moment."

Mrs. Wardle assured him with a brisk nod. "The owners can accommodate your wishes, I'm quite certain of that."

"Ah, then the staff and ... er ... the owner's mother have contingency plans." Mrs. Wardle hesitated. "I don't quite understand."

"What I mean is, do you and the groundskeepers have other positions lined up when a sale is completed, and does the elderly lady have a place to go?"

Mrs. Wardle's eyes narrowed. "Some of us will go to the owner's other homes, and some of us who live locally will be available to the new owner." She gestured toward the staircase. "As for her, I have no idea what they ... what she will do, but that should be no problem so far as your taking possession of the property is concerned."

Amanda and Ali thanked Mrs. Wardle before retreating down the staircase to the entranceway and the verandah beyond. No sooner did they settle themselves in the car than Amanda's cell phone rang.

"Amanda? ... This is Robin ... Burke Cameron needs to speak to you. He's out of the office. Here's the number where you can reach him."

The phone rang only once before Burke answered. Not pausing to question Amanda's identity, he said, "Ms. Prescott, there's been a postponement. You were scheduled to take Mr. Ahmed to Crestmont in mid-afternoon, but the owner called to say that something's come up and she can't be there to show you and your client around until after eight. Can you stall?"

"No problem," Amanda said. "I've scheduled two more showings in the area. Afterwards, instead of going directly to Crestmont, we can have dinner in Warrenton first."

"That should do it. Where do you plan to eat?"

"Where?" Amanda thought a moment. "I suppose we can try The Depot. Your mother recommended it."

"That's a good choice. Stay close to your cell phone. In fact, keep it with you at all times. If there are any changes, someone will be in touch."

Ali searched Amanda's face. "A problem?"

"Nothing urgent. Just a shift in our schedule. The owner of Crestmont can't be home until later this evening, so we'll eat after seeing the other two listings. I hope it won't be too dark for you to see the layout of the grounds by the time we arrive."

"If so, we can come back another day." Ali cast one of his penetrating glances in Amanda's direction. She shrank away involuntarily, sensing that he was trying to excavate a passageway into her thoughts.

The Depot had scant resemblance to its original guise. The short-line tracks visible from a large picture window were the sole reminder of a once-bustling transportation hub on an active branch of the Chesapeake and Ohio Railroad. Time and the advent of Interstate highways and the burgeoning trucking industry had hastened its abandonment, but its reincarnation was a delight to behold.

Inside, the stationmaster's counter held a spray of flowers, while the ticket office beyond had been transformed into a cozy dining alcove that Amanda envisioned as all the more appealing in the depths of winter when logs blazed in the stone fireplace. Oriental screens and banks of fresh greenery partitioned the rest of the building into intimate niches, each accommodating no more than three or four tables to convey a feeling of privacy.

As the ancient clock in the county courthouse struck six, Amanda began studying the blackboard menu with an eye to determining which among the ingenious dishes listed would take the least amount of time to prepare. Hungry as she was, her primary objective was to deliver her client to Crestmont on time. Ali, on the other hand, stretched back in his chair, unbuttoned his jacket, and riveted his eyes upon her. He seemed unconcerned about their delay, effecting a pose that matched Amanda's mental image of an Arabian prince lolling in his palace on a damask divan surrounded by submissive dancing girls.

"I'll have the sea bass, if it won't take long," Amanda told the waiter.

"Time matters not," Ali's lips curled mirthfully. "I'll have the roast lamb." The moment the waiter moved out of hearing range, he leaned forward. "Tell me, why are you so business-like? This is the time to relax and enjoy oneself. If we miss the appointment, we can always make another. Besides, I'd like to get to know you better."

Amanda tensed. "Mr. Ahmed, you must understand several things. First of all, I am here to help you find the perfect place to live. If I take time to socialize, I do the Cameron Agency a disservice. Secondly, the places meeting your needs in the area are very limited. Someone else with the same requirements could be making an offer right now on a farm that would be perfect for you."

Ali smiled patiently. "Ms. Prescott, I have discovered that when one is in a great hurry, he misses the beautiful sights along the way. If you will pardon my saying so, you are one of the most beautiful sights I have seen in many a day, and I wish to spend as much time with you as possible."

Not pausing to blink, Amanda continued as if she had not heard Ali. "And thirdly, Mr. Ahmed, I am obligated to my agency to conduct my relationships with all of my clients on an impersonal basis."

With that, Ali laughed aloud. "I thought that this was a free country, one where a person's thoughts and actions aren't dictated by a police state. If you choose to spend time with me over and above your job, that should be your affair, not your employer's concern."

"The key word is 'choose,' Mr. Ahmed. I do not choose to have a social relationship with you. The end."

Ali's smile faded. "If that is your decision now, so be it, but please be aware that I intend for you to change your mind." His eyes searched Amanda's as he passed her the basket of hot mid-Eastern bread aromatic with yeast and stone-ground flour.

Amanda selected a piece, broke it in two, and lathered its pocket with butter before looking him straight in the eye and replying, "Mr. Ahmed, if you use my sincere efforts to locate a horse farm for you as a means of trying to engage my affections, I shall be obliged to turn your account over to another agent."

Ali imitated her serious expression. "That would be a fate worse than death."

He had touched a nerve. "For a newcomer to this country, you're very familiar with our idioms."

"I'm not such a newcomer as you seem to believe. My family has traveled here many times, and I studied two years at Princeton. You might call me a second-hand American." Abruptly, Ali fell thoughtful. "Since you seem determined to change the subject, let me retreat to what we saw today. I must say, I don't know what to make of the old woman. Is it an American custom to put grandmothers in attics?"

"That was strange, I agree." Momentarily, Amanda tabled her righteous refusal of Ali's intentions in favor of the puzzle at hand. "It almost seemed as if she were a prisoner there. But of course that's ridiculous. Nobody in this day and age hides relatives away in an upstairs room. That happened a hundred years ago when there was no medical help for dementia. Things are much different today."

"Or should be," Ali said.

"Surely it must be exactly as Mrs. Wardle said, that the old lady likes to be alone."

Ali frowned. "Maybe. Maybe not. Wouldn't she rather be downstairs in that beautiful house? With nobody there but the housekeeper, she would still be alone, if that's what she enjoys, but without the isolation."

"There wasn't much in that attic to keep someone's mind occupied," Amanda said.

"Exactly." Ali leaned across the table. "The room was so empty that I believe the woman was placed there either because she already has lost her mind, or to make sure that she does lose it."

"Why would anyone do that?"

"If I knew, I'd have the answer to many questions. There is one other possibility ..."

"Yes?" Amanda's voice dropped to a whisper as she became caught up in the drama of the moment.

"Perhaps she knows something someone else wants to know, or maybe she's hiding an object others are looking for. She won't tell them or give it up, so they put her there to make her change her mind."

"You make it sound positively felonious. Still, why would they let us go through the house alone? We were bound to find her."

"You forget that we weren't supposed to be up there," Ali said. "Mrs. Wardle called us down."

"Yes, but she didn't make an effort to monitor us. If she had really wanted to prevent us from seeing the woman, she would have gone through the house with us. She could have told us that the door led to a closet or made some other excuse."

"Wait a minute." Ali's dark eyes blazed. "Maybe they *did* want us to see her. That would arouse our suspicions and we might start our own investigation to find out what secret she's hiding. If they monitored us, and if we happened to stumble over the answer, they could benefit from our efforts without exerting a finger."

Amanda shook her head. "That's too far-fetched. Why would a real estate agent and a client bother to investigate the story behind an old woman in a rocking chair? The owners had no idea we'd be there. We could have been anyone."

"Didn't Mrs. Wardle say the owners know the Camerons?"

"She said they're good friends of Sheila, but what does that have to do ...?"

Ali shrugged. "I have no idea, but no matter how I look at it, I believe there's some kind of connection."

At that moment, Amanda's attention was directed to the waiter bearing their platters, each topped by a silver warming dish. With a flourish, he placed one before her and whipped off the cover to reveal an immense fish sizzling between curly parsley sprigs and roasted zucchini slivers. Golden duchess potatoes nestled in a gilt-edged side dish.

"It looks lovely," Amanda said.

"And so does mine," Ali said, as the waiter place before him a fan of thinly sliced lamb, faintly pink, surrounded by tiny eggplants stuffed with sweet peppers, tomatoes, pine nuts, and currants. The scent of chopped mint and dill sprinkled over the roast lamb mingled with the aroma of cinnamon and cloves emanating from the stuffed vegetables. Solicitously, the waiter scooped fluffy rice onto a small plate, topping it with a dollop of butter and a quick squeeze of lemon.

Ali rubbed his hands together. "Begin, begin," he urged Amanda. "Food for thought. Perhaps it will help us solve the puzzle."

Managing a silent truce, Amanda smiled back at him. Her mental image of Ali's harem sailed off upon the evening breeze and she pierced her bass with nothing more important on her mind than devouring each succulent forkful. She savored its delicate flavor, scarcely noting the two men being seated by the maitre d' at a table behind the nearest oriental screen. Then something registered and she mumbled, "The strangest thing ... that looked like someone from the Cameron Agency sitting down over there. Of course it couldn't be."

Ali was enjoying his repast too much to notice her frown.

By the time she finished the main course, Amanda believed that she could not eat another bite, but Ali—undaunted by his enormous serving of roast lamb—commanded the waiter to wheel in the dessert cart.

"What will the lady have?" The waiter passed his hand provocatively above three tiers of delectable concoctions.

"Nothing, thank you," Amanda said.

"Of course she'll have something. You must try the baklava," Ali insisted.

"No, really ..."

Ignoring her feeble protest, Ali pressed, "Do you prefer chocolate? The Black Forest cake looks tempting." He accepted a slice from the waiter and held it before Amanda.

The aroma was her undoing. She relented. "Maybe a tiny bite."

"You must take the entire serving. Eat what you can. It's a treat you cannot turn down. The next time we come, we'll try another of these wonderful sweets. The baklava for me," he told the waiter.

Amanda signed deeply. Ali *was* persistent. Much too persistent. Against her good judgment, she sampled a bourbon-soaked cherry topping the cake. Luscious and rich, its spell rapidly blanketed some of her concerns about Ali and induced her to consume more of the cake than she had intended.

When the bill arrived, Ali reached for it gallantly, but Amanda maneuvered her credit card onto the waiter's tray. "This is on the Cameron Agency," she reminded him. "All part of our service." She hoped her aggressive move further riveted on his mind the fact that theirs was strictly a business relationship.

"If you insist," Ali said, rising to usher her out of the chair with a sweep of his hand.

As they headed toward the door, Amanda strained to get a better view of the secluded table. The man who had caught her eye was no longer there, although his companion was seated with his back to her. Where had he gone?

The answer came with a rush as she turned toward the door and someone grabbed her elbow. A rough voice in her ear said, "Ms. Prescott, I thought I heard you across the room."

Amanda's head snapped around. It *was* Burke Cameron. Did he drive to Warrenton after they last spoke? Or had he been tracking her all along? She hoped her facial expression was sufficiently daunting as she demanded, "What are you doing here?"

"The same thing you're doing. Having dinner." Burke extended his hand to Ali. "Mr. Ahmed, nice to meet you. I'm Burke Cameron, Ms. Prescott's employer. I hope she's helping you locate the ideal home."

Amanda detected a thick serving of sarcasm in his voice.

Ali accepted Burke's handshake and returned the pleasantries. "She has been most helpful, and the dinner was excellent."

Burke consulted his watch. "Glad to hear it. May I suggest that you hurry on to your next appointment. The sun sets shortly. You want to arrive in daylight for the best impression."

"By all means," Ali said. He moved dutifully ahead to the doorway where a silver bowl filled with mints caught his attention.

Bristling, Amanda turned to Burke. "Do you plan to follow us there to make sure we arrive safely?"

Burke looked amused. "Why would I interrupt my meal to follow you? I can assure you, Ms. Prescott, that my only concern at the moment is your ability to please our client with a home that suits his taste."

Defensively, Amanda persisted. "Then why did you come this far for dinner?"

"If I told you I lived nearby, would you believe me?"

The response escaped her lips before she considered Burke's possible reaction. "Not in a pig's eye."

Instead of firing her on the spot, he laughed aloud and squeezed her arm. "Good for you, Ms. Prescott. Don't believe *anything* you hear. I'm glad you're on our team."

Tossing her employer a look that teetered between astonishment and respect, Amanda joined Ali at the threshold. As they left the restaurant, she sensed Burke's eyes burning into her back. Once again, she wrestled with the recurring feeling that she was being manipulated as surely as if she were a puppet on a string.

The area map printout told Amanda that Crestmont was situated at the base of the Broken Hills, the tantalizing ridge of blue that once beckoned settlers into the untamed wilderness. She drove purposefully down the Little River Turnpike, determined to reach the estate before the sun dipped behind the hills. But as she turned onto Beverley Mill Road, an explosive report from the rear tire signaled disaster.

"Oh, no." She steered onto the shoulder.

"Sounds like trouble," Ali said. He got out to inspect the problem and soon called back, "It's a flat tire. Looks as if you went over something sharp. Slashed the tire right through."

"What can we do?" Amanda tried to camouflage the fear in her voice. "I didn't see any service stations along the main road."

"If you have a spare, I'll change it. It'll take some time."

Joining Ali at the rear of the car, Amanda unlocked the trunk. It popped open to reveal the precious spare tire and some tools.

"Exactly what we need," Ali confirmed.

"While you're taking care of that, I'll call Crestmont so the owner will know we haven't forgotten the appointment." Amanda returned to the driver's seat to retrieve her cell phone. She rummaged through her purse, but it was not there. Frantic, she searched the crevices of the seat and the length of the floorboard in case it had fallen and drifted to the passenger side. Nothing. She called to Ali, "I'm sorry, but I can't find my phone. Have you seen it?"

"Afraid not."

"I can't imagine where it went. I'm certain I put it in my purse after speaking with the office."

Ali seemed unperturbed, but Amanda felt isolated and inexplicably frightened. Now she wished that Burke Cameron *had* followed them. Summoning what common sense she could muster, she began exploring the lay of the land, leaving Ali to contemplate the tire. Her first thought was to mount the embankment to attract attention and flag a passing motorist. Several minutes passed. Not one car appeared, only a military helicopter. The whir of its rotors overhead was deafening. As it moved away, it nearly skimmed the roof of a stone church perched on a rise no more than a hundred yards distant. Then it disappeared from sight.

Perceiving salvation in the presence of the church, Amanda called back to Ali, "I'm going over to that church. There might be a pay phone in the lobby."

"Suit yourself. Be careful crossing the road," he added.

Amanda scurried across the highway and along the shoulder toward the church. Passing a historical marker that read: *Broad Run Church Established 1742*, she mounted the bank. There she came upon a path that cut through the graveyard. Already shrouded in shadows comfortable only to the inhabitants of the crude coffins beneath, it was overhung with willow trees, their transient roots thrusting wildly up through the soil. Some of the headstones stood askew, misplaced by tree roots seeking solace from the adjacent stream whose banks were populated with peep toads broadcasting their mating calls in chorus. Glancing back toward the west, Amanda was nearly blinded by the great red ball suspended between the horizon and the ebony nether world of forested hills. It was sinking rapidly, flinging triumphant coral rays heavenward to penetrate the ether and reflect in the clouds moving lazily eastward above her head. An icy jet trail dissecting them was limned in a darker hue of magenta. The vivid tapestry, deepening in intensity by the moment, commanded the earth's attention by wresting the color from everything below. Only their black outlines etched against the brilliant backdrop verified the existence of the trees and the church.

A catbird perched on the stone cemetery wall squawked a warning to Amanda before winging off to its nest. From the sanctuary of the church eaves, a mourning dove's doleful cry seemed to call, "Oooooo, Amanda Prescott, Oooooo."

Shivers cascaded up and down her spine. Stumbling over a trailing honeysuckle vine, she grabbed a tilting headstone for support.

The cry came again, this time nearer. "Oooooo, Amanda Prescott."

Her heart pounding, she inched toward the church, all the while cautioning herself to ignore her runaway imagination. Occasional headlights on the highway flashed by, no more real to her than if they were displayed on a movie screen. Pressing on through the eerie twilight, she was determined to locate a telephone, whether or not local ghosts were stirring.

She had just reached the final row of tombstones when she saw him.

A statuesque figure, garbed in what appeared to be a long black cloak, moved fluidly across the footpath no more than ten yards ahead.

Alexandria, Virginia, 1765

Reverend Henry Conyers stood at the door of Pohick Church greeting the congregation leaving the sanctuary. He offered his hand to the last in line, a middle-aged gentleman with a friendly smile. "Good morning, friend. What brings you to our church?

John Davis grinned. "I'm not a spy, if that's what you thought."

Reverend Conyers relaxed. "Your handshake confirms that we are brothers."

"That I am, in heart, soul, and determination to oppose the outrage of taxation King George wants to impose on us."

"You speak bravely brother. What brings you at this time?"

"In truth, I come in place of my father, Thomas Davis. He is pastor of the Short Hill Meeting west of Leesburg. We heard of your inspiring sermons. Since he has his own obligations each Sunday, I came to hear what you have to say, although I hasten to emphasize that neither my father nor I feel close to the Church of England."

The vicar nodded. "You realize, I feel certain, that I no longer speak for the Church of England, but for our colony, all of the colonies, in truth. The time has come to break the bonds."

"And not a moment too soon. The word is spreading that you are inspired by unseen powers. I had to see for myself. Now I can confirm to my father and members of our meeting that the rumors are true."

Later that week, Thomas Davis passed a sheaf of papers across the desk to his son. "Here is a draft of my Sunday sermon. Do you have any suggestions?"

John Davis studied the sheets for several minutes, smiling occasionally as a phrase struck his fancy. At length, he looked up. "You've said it well, Father, exactly what I heard last Sunday at Pohick. The vicar is barely more than thirty, but he is wise beyond his years. He speaks and walks with the air of someone who is ... almost holy."

CHAPTER TEN

Amanda clapped her hands over her mouth, but the figure paid her no heed. He traveled rapidly across the lawn, rounded the far side of the church, then disappeared from view. Shedding her temporary paralysis, she continued toward the church. Surely there was a telephone in the vestibule.

The gravel crunched beneath her feet as she made her way along the path from the graveyard to the building. An ancient, musty odor emanating from the damp stone walls mingled with the scent of the gnarled wisteria vine crowning the doorway.

The wooden door stood ajar. Pushing it wider, she slipped inside and groped the nearest wall until she located an electric switch. The bare bulb cast a dim light that revealed nothing more than a solitary table holding only some pamphlets, a guest book, and several outdated church bulletins. There was no telephone. In the sanctuary beyond, rows of primitive benches faced the chancel. It held only a stone altar, an upright piano against the wall, and slat-backed chairs for clergy and choir. A short curved stairway led to the elevated pulpit. Clearly, the modern world had swept past Broad Run Church. The telephone company, in particular, had not invaded its solemnity to service either the congregation or wayfarers.

Dismayed, Amanda was preparing to leave when a door behind the pulpit creaked open. Despite the gloom, she recognized the form that emerged as the very one she had seen in the churchyard. Obviously a clergyman, hardly the specter she initially believed, he mounted the steps to the pulpit and flipped several pages of the oversized Bible as if searching for notes he had left there earlier. He seemed so absorbed in his task that she hesitated to disturb him, but he quickly detected her presence.

His voice echoed through the empty sanctuary. "Yes? How can I help you?"

"I beg your pardon. I was looking for a phone. My car had a flat, and …"

He interrupted her hasty explanation. "Sorry. I can't make out what you're saying. One moment please, I'll be there."

She could not see his face in the gloom, but his melodic baritone voice was unmistakable. Her words fairly fell over one another. "Henry, it's Amanda."

"Amanda? What a nice surprise. But shouldn't you be practicing?" Henry descended the pulpit stairs and strode rapidly up the aisle as he spoke, the long cloak flapping about his ankles. His footfall resounded on the stone floor, erasing Amanda's fear that Henry could be the Pohick priest Sybil Clyde had described.

"To answer your question, Henry, I'd love to be practicing, but I have a new client. We had dinner in Warrenton and were on our way to see a house nearby when I had a flat tire. Mr. Ahmed, my client, is repairing it."

"And you decided to tour the local historical sites of interest while he's slaving away?" His laugh was gentle.

"Hardly. I have to confess that I'm here because of my own stupidity. Somewhere between here and the restaurant I misplaced my cell phone, so when I saw the church, I came in desperation hoping to find a pay phone to let the owner know we'll be late. But what on earth brings you here?" The harder Amanda strained to see Henry's face, the deeper he seemed to retreat into the shadows.

"I'm filling the pulpit while the regular minister is away," he said.

"You seem to gravitate to historic churches. According to the marker outside, this one is even older than Pohick."

He chuckled. "And to think that if we hadn't met there I would have been denied the pleasure of sending you back to the keyboard. Have you had time to revisit those Gershwin preludes?"

"Only last evening after an hour devoted to Grieg. I called it a day with a dash of Steve Reich for a contemporary flavor."

"You're not abandoning the French romantics, are you?"

"Never, but it's refreshing to move into the 20th century. With luck, as the years go by I'll discover new composers to champion."

They fell into another of the cozy conversations Amanda adored, chatting about music for perhaps ten minutes when he suddenly pointed toward the rear of the sanctuary. "I believe your car's ready," he said.

"Really? How do you know?"

"See for yourself."

Amanda rushed to the door and found Ali standing in the dark. Henry must have heard him coming.

"So here you are, Ms. Prescott," Ali said. "We're ready to go. Right after you left, a very helpful fellow pulled up and gave me a hand. I would have driven over to pick you up, but you took the keys."

"Sorry. I hang onto my purse and car keys by habit."

"A good habit to have," Ali said. "It's so dark here, I'm surprised you found a telephone."

"I didn't."

"No? Then what took so long?"

"I ran into a friend and we got to talking." Amanda swiveled around, expecting to introduce Henry, but there was not a soul in the sanctuary.

"Must be a slippery fellow. I don't see anyone."

"That's odd. He was right behind me. He does move quickly, though."

"And so must we if we want to see Crestmont." With that, Ali took Amanda's arm and steered her toward the highway and her car.

Crestmont was nestled comfortably between twin hillocks a few miles off the main road. At the end of a winding driveway, welcoming house lights pricked out in the deepening night to assure the homing traveler of a warm welcome.

"It looks inviting," Amanda said.

The car headlights forged ahead to warn of sinewy curves that narrowed in the approach to a small creek. Its metal bridge clanked alarmingly as the car bounded across.

"They must know when company's coming," Amanda said.

"I'd replace that right away."

Even in the dark, she could tell that Ali was frowning. "If you like history and classic architecture, you can't do better than this," she pointed out. "Thomas Jefferson designed the windows. They run from floor to ceiling."

"All the better for enjoying the view ... and seeing who is approaching." Ali observed.

"The house is maintenance-free brick," Amanda continued, determined to emphasize its selling points, despite Ali's nonchalance. She could not decide if he was truly indifferent or cunning. "And if you enjoy sitting by the fire in the wintertime, there are four large chimneys and sixteen fireplaces, eight on each floor."

"The only warmth I require is the presence of a lovely lady like yourself," Ali said, regarding Amanda with an amorous expression she had no intention of acknowledging.

"Here we are." Amanda braked, cut the engine, unhooked her seatbelt, and stepped from the car in one continuous motion to deflect his arm. Sternly, she shook her finger as he approached from the other side of the car. "I have the impression that you're not going to take this walk-through seriously. Would you rather I make apologies and tell the owner that we'll come back another day?"

Hastily, he said. "No, no. You must forgive me. I'm afraid that my bout with the tire robbed some of my enthusiasm for large impersonal houses. At this time, I'm far more inclined to favor a cozy *tête-à-tête* with my present company, just as the poet said, 'a jug of wine, a loaf of bread, and …'"

"And your favorite steed," Amanda said, trying to refocus Ali on his original purpose. "Come along. We mustn't keep them waiting."

Ali was so near she felt his breath on the nape of her neck as she pressed the front doorbell. Chimes resounded through the hall beyond and re-emerged through the open windows.

Amanda had expected either a prim servant or a dignified dowager, certainly not the young woman who responded to repeated pressure on the bell. Dressed in riding boots, jodhpurs, and a designer shirt, her platinum hair twisted into a pony tail, she appeared to be in her mid-thirties, but the aging process may have been deferred by a deft cosmetic surgeon.

"I suppose you're from the Cameron Agency," she said, her voice heavy with weariness. "I expected you much earlier."

"I'm terribly sorry to be so late," Amanda said. "We had a flat tire along the way. I misplaced me cell phone and couldn't find a pay phone, so we just took a chance and came on as soon as we were road-worthy."

The woman waved away Amanda's concern and beckoned them into the house. "It's okay. I found the message on my answering machine when I came in from the stable. I've been busy with my foals and just got back to the house a little while ago myself. Thought I'd missed you."

Amanda frowned. What message? And who sent it? She thought it imprudent to interrogate the woman, who probably knew more than she did. Rather than expose herself as an incompetent greenhorn, Amanda played it cool and introduced Ali. "Mr. Ahmed is looking for a place to raise thoroughbreds."

"Glad to meet you. I'm Bunny Phelps. Any horseman's a friend of mine." Bunny extended her hand to Amanda, all the while appraising Ali. Her manufactured smile blocked the bitterness Amanda marked bubbling beneath the surface.

Ali oozed continental charm as he clasped Bunny's hand for longer than either woman anticipated. "You're a breeder?"

"Occasionally. With me, it's a hobby. With my first husband, it was a business. He had a couple of Derby entries that did well. He also met a lady jockey who demanded more of his time and money than I cared to forfeit. My second husband was no better. He romanced me for two months, rushed me to the altar, and showed his true colors a week later by admitting that he married me for rumors of a fortune that probably doesn't exist. I'll do everything in my power to make sure it doesn't materialize in his favor. All of which explains why I'm here by myself. My next move is to get rid of this albatross." She gestured broadly, the sweep of her hand visually encompassing the huge house and its environs.

"I certainly don't see this beautiful place an albatross," Amanda said. "Most people would think it a joy to live here."

"Oh, don't take me wrong," Bunny said. "I'm actually fond of it. I was born and raised here, so it's home. But at this point in my life, I'm exploring other options. I've applied to the University of Virginia law school. If they accept me, I want to be ready to go, no strings attached. A law degree should come in handy, especially if I meet any more cads and fortune hunters"

Bunny's willingness to discuss her private life with strangers was making Amanda uncomfortable. To change the topic, she asked, "Do you mind if we look around?"

"Be my guest. Except for my housekeeper who stations herself in front of the television in her room when the basic chores are done, I'm the only one living here, so you can wander around to your heart's content. I expect you'll have to come back during daylight to see the out-buildings. There are two barns, a stable, a guest house, an office, and a pool with dressing rooms adjacent."

"Splendid." Ali bowed graciously and moved ahead into the parlor.

Amanda started to follow him, but Bunny pulled her aside. Her bony fingers dug into the flesh of Amanda's forearm as she asked, *sotto voce*, "What are his credentials?"

"What do you mean?"

"Can he afford this place?" Bunny's slow deliberate question dripped with suspicion.

"So far as I know, he can. The Camerons investigate their clients' backgrounds thoroughly enough to know their financial limits. Judging from the sheet the office gave me, I'd say that Mr. Ahmed has none."

Bunny relaxed. "Good. The sooner I can sell this place, the better. Between the taxes, the upkeep and the spookiness, it's a burden I need to unload."

Amanda drew a long breath. "Did you say 'spookiness'?"

"I sure did. Have you any idea what it's like to live alone? In a place this size? Talk about creepy! This house shivers and shakes all night. You'd think the ghosts from the family plot were having a convention. The sounds never bothered me when I was growing up, not even after my parents died, or while I was married to those rats, but now it's enough to send me to the funny farm. It must be the curse I inherited from my Davis ancestors."

"Davis? The house I sold near Purcellville was built by a Davis family, but I imagine it's no relation. Davis is a fairly common surname."

Bunny's eyes lit up. "Not around here. There was only one Davis family among the early Loudoun County settlers."

"Then we're talking about the same family?"

"The one and only. I inherited that house and sold it to a local builder named Tom Grigsby five years ago." Pouting, Bunny placed her hands on her hips. "Don't tell me he sold it again."

"Yes, it hasn't been two weeks since the closing."

"Who's the buyer?"

"A man from Chicago. His wife likes very old places."

"Well, she'd better like it. It's the oldest house in Loudoun County."

"I gather there's a fascinating story about it and the people who built it."

"You gather exactly right. My ancestors weren't like most immigrants coming here to seek their fortune; they brought theirs with them."

Amanda was hooked. "Really? What sort of fortune?"

"Everything they could gather and take on board ship when the first King George's men hounded them out of Wales. Tradition says they arrived with barrels and chests filled with gold, silver, and pewter, wealth far beyond what their neighbors had."

"Were they criminals.?"

Bunny laughed. "Not by today's standards. Their crime was founding a church that defied the Church of England. That didn't sit well with those in power, so my ancestors came here to worship as they pleased."

"They must have fit right in. Many of the early settlers came seeking freedom of worship."

"That's true, although few had assets to compare with my family's. Even so, they weren't snobs. They lived and worshiped very simply. The meetinghouse they built near their home is very plain, not the least bit elaborate inside, and the house is very ordinary as colonial homes go. Since seven generations have lived in it and examined every nook and cranny without finding the fortune, folks believe that the meetinghouse is a more likely spot. The way I look at it, if the fortune had been hidden in either place, it would have been discovered by now."

"It couldn't simply vanish," Amanda said.

"I'm sure it didn't. I'm inclined to think it's in a third location nobody has considered. Wherever it is, I'm sure it's waiting patiently for someone to solve the clues the immigrants left behind."

"Clues, you say? What kind of clues?"

Bunny rolled her eyes. "That's another story. They're hidden in a few written lines that make no sense, but they must have meant something important to the person who left them for his descendants. The clues have been passed down to each generation. So far, nobody in our family, including me, has understood them."

"Are you the only family member today with access to the clues?"

"I'm the only family member, period. Most families multiply from one generation to another. Ours is the exception. Every family line has died off. I'm the last surviving member of that Davis line."

"I see. Then it really is your responsibility to solve the clues. If you don't, the fortune may be lost forever."

Bunny heaved a sigh. "That's why my so-called husband is desperate. He thinks I know more than I do. At first, he tried to sweet-talk me into telling him where it's hidden. When he realized that wasn't working, he became abusive. I ordered him out and got a restraining order."

"Fortune hunting certainly brings out the worst in people." Amanda drew a deep breath. "Perhaps I should tell you I'm beginning to suspect that the man who just bought the house knows about the fortune."

"Really? Why do you think so?"

"As soon as he became aware of the house, he became very excited. He even brought up the topic of a church nearby. From what you say, I imagine he meant the meetinghouse. Since he's new to the area, how do you suppose he learned about it?"

Bunny shrugged. "Stories about hidden fortunes make the rounds. All the old-timers in Loudoun County know about it. Someone could have easily passed along the word to their friends and relatives in other parts of the country."

"I suppose that's possible," Amanda said. "So if my client bought your ancestral home, the meetinghouse can't be far."

"It's less than a mile away."

"Is it still in use?"

Bunny shook her head. "Goodness, no. Hasn't been used for two hundred years. Right after the Revolution, the members built a larger one in Leesburg."

"If it's been abandoned that long, it must be in dreadful shape."

"Not so bad as you'd expect. In those days, folks built things to last."

"Is it possible that the fortune is in the newer meetinghouse instead of the original?"

"Anything's possible, but the rumors about the first meetinghouse persist, like the stories of a secret room in the house. If there were any truth behind that, someone would have proved its existence by now."

Had it not crossed Amanda's mind that Bunny could be an important ally, she never would have uttered her next remark. "The room does exist. Tom Grigsby showed me the staircase leading to it."

Bunny's mouth flew open. "You're serious?"

Amanda nodded. "He made me promise not to tell the buyer about the room."

"Good for him. How did he find it?"

"By comparing the inside and outside dimensions."

A wry smile crossed Bunny's lips. "Sounds like a clever guy. I should meet someone like that for a change."

"Tom Grigsby told me he felt obligated to honor the secret."

Bunny moved closer and lowered her voice. "Did you get the impression he found anything of value there?"

"No. He was pleased simply to have figured out how to reach the room. Besides, Burke Cameron vouches for his honesty."

"Burke Cameron? That name isn't familiar."

Amanda reddened. "No reason it should be. He's the son of the agency's owner."

"Is he reliable?"

"Yes. I believe he is."

Turning aside, Bunny spoke softly, as if addressing an invisible presence. "So the secret room really exists. Then there's a chance the code *is* valid."

Even as she spoke, a faint ghostly moan wafted through the open windows.

"I see what you mean about this place being spooky," Amanda said, forcing a laugh. She dismissed the sound as nothing more than the evening breeze titillating the chimney tops.

Bunny responded sharply. "It's no joke. Lots of ghosts haunt this house. Before the British burned down the White House in 1813, Dolley Madison sent some of the treasures here. Then during the Civil War, Union officers fleeing the

Confederate soldiers were brought here by a young minister from the church down the road. He hid them under hay in his wagon."

"You must be talking about the Broad Run Church. I was just there looking for a phone."

"Were you? Then you might have noticed the graveyard. The minister is buried there. They say he died of a broken heart."

"From the trauma of the war?"

"In a roundabout way. He was engaged to Lisette, daughter of the owner of Crestmont, and he knew the family would hide the officers. Unfortunately, Lisette fell in love with one of the officers and eloped with him."

"Leaving the minister at the altar, so to speak."

"Yes. I've always felt bad about it. Lisette and the officer settled down here after the war and were members of the church where the minister continued to preach until his death. They were my great-grandparents." A sad smile crossed Bunny's face. "I inherited a tintype of the minister that Lisette cherished until the end of her life. Perhaps she never fell out of love with him. He was a handsome man with the kind of smile that would curl your toes if you were young and single. To tell the truth, I wouldn't mind meeting him, even if he were the ghost I blame for all the noise around here." She threw back her head and laughed aloud.

At that precise moment, Ali reappeared. "Very interesting atmosphere," he said. "When I was in one of the upstairs bedrooms, I could have sworn I heard someone tapping on the window. I looked out, thinking it was a tree limb, but there was nothing there. Is this house haunted?"

Bunny and Amanda exchanged glances, signaling a joint decision to say nothing to Ali about their conversation.

"You have an active imagination," Amanda told him. Thanks to her encounters with Tom Grigsby, Henry Conyers, and now Bunny, she almost believed that the sounds Ali heard had *nothing* to do with his imagination.

The Short Hill, Loudoun County, Virginia, 1775

A solitary candle illuminated the room. Outside, rain splattered the window pane. Occasional streaks of lightning and rolls of thunder dominated the gloom. The man on the bed sought to speak, but his voice was weak, his effort to rise fruitless. He beckoned to his eldest son.

The younger man rushed to the bedside. "What do you want to tell me, Father?"

Thomas Davis grasped his son's arm. "The treasures ... are they ...?

John Davis covered his father's hand with his own. "Fear not. I know what to do when the time comes."

"Good, good." Thomas Davis fell back on the pillow, his body wracked by coughing. Just before his eyes closed for the last time, he muttered, "Hiraeth ... Gwlad."

John Davis searched his mother's face. "What does he say?"

A sad smile crossed her lips. "He longs for Wales."

"Wales? But why? His life was so much better here."

"So it was. The journey to America brought your father all the good fortune wished upon him at our departure, and yet I know that deep in his heart he dreamed of fulfilling the promise."

John Davis stroked his chin. "The promise, you say. Now I understand."

He stood abruptly and walked toward the window. Somewhere in the dark Eastern sky, at that very moment, his father was realizing the promise. Until his own turn came, he was responsible for furthering the ministry that drew his father to the colonies and far away from his homeland, the Gwlad.

CHAPTER ELEVEN

The next morning, Amanda stopped at the Cameron Agency before collecting Ali for their next foray into the countryside. She was still mulling over the strange events of the previous evening when she noticed a package on her desk. The attached card bore Burke's aggressive handwriting:

> *Ms. Prescott: Here is your new cell phone. Please hang onto it. Your number has been changed to prevent unauthorized people from receiving your messages. BC*

How did he know she had misplaced her phone? Earlier, a thorough examination of her car failed to locate it wedged under the seat, as she had hoped. Shoving that puzzlement into the background, she rang up Bunny Phelps. After setting a time to view Crestmont's grounds and out-buildings, she arranged to stop first at Maplelawn, an estate that had just come on the market. The new listing caught her attention as she scanned the realty website. It sounded like a close match with Ali's needs.

Before turning off the computer, she satisfied her curiosity about Bunny's latest estranged husband by accessing the recent Loudoun County marriages. She did not have to scroll far to find the marriage license application of Elizabeth Phelps, 37, and Jerry Ewing, 49. Did Bunny realize the day she filled out the form that she was promising her heart to a scoundrel and was destined to be single once again within a few months?

Amanda was gathering her belongings to leave when Burke's voice came over the intercom, whisking her back to reality. "Ms. Prescott? Are you still there? Mr. Ahmed just called. He's wondering why you haven't shown up yet."

Before she could reach the desk to flip on the answer switch, Burke was blocking the doorway. "You have a habit of appearing silently ... like the Pohick priest," she said.

Burke's cocky grin vanished. Feeling in control, Amanda added, "It so happens that I'm on my way to pick up Mr. Ahmed, but it's lucky that I stopped here first. You may be interested to learn that a listing I happened upon a few minutes ago sounds even better than the estates he's seen."

He appraised her sternly. "Ms. Prescott, your ability to take matters into your own hands is admirable, but I *must* know where you are at all times."

"For the client's safety, or mine?"

His eyes were hard as steel. "Spunk becomes you. Please do not leave without giving Robin your new itinerary."

"I gave it to her a few minutes ago. And thank you for the new cell phone, Mr. Cameron. How did you know I'd misplaced mine?"

A half-laugh. "Are you into the paranormal sufficiently to believe it was ESP?"

"That's as good an explanation as any." It was difficult to suppress a smile as she gathered her briefcase and bag. That accomplished, she swept past him, mindful that the glances they exchanged were conspiratorial.

She met Ali at the Vienna Metro Station, as he had instructed. He swung into the car, his engaging grin leading the way. "I hope you don't mind my calling Mr. Cameron, but I didn't want to lose any time with you. I can't remember when I've enjoyed being with someone as much as I enjoyed our time together yesterday."

Warily, Amanda eyed his subtle attempt to edge closer before adjusting his seatbelt. She pulled away from the station focused on the road ahead and hoping her measured response masked her annoyance. "The Cameron Agency appreciates your patronage. However, you need to understand that my job is to locate the perfect setting for your horse farm. Period."

"And so far, I'm delighted with your service," he said.

Ali's suavity troubled Amanda, but she had little opportunity to assess his intentions. For the next half-hour, she was preoccupied with locating the most efficient route to Maplelawn with the least number of stoplights. It seemed forever to her before the commuter traffic ebbed and they were moving apace along the highway. Upon nearing Dulles Airport, her attention drifted to several jumbo jets slowing dramatically, seeming to hover aloft as they awaited landing instructions from the tower.

Their presence jogged Amanda's memory of her mother's excitement in describing the days of yore in Northern Virginia. She had not spared her daughter a single detail. Those impromptu lessons, Amanda knew, were every bit as detailed as those her mother planned for her university students. Off to the right, she recalled, the airport's vast acreage now owned by the transportation authority and surrounded by electronic fences had been the site of thriving plantations two centuries earlier. The homesteads, slave quarters, out-buildings, and adjacent graveyards were bulldozed for lack of information about descendants to facilitate airport construction before historians could halt their destruction.

Amanda smiled to herself, envisioning the reaction those early settlers would have if they returned today. Educated in the quaint rural traditions and religious beliefs of an agrarian age, they would be terrified and regard the jets as fearsome omens. So, too, would they be puzzled by the brick townhouses and shopping centers bordering the highway for as far as the eye could see. An extension of suburbia to accommodate the new hires of the burgeoning government and private offices, they were rapidly obliterating what remained of open land from Bull's Run to the Potomac River. Idly she wondered what changes would be observed by those traveling the same route two centuries hence.

As she maneuvered away from the industrial center toward the countryside, Amanda found it every bit as challenging to make small talk with Ali as it was to ignore his pointed remarks and references to the pleasant times he foresaw in the future for the two of them once he was established in the area. When finally she grew too uncomfortable to parry his verbal thrusts, she switched on the radio to search for a good music station. The radio in her own car was programmed to her favorite music stations, but now she was reduced to hunt and peck. She quickly discovered that a large chunk of morning airtime was inundated by country, rap, or hip-hop recordings, while most of the remaining stations were outlets for noisy talk-show discussions of hot-button topics chosen to generate phone calls from listeners whose hazy qualifications provided scant basis for the opinions they dispersed with zeal.

After twirling the dials for several minutes and despairing of tuning into anything worthwhile, she finally hit the classical music station. No sooner had she settled back, content, than Ali began fidgeting in his seat, annoyed by the repetitive notes of Chopin's "Raindrop" prelude.

"That's very depressing on a sunny day," he said. "Do you really enjoy it?"

"Sorry." She turned off the radio. "I should have asked. It's not one of my favorite pieces, but it was a big improvement over the other options." She feared the silence would revitalize Ali's romantic musings, but for once he seemed content to gaze at the passing scenery. She almost wished she knew what was going through his mind. Then again, she was glad she was not that perceptive.

At the exit highlighted on her map, she abandoned the highway for a pastoral road bordered by the potpourri of lush, aromatic shrubs that run riot throughout Virginia's gentrified countryside. She turned off the air-conditioning and rolled down her window to drink in the atmosphere.

"That delicious perfume sets the stage for Maplelawn, Mr. Ahmed. The photographs I saw this morning are stunning."

"As is my present companion," Ali said, artfully twisting the topic back to Amanda.

Before she could conjure up a safe response, the estate entrance loomed directly ahead. She eased onto a formal drive lined with ancient maples. The pristine columns of a sprawling neo-classical house were visible at a distance.

"The wing on the right is the servants' quarters. It adjoins the kitchen," she explained.

"And the wing on the left?"

"I believe there's a library and some sort of recreation room."

"So it's fairly modern," Ali mused.

"As modern as a restoration can make it. Of course the house itself goes back several decades before the Civil War, so if you like old places you have a documented historical building. At the same time, you have all the plumbing and electronics of the space age."

"The outbuildings look serviceable enough," Ali said. Amanda noted that he was observing the barn and paddock visible some distance to the right. They were designed like miniatures of the main house. "Will we drive over there later?"

"Let's go now. We're a few minutes early." Abruptly, Amanda turned onto a gravel lane.

When she could proceed no further, she parked between the buildings. Ali climbed from the car and hurried around to her door, a gentleman without dispute. As they walked toward the paddock, they heard the whinny of horses and a man's voice deep in a monologue as he tended to his duties.

Amanda sought to grab his attention. "Hello, there,"

The speaker turned toward them slowly, exuding the orneriness of a native son of the land with an innate dislike of city slickers. Amanda hoped that her crisp suit with the Cameron logo embroidered on the jacket pocket would exclude her from his mental category of giddy society women who visit horse farms for unprofessional reasons.

The man's leathery skin, the product of years spent outdoors, contrasted with rheumy blue eyes that seemed bleached by the sun. "This ain't the main house, even it if looks it," he warned, revealing some missing teeth as he spat tobacco juice onto the ground.

The projectile landed inches from Amanda's feet, but she stood firm. I'm Amanda Prescott from the Cameron Agency. My client, Mr. Ahmed, would like to inspect the facilities before we look at the house."

Ali extended his hand. He was obliged to hold it outstretched for several moments while the other man pondered the wisdom of acknowledging the newcomers.

Relenting, the man pumped Ali's hand several times to signify approval. "Okey Luckett here. I'm the Maplelawn trainer, just like my daddy and his daddy before him."

Ali smiled broadly. "You have a good heritage. Can you show me around?"

Okey frowned and consulted the bare space on his wrist where a watch might be expected. "Five minutes is all I have."

"That's about all we can spare, so this will work out just fine," Amanda assured him.

Okey studied her critically. "You're welcome to follow along, missy, just so you don't step where you hadn't oughta. Mind you, look out where you go with them heels."

"They're no higher than the heels on riding boots," Amanda said, amused by his provincialism.

Okey scratched his chin. "Hmmm. So they're not."

"Ms. Prescott is a very wise lady," Ali said, as he took Amanda's arm and guided her gently past the horse stalls.

The tour was swift, as Okey had promised, but concise, with Ali learning everything he seemed to want to know about the training facilities, as well as the fact that Okey and his wife occupied the servants' quarters and were included in the purchase deal. Okey's field of operation was limited to the horses, while his wife ruled over the main house. Amanda gathered that Mrs. Luckett was a combination caretaker and cook.

"The gardener lives in the small house at the end of the lane near the back entrance," Okey said. "The rest of the folks on the staff work by day. They come from round about."

"You mean they live locally?" Ali asked.

"That's what I said, didn't I?" Okey provoked a grin that Amanda shared with Ali. As he turned to help her into the car, Ali said, "It's been a pleasure meeting you, Mr. Luckett. I'm impressed with your operation, and if I decide to purchase the property, I'll be delighted to work with you. Since I travel a great deal, I'll appreciate knowing that you're in charge."

"So? You think you'll buy this place?" Okey looked Ali squarely in the eye.

"It's a strong possibility. Of course, I'll have to see the house, compare it with the other places I'm considering, then think about the advantages and disadvantages of them all to make the best choice."

Amanda slipped into the driver's seat. "We do thank you, Mr. Luckett."

Okey was not ready to relinquish Ali. "Where else are you looking?"

Ali glanced toward Amanda for help. "Can you tell him? I'm not familiar with the area."

"We've been to two estates this side of Warrenton," she said.

"Betcha I know which ones they are." Okey looked as if a secret inside his head was about to explode.

"You probably do," Amanda said. "I imagine all the horse breeders stick together."

"No, can't say they do," Okey said. "Most of 'em are loners. Always trying to develop a filly that'll knock the others out of the race. Like the guy that used to be up at Crestmont."

"You mean Phelps?"

"Yep. That's the guy. A real schemer."

"He's not there any longer since his wife divorced him," Amanda said.

"Yep. But some women never give up. Darned if she didn't marry again. Another bad egg. Never did know his name."

"He's out of the picture also," Amanda said, hoping Okey would drop the subject.

"Don't she wish." Okey chortled to himself and ejected another arc of tobacco juice. "Heard he's after the Davis fortune. 'Course two hundred years are gone and nobody's found it yet. Folks hereabouts think she knows where it is, though. Maybe has it hidden in her safe. When he got wind of that, he married her, but she's a smart cookie. Didn't take her long to figure him out. Lucky she never bothered to change her last name to his before sending him packing. He ain't giving up, though."

"If his name's not on the deed, he'll have no claim to ownership when Bunny gets a buyer," Amanda said, aware that Ali was listening intently.

Okey would not give up. "Don't you believe it. He's a real operator. Looks to me like one of those blasted skinheads who go around beatin' up innocent people. Friend of mine out near Purcellville saw him driving around the back roads with a couple of other tough birds. Thought they might be up to some kind of dastardly plot." Okey spat again. "But no sense bashing him around. You've got to get up to the house. My wife has lots to do so she can't sit around waitin' for you to show up."

Upon arriving at the house, Amanda realized at once that Okey had not minimized his wife's impatience. Like her husband, Nettie Luckett "put no truck in city folk." Clearly, she was intent on serving her absent master by keeping the premises spotless in case he chose to vacate his Georgetown townhouse for a sporting weekend. From the family history Nettie divulged as she led them through one exquisite room into the next, Amanda deduced that the recent death of his wife had changed the banker's outlook on life. Since the horses were her hobby alone, he had decided to dispose of the property—house, stables, and personnel—in one fell swoop.

Amanda sensed that Ali was impressed by Maplelawn and would be happy to meet the asking price with no questions asked. Still, there was the promise to Bunny Phelps. As they pulled away from the house, Amanda reminded Ali that Bunny was expecting them.

"By all means. We must go there now, but before we go back to your office, I insist on taking you to lunch."

"You know I can't accept your invitation to lunch. I'll be happy to treat you, though, as a guest of the Cameron Agency."

Ali spoke sharply. "In my culture, women are women, not businessmen. Instead of defying nature, you must become dependent on a man."

"Mr. Ahmed, in my culture, many women must work to support themselves. I am one of them. My goal is to help clients purchase a home, not to socialize. I thank you to keep that in mind."

"We shall see, we shall see," Ali murmured.

When they passed Broad Run Church, Amanda cast a wistful glance in that direction, half expecting to see Henry Conyers strolling through the grounds, but they were deserted save for a solitary mourning dove perched on the roof.

In daylight, the approach to Crestmont was unremarkable. The pasture, green and rolling, was pleasant enough, and the out-buildings, though not as dramatic in appearance as those of Maplelawn, were clean and respectable looking. As they pulled up before the house, Amanda was taken aback by drawn shutters masking the long, formal windows that had glowed so invitingly the previous evening.

She turned to Ali. "Strange, isn't it?"

He smiled, an enigmatic grin that struck her as bordering on derangement. Before Amanda could react, he bolted across the seat, seized her roughly, then began kissing her with an ardor she had anticipated from the moment they met and had tried desperately to avoid.

Summoning reserve strength, she beat his chest with her fists. That had no effect, but when she bit his lip, he relinquished his hold. His hand shot up to stem the bleeding. Enveloped in fury, feeling no remorse, Amanda hissed, "I told you this is strictly a business relationship."

Unbridled anger flashed through Ali's eyes and a vein bulged at his temple. Amanda drew back, believing he was about to hit her. Just as quickly, the vein ceased pulsating and he grinned evilly. "A spitfire, are you? Women in my culture know better than to resist."

"Women in my culture call the police, and that's exactly what I'll do if you dare touch me again."

Amanda bounded onto the gravel trace, slammed the car door with finality, and marched up the front steps, Ali at her heels. The chimes echoed through an empty house, defying her repeated attempts to rouse Bunny. "That's very strange. When I spoke with her this morning, she promised she'd be here."

As Amanda moved to leave, Ali grasped her elbow forcefully. "Come. We'll try the stable. Remember, she was there last evening."

They proceeded to the stable in silence. Inside, several mares and their foals stood in the stalls. There was no sign of Bunny.

"This is really odd. I can't understand where she ..."

At that precise moment, they both saw a riding boot protruding from the far stall. Bunny Phelps lay on the floor, motionless.

Ali lunged ahead, blocking Amanda's path. By the time she reached Bunny, Ali was rising from a kneeling position. He muscled Amanda away, saying, "You don't need to see this."

Out of nowhere came a power Amanda never knew she possessed. Screaming, "Get out of my way," she shoved Ali with such force that he lost his balance and toppled into the straw.

The Short Hill, Loudoun County, Virginia, 1785

John Davis held the paper over the candle flame. As if by magic, the secret writing appeared. He studied the text, smiling to himself. Now that the strife with the British was over, he felt comfortable about revealing the message his father had written in invisible ink—a mixture of a ferrous sulfate and water—between the lines of his final sermon.

It was in code, a caution his Freemason training emphasized. Until his own death, nobody else would be privy to the sheet, not even his son and namesake who had faced defeat by the British redcoats at Guilford Court House and earned victory when Cornwallis surrendered at Yorktown.

Because the Treaty of Paris ending the strife had been in effect for more than a year, John Davis was convinced that his new nation would endure. And yet there was ample reason for him to harbor the secret that he and his father had shared for two decades.

CHAPTER TWELVE

Amanda dropped down beside Bunny to check her vital points. Despite a severe blow on the head, she was still breathing. In the adjacent stall, a horse whinnied. Amanda groped for her cell phone and dialed 911, all the while monitoring Ali's facial expression. Within the fraction of a moment, it had shifted from authoritative to unabashed hatred. Even as he scrambled to his feet and tried to feign composure, Amanda knew she had overstepped the rigid boundaries drawn for women in his culture.

Removing herself from his volatile presence, she rushed outside to dial the office. Too late, she realized that the number was not programmed into the new phone. Even worse, her thoughts were so muddled that the familiar combination eluded her. With every attempt, her trembling fingers hit at least one incorrect numeral. After several futile tries, she knew that her only hope of contacting Sheila—or Burke—was to retrieve the sheet of phone numbers in the glove compartment.

She raced down the slope to the car, yanked open the door, and located the blessed sheet. Frantically, she dialed once, twice, perhaps a dozen times. No matter how often she tried, it was impossible to get through. The line was continually busy. Robin chatting with one of her girl friends, she surmised.

Abandoning all hope of contacting anyone at Cameron Agency, she climbed back up to the stable. Ali stood by the entrance squinting at a slip of paper.

"What do you have there?" Amanda asked.

It was too late for him to secrete his find, so he shrugged, as if to dismiss its presence. "It's nothing at all, just a scrap she was clutching in her hand. Doesn't make any sense."

"Let me see. Maybe there's a clue about who did this to her." Amanda snatched the crumpled sheet from his hand and read it, quickly at first, more deliberately a second time. Her heart pounded. Every nerve of her body shouted that this was the mysterious code Bunny had mentioned.

> *Drop the plumb line of truth to the all-seeing eye,*
> *Find the key to the secrets wedged halfway between.*
> *Follow ten degrees west, fifty perches now south,*
> *Neath the hickory tree, reason measures the sky.*

Ali frowned. "Do you make anything of it?"

Amanda feigned nonchalance. "Bunny told me her hobby is writing. This must be one of her poems. I'm not a proper judge, but it doesn't strike me as being very good."

Ali accepted her explanation. Knowing it would be far safer in her hands than in his, she vowed to retain it until Bunny recovered. The moment he turned back into the stable, she tucked it into her jacket pocket and fled outside to await the police.

It was then that she noticed a sudden shift in the weather. The sun, riding high above the Blue Ridge range, was sliding behind dark, scudding clouds. Raw breezes whipped tendrils of hair across her cheek. Was this the vanguard of a summer storm?

Even before the police car topped by a revolving red beacon rumbled across the metal bridge and swept around the final curve of the driveway, the piercing siren of the ambulance directly behind pained Amanda's eardrums. Both vehicles halted before her in a virtual tie.

While the medics tended to Bunny, the officers—every inch professionals—conducted their business. They questioned Amanda and Ali, recorded their responses, and sketched the scene. Soon after the ambulance left for the hospital, they told Amanda she and Ali were free to leave.

Back on the main road, still shaking, Amanda was astonished by Ali's quick recovery. All smiles, his dark eyes glinting provocatively, he pressed her about lunch. "At times like these, companionship is important."

She shook her head. It should have been obvious to him that she was in no condition to socialize or to conduct business. "No thank you. I need time to pull myself together. We'll talk tomorrow about the houses we've seen."

To Amanda's relief, he did not protest, and by the time she pulled into the Cameron parking lot after dropping him off at the Metro station, she had drummed him and his courteous parting bow from her mind.

Robin met her at the door. "How awful for you, Amanda."

"You know?"

"Of course. The authorities have already been here talking to Mr. Cameron."

"How is that possible?"

"Word travels fast, especially when a Cameron agent is on the scene."

"I see," Amanda said.

Burke Cameron's voice broke into her thoughts. "Ms. Prescott, please come with me."

He had arrived quietly and dominated the doorway opening onto the hallway. Obeying without question, she let him escort her to his office. He closed the door carefully, then positioned a leather chair across the desk from his. He motioned her to sit down. Was he going to berate her for getting into a sticky situation? If so, she had ample ammunition ready to convince him that she had not knowingly driven into the scene of an attempted murder.

Burke removed his glasses. His steel blue eyes looked straight into hers. "Please don't be afraid, Amanda. I need your help. From the top, tell me exactly what happened."

Amanda recognized a sincerity, even a vulnerability, in his expression. The instant he spoke her name, she felt protected. Breathing much easier, she began to describe the meeting with Bunny Phelps the previous evening, endeavoring to recall every remark she made in case it was significant. She concluded with a vivid report of the scene they came upon earlier. All the while, Burke sat with his elbows on his desk, his chin resting on folded hands. Occasionally he nodded, evaluating each statement far more carefully than would the typical employer.

When Amanda finished, he sat quietly, thoughtfully, his eyes still riveted on hers. Finally, "Anything else?"

"Connected with Bunny, you mean?" She thought a moment. "Her revelation about the hidden treasure caught my attention."

"Treasure?"

"The family treasure hidden by the immigrant. She thinks her second husband believed she knew where to find it, but she doesn't."

"I see," he said. The corner of his mouth twitched, then rose into a half-smile. "You needn't limit your thoughts to Bunny. What about our friend Ahmed?"

"Ali?" He had caught her unaware. She masked her nervousness with a laugh. "He's probably perfectly harmless, but I'll be glad to make a sale and get as far from him as possible."

Burke did not smile. "Tell me exactly what you mean."

"Maybe it's woman's intuition, but he frightens me. He's a perfect clone of Hollywood's version of a wealthy emir. I can't help thinking he must be a professional actor."

Burke tilted back in his chair and smiled. "You're a born detective."

"I don't understand."

"What I mean, Amanda, is that you're exactly right."

Now it was her turn to probe. "Are you telling me he's not a legitimate client?"

There it was again, the enigmatic smile. "I'm saying nothing you haven't thought. He lifted your cell phone, you know."

"No, I didn't, but how do you …?"

"I saw him take it from your bag at The Depot."

"Then you *were* following me. Because I was in danger?"

He nodded. "I'm sorry I got you into this. I'll explain my selfish reasons in good time. When he took that phone and you were left without any way of contacting the office, I knew we were heading for pay dirt."

Expelling what breath she had left, Amanda clutched the arms of her chair. "Mr. Cameron, this huge charade has nothing to do with real estate, does it?"

"Not in a pig's eye, Amanda." Grinning, he tossed her a sly wink before he grew serious once more, his eyes piercing hers. "Would you mind if I examine your purse?"

"My purse?"

"In case he's bugged it and can track you."

She gasped. "You think that's possible?"

"Everything's possible in this business."

Without hesitation she handed him her purse and watched him check every item, every crevice in a thoroughly professional manner. "You're clear." He handed it back. "Now we have to make certain he has no more opportunities to be near you."

Amanda trembled, remembering how Ali had grabbed her that morning. "I thought my main concern was repelling his romantic advances. What do you know that I don't?"

"More than you can begin to guess, Amanda. Think now, is there anything you've forgotten to tell me."

"I ... I'm not sure."

"Connections. That's what we're after. Can you make any connections between the places you've been and the people you've met?"

"Maybe." Her thoughts flew first to Henry Conyers and Tom Grigsby. "The coincidences are there all right, but I don't know what you're looking for."

"I'm not surprised. It's time to set you straight. Once we compare notes, other important clues should come to your mind." Burke scribbled something on a notepad. He ripped off the top sheet along with several underneath that still bore an imprint. Shoving the original into her hand, he pocketed the others.

The message read: *Can't talk here. Meet me in the Leesburg parking garage at 6 p.m.*

Amanda was about to blurt a comment when his eyes cautioned silence. "By the way, Martin's Service Station dropped off your car. It's in the parking lot."

Her hands flew to her hips. "Well it certainly is about time. Did he leave the bill?"

"There's no charge, Amanda. It's on the house, part of the whole package." He grinned at her reaction. "I do suggest, however, that you leave the company car here and take your own ... if you plan to do any shopping this afternoon."

"Shopping?"

Again his eyes pierced hers. "You mentioned that you might be going out."

She considered the note in her hand. Was their conversation being monitored? Certainly something curious was afoot. "Are you hinting that someone might be after me and gunning for the company car?"

His broad smile signaled relief. "Exactly. And don't stop by your apartment for any reason."

Amanda frowned. He had just foiled her plan to hurry home and change into something a bit more attractive for their meeting in Leesburg. "No?"

"No." His stern expression sealed the non-negotiable order.

Softly, she said, "It must be the Gallows Road curse."

"Gallows Road curse?"

She smiled up at him. "I don't know that there is such a thing, but from my very first night at Cameron Terrace, I've wondered if ghosts from the past are still cavorting through the neighborhood and causing havoc. I certainly have had my share of mishaps."

He smiled back. "That's out of my domain, Amanda. I prefer dealing with tangible adversaries, but since we have to separate temporarily, there's no harm in keeping in touch vicariously."

With that, he reached into his CD collection, selected one, and placed it on the turntable. The moment the music began, Amanda gasped. "That's *my* recording of Faure's 'Pavane.'"

Burke's expression softened. "One of my favorites. You give it such a plaintive touch that the listener wants to reach out and hug you. I'm sorry I wasn't able to deny Ali that pleasure." As Amanda felt herself turn a brilliant shade of red, he added. "In the meantime, your interpretation of the Gershwin Prelude gives me energy I never knew I had. Without your CD, I'd be lost."

Amanda's voice was stuck in her throat. "But how? Where …?"

"I bought it in the Strathmore lobby. After your concert."

Her head began to swirl. "You were *there*. It *was* you. It *had* to be you." She put her hands to her face. "Oh, Mr. Cameron … Burke, I should have known. I made a horrible mistake."

He came from behind the desk with a bound. Taking her hands gently in his, he whispered, "We'll set it right, Amanda."

She smiled up at him through tears, charged by the electricity flowing from his hands into hers. "By jumping to the wrong conclusion, I took the long way home."

His voice, that wonderful voice, soothed her. "Sometimes we need to go astray to find the road we were meant to take. Even though I'm stuck here for the next few hours, I'll spend every minute looking forward to this evening."

He produced a tissue and dabbed at the tears rolling down her face. For a moment, she expected him to gather her into his arms. Instead, eyes hooded, he took a deep breath and gave her hands a final squeeze. Drawing her from the chair, he opened the office door and spoke in a voice loud enough for Robin and anyone else down the hall to hear. "Thank you, Ms. Prescott. I can't express how much I appreciate your valuable help. Please take the afternoon off to settle your nerves. We'll see you tomorrow."

Amanda left him filled with wonder and a litany of questions. By the time she found her trusty jalopy, her brain had sifted through a multitude of scenarios.

Miraculously, the dreadful weights of the past were lifted and everything fell into place, even the key that Martin, the trustworthy repairman, had left in the ignition.

Still clutching Burke's note, she automatically tucked it into her pocket. In so doing, her fingers touched the crumpled sheet she deposited there earlier. She drew it out and examined it closely. Should she have mentioned those cryptic lines to Burke? Too late. This evening would be soon enough.

With a flip of the ignition key, the motor began to purr. It occurred to Amanda that Martin had done a pumpkin-to-coach kind of job on her old heap. Not bad for what once had seemed a hopeless case.

She maneuvered through the Tyson's Corner traffic, not quite sure where she was headed next, but her car seemed to know. Once she entered the Dulles Airport Toll Road, she coursed westward toward Leesburg at the speed limit. Three hours to kill before meeting Burke. Then why was she rushing to reach a rendezvous she could make in a half hour? Perhaps it was the oppressive heat. A brief rain shower had done little to relieve the humidity, a sure signal that it would be followed by a second storm already building in the west. Had she thought rationally, she would have stopped somewhere for a tall glass of iced tea and reconsidered her options.

But forces beyond her power were spurring her to investigate another segment of the puzzle. After all, she was the only one who had the slightest suspicion about … or was she? No matter, she had learned early in life that she must answer when destiny calls, even for small emergencies. It all went back to the times her parents emphasized the importance of taking responsibility for a situation and doing everything in her power to solve the problem. She had always endeavored to do just that, even when common sense told her it would be wiser to sit back and let someone better equipped handle the basics.

This time though, she had no doubt that it was her move. She was playing a game of chess with higher stakes than she had ever dreamed possible. A pawn no more, she was joining forces with the king, but first she had to reach the castle and find the rook … the crook.

She switched on the car radio to numb her brain with easy-listening melodies. Hurtling toward an unknown destination, she assured herself that everything would work out perfectly. With a large chunk of time on her hands, she could make it to her goal and back to Leesburg in plenty of time to meet Burke. By then, she should have unearthed more facts to capture his interest.

Before long, she crossed over Goose Creek and merged into the traffic generated by the quaint town of Leesburg. Just beyond the red brick courthouse she saw the public parking garage where she would meet Burke later in the afternoon. Why was she pulling into an empty space far ahead of the appointed hour?

She thought about her introduction to Sybil Clyde. When she accepted the author's card and acknowledged her invitation to drop in for a visit, Amanda had no idea she would be in a position to respond so soon. Now without giving Sybil the courtesy of a telephone call, Amanda anticipated finding the psychic at home just down the street.

The stone house Sybil renovated several years earlier was easy to locate, a sturdy reminder of the talented masons who began transforming the wilderness into a bustling market town several decades before anyone thought of launching a revolution. Boldly, Amanda approached the threshold and set the heavy brass knocker to work. Almost immediately, she heard footsteps from within tapping briskly in her direction.

As the door swung open, Sybil smiled broadly. "Do come in, Amanda. I've been expecting you."

Leesburg, Virginia, January 1792

The widow and children of John Davis gathered in a small anteroom of the Loudoun County Courthouse for the reading of his will. Dated November 7, 1791, it allotted his widow and each child ample inheritance for their lifetimes, but one final bequest raised several eyebrows in the room:

"I give and bequeath to the Baptist Church, whereof I was a member before I emigrated to America, the said is in the Principality of Wales, which met at the White House names Cilfowyr in the County of Pembroke and Parish of Manordeifi, the sum of one hundred pounds Virginia currency in Trust to the Elders of the said Baptist Church for the time being and for the proper use of the said Church forever."

John Davis, Jr. slammed his fist on the table. "Why did he do that? That place means nothing to us."

His mother blinked black tears. "Hiraeth, my son. Hiraeth for Gwlad."

The attorney cleared his throat. "There is one more item. Your father left instructions that you retain this paper in strict confidence."

The young man reached out to accept an envelope. In it was a wrinkled sheet, the secret code now evident between the lines of his grandfather's final sermon. He studied it for some minutes, his brow furrowed. "It makes absolutely no sense. What does it mean?"

The attorney shook his head. "That is for you to discover. Perhaps you will uncover the explanation when you look through your father's papers. If you have not solved it when the time comes to prepare your own will, then you must follow his instructions and pass it on to the next generation."

During the days, months, and years that followed, John Davis, Jr. read and re-read everything in his father's possession, but the solution evaded him.

CHAPTER THIRTEEN

Amanda followed Sybil into her cozy sitting room. Sybil motioned her guest into a deep, inviting chair, then bustled toward the kitchen to prepare tea.

"Honey and lemon, or cream?" she called over her shoulder. "What do you like?"

"Honey and lemon please," Amanda replied, all the while mesmerized by the eclectic collection of memorabilia before her. Dowsing rods were propped helter-skelter on dusty shelves. Dog and cat skeletons and rattlesnake skins inhabited a glass bookcase in company with jars of dried herbs she could not readily identify. Subduing the thought that the other woman might be concocting a witch's brew on the stove, Amanda let her gaze wander toward Sybil's desk where the ebb and flow of a multi-colored screen saver on the computer monitor confirmed that sorcery and fuzzy telepathic communications are outmoded in today's world of smart, swift electronic networks.

"Here we are." Sybil came through the doorway bearing a silver tray laden with a steaming teapot, tempting cakes, and dainty bone china teacups. She poured Amanda a cup of fragrant Earl Grey and proffered sweets that could not be refused. That ritual observed, she served herself generously before easing into an adjacent chair, "Now tell me, what brings you here so soon after our meeting?"

"It's not your theory about walk-ins, although I understand why that intrigues so many readers. What I'm after is far more immediate."

Sybil sipped her tea and nodded. "Go ahead."

"When I was working on the Hill, several articles about the projects you undertook for the government came to my attention. It occurs to me that you're one of the psychics who had a meeting of minds with astronaut Edgar Mitchell while he was in orbit."

"That's right," Sybil said. "He was so impressed with the power of mental collaboration that he established the Institute for Noetic Sciences in Palo Alto."

"But that was quite a few years ago, right after he retired from NASA. The articles indicate that you've been applying your mental powers ever since then to help our government detect and squash foreign conspiracies."

Sybil's cool eyes burned into Amanda's. "And?"

"Frankly, I believe I'm a pawn in one of the plots." There. It was out. Amanda sighed deeply and awaited confirmation.

The muscles in Sybil's jaw slackened and the corners of her prim mouth turned faintly upward. "Senator Shellenberger's prize gift," she said.

"You mean ...?"

"You were set up, Amanda. And for very good reason. As a member of the Senate Select Committee on Intelligence, he needed to have a link with possible infiltrators. When I received a psychic impression that they were establishing a base in the Northern Virginia countryside, it was obvious that their first contact would be with a realty company."

"A realty company? Whatever for?"

Sybil cast Amanda a look implying pity for not having figured that out herself. "Simply because their first need was a place of operation that would be shielded from the public, and yet not suspicious by nature. Since funding for these kinds of groups comes from interested political supporters around the world, money is no object. In this case, the location offers plenty of secluded choices in prime areas.

"As soon as I approached Senator Shellenberger with my impressions, he went immediately to the CIA and they contacted Sheila. Their goal was to identify and key in on men of suspicious backgrounds and motives in search of large, isolated properties. Everyone in that category would automatically be prospective Cameron clients because the company deals exclusively with fine estates. The only thing lacking was the bait."

"The bait?"

"An unsuspecting, yet trustworthy, agent, and so ..."

Amanda finished Sybil's sentence. "... and so Senator Shellenberger zeroed in on me because I'm single."

"There was far more to it than that," Sybil countered. "Think now. You, of all people, understand how the clandestine community operates. Who better to select for a mission of this nature?"

"Perhaps I do have a better understanding than the average person on the street, but knowing and doing are worlds apart," Amanda said. "When it comes to volunteering to place myself in danger, I'm basically a coward. That in itself should have ruled me out as a reliable undercover agent."

"For that very reason, you're perfect. You're also reserved, businesslike, attractive, and industrious. Because you weren't aware that your security upgrade was already approved, you were perfect for the intricate plot they concocted."

Amanda was jolted back to the day her escape from Washington was aborted by circumstances that had seemed at the time to be little more than bad luck.

"Best of all," Sybil continued, "because of your career in the arts, there was nothing about you and your past to arouse the suspicion of terrorists."

Amanda nearly dropped the expensive teacup.

Sybil tossed her a smile meant to calm. "Don't let me scare you. You've been protected in more ways than you could ever imagine. Someone has been able to see or hear you at all times."

"Then the Cameron Agency is ..."

"Oh, it's perfectly legitimate. As a realty company, its impeccable reputation goes back many years. That's why it's an ideal setting for covert operations, even though its prime purpose is unchanged. My friend Sheila is the part-owner of the company, but she also is the widow of a CIA operative who lost his life in the Middle East. Because of her determination to revenge his death, she turned over part of her Tysons Corner office to the other 'company.'"

"Obviously, you mean 'the company' in the sense that people refer to the CIA."

"I do. Now I must make another point clear, however, and that's the relationship between Burke Cameron and Sheila. He's not her son, not even a relative in the remotest sense. He's simply one of the best agents around. He also was very enthusiastic about utilizing your services."

Sybil laughed aloud at Amanda's expression and popped a morsel of cake into her mouth. "I'll have to tell Sheila that her flair for dramatics worked. She dabbles in amateur theatrics when she's not amassing a small fortune from her company's sales and polishing Pohick's silver. Oh yes,"—this to Amanda's incredulous stare—"she really is on the Altar Guild. That was critical to waylaying you."

"Exactly how did she manage that?"

"Senator Shellenberger knew you'd be heading down Route One to get on the Interstate at Woodbridge and avoid the usual backups in Northern Virginia. But it doesn't matter which road you travel that time of day. Since the traffic moves slowly for miles, it was simply a matter of keeping you in sight until you could be stopped 'accidentally' and permanently with a fender-bender of some kind. The bad weather turned out to be an unexpected plus."

"Okay. That explains what happened to my car, but what about Martin? It took him long enough to finish the repairs. Judging by an exchange Burke and I had this afternoon, I gather that his identity is slightly bogus."

Sybil smiled, pleased with herself. "You're catching on. Another agent just doing his duty under the cloak he most enjoys. He's an antique car buff who knows his way about body shops. As you've guessed, he didn't make your repairs. That was up to the real 'company' mechanics. Since you ended up with more than adequate transportation, a speedy repair was not a priority. The cost of repair was merely another minor budgeted expense in the scheme of things, as is your 'company' car, which is equipped with hi-tech surveillance equipment."

"And the story Martin told me about Burke being some kind of prodigal son, that was pure nonsense, I gather, simply to justify his presence in the office."

Sybil chuckled. "You fell for it, didn't you? Just like the rest of the Cameron Realty staff. There had to be a plausible explanation for bringing a long-lost family member into the fold in a prominent position. One of the lighter moments was a dramatic scene Sheila staged so Burke could convince the staff that he's slightly mad."

Amanda grinned. "That must have been the time he screamed at a new hire and frightened her away. It certainly did make an impression because Janel mentioned it my very first day. Nothing surprises me now, not even the attack on Bunny."

Sybil nodded. "That was unexpected, an early show of strength."

Without asking, Amanda sensed that the other woman knew every detail. "Was Bunny in on the plot?"

"My goodness, no. She simply was in the wrong place at the wrong time."

"Or married the wrong man," Amanda murmured.

Sybil looked up sharply. "What are you thinking?"

Amanda laughed nervously. "I could be way off base, but I believe that her second husband is my first client, Justin Elmont. I suspect that he's the one who attacked her, and I'm certain that's not his real name."

"And your reasoning ...?"

"First of all, he doesn't come up in any data base I've consulted. Secondly, his initials are the same as the man she married four months ago, Jerry Ewing. Many people adopting false identities keep their own initials. Thirdly, even though the Davis house didn't meet the original criteria he presented the Cameron Agency, he leaped at the chance to buy it when it practically fell into his lap. In addition, Elmont and Ewing are both bald. Now that I know Jerry Ewing's goal in marrying Bunny was to get the code to the rumored Davis fortune, it seems too great a coincidence to ignore."

"Knowledge can be dangerous. Still, I sense that your reasoning is valid."

Amanda swallowed the last drops of her tea. "You've explained a great deal and given me the courage to follow my nose. What else can you divulge about this project?"

"I'm not a major player, if that's what you're asking. Sheila and Burke, as you know him, have filled me in on a few facts out of necessity, but most of it comes directly from my contacts in the ether." Sybil passed her hand through the air in a mystical, catch-all swoop to designate her sources, whatever they were.

Amanda hoped her silence would prompt Sybil to elaborate, but the other woman was intent on reaching for the teapot and offering a refill.

Amanda glanced at her watch. "Thanks, but I'd better be going. I'm meeting Burke in a few hours, and before that I'd like to check out something while I'm in the area."

Sybil gave her a hard look. "Don't place yourself in any more danger."

Airily, Amanda said, "Oh, I doubt that there's any danger in what I've planned." She was confidant that the note Ali pulled from Bunny's fingers had nothing to do with terrorism. Instead, it offered a solution to the whereabouts of the mysterious Davis house fortune, the reason Justin Elmont wanted Tom Grigsby's house so badly and his other persona, Jerry Ewing, married Bunny. Even Sybil's tiger cat, who had been curled up contentedly on the window sill, twitched his ears in alarm when that thought surfaced, as if he, too, could read minds.

Sybil noticed. She repeated her warning.

"Sybil, I have no intention of putting my life on the line," Amanda said. "Considering what happened today, I've probably reached the end of my usefulness for the Camerons. The truth is, I'm a sucker for historical mysteries. What fascinates me now is one that goes back to Revolutionary days. If things come together the way I believe they will, there might even be a connection with this undercover work."

They rose from their chairs in unison. "If you must get on with it, then I can't stop you," Sybil said. "Sometimes things happen because of fate's larger plan."

"There you go," Amanda said, brightly. "My future is in the hands of fate. At the very least, that may be better than letting 'the company' set me up again. That was one fender-bender to behold. And to think, had none of this happened, I could be soaking up Florida sun at this very moment."

Stooping to stroke the cat as he arched against her leg, Amanda thanked Sybil for her hospitality. The visit had been time well spent, not only for the clarification of everything that had happened to her over the past months, but also for the tacit confirmation that she was on the trail of the past—and her future.

As she retraced her steps to the parking garage, darkening clouds coursed briskly eastward from somewhere behind the Blue Ridge confirming her suspicion that a storm already was gathering. There should be just enough time to test her theory before the rain swept into Loudoun County.

Once past Leesburg's outer fringes, Amanda drove purposefully toward the rising hills, meeting very few cars other than family vans driven by mothers chauffeuring children to soccer practice or headed to the supermarket for a forgotten item, the usual afternoon errands. Where the Leesburg-Snicker Gap Turnpike abruptly widened to four lanes, she overtook an ancient stake truck laden with empty crates, probably returning home with jingling money bags from wares sold at the weekly farmers' markets in Fairfax, Vienna, and Herndon. Toward evening, the road would be clogged with commuters who had bartered the luxury of living close to nature for the inconvenience of battling miles of traffic between their homes and Washington. For now, though, Amanda could travel easily, her car buffeted by occasional wind gusts that teased the maple leaves into revealing their silver undersides.

At Clarks Gap, the by-pass led her around the village of Hamilton, then back through Purcellville. A mile or so beyond the town, she braked cautiously to accomplish the sharp turn onto Short Hill Mountain Road, hardly a route to tempt folks out for a pleasure drive. Loudoun County residents, Sheila had told her, prefer the contrived isolation of unimproved lanes as a privacy guarantee.

She edged her car onto the track. It was even more narrow and desolate than she remembered. By now the approaching storm covered the last vestiges of sun with churning mackerel clouds. Wild black locust trees, their blossom clusters whipped by determined breezes, permeated the air with a heady jasmine scent.

Several hundred yards ahead, she braked at a fork in the road. She could not remember having to make this choice the day she drove Justin Elmont to Grigsby's house, but now two distinct options presented themselves. Which should she take? The lanes merged at a grove of sycamore trees, its green canopy towering above dogwood and redbud interlopers. Tall weeds flourishing alongside the drainage ditches obscured whatever natural markers the occasional traveler might recognize.

Unable to decide from the clues at hand, Amanda followed the lead of a rabbit scurrying through the underbrush and selected the road most recently traveled. It seemed a logical option; tire treads, still distinct, told her someone had driven this way in the recent past. Even before mastering the next sharp bend, she realized her mistake.

There the road narrowed abruptly, and what had been a relatively smooth gravel surface took on the contours of moon canyons. The deep ruts canceled out the possibility of turning around; there was nothing for it but to continue. Instinctively, she believed that something up ahead must justify the road's existence. Accordingly, the prospect of the hunt obscured her usual caution. With a lurch, a shimmy, and the sickening crunch of its tailpipe making solid contact with a boulder, her car bottomed out on the hateful trail.

Broad Run Chapel, October 21, 1863

The minister hesitated outside the chapel. Perhaps he had imagined the sounds. When the Rebel company marched up Little River Turnpike earlier in the day, their commander had stopped to warn him of Yankee stragglers in the vicinity. Unarmed, yet cautious, he pushed open the wooden door and peered inside.

"Hello," he called. "If anyone is here, be assured that your secret is safe."

There was no answer, merely the faintest shuffle. Perhaps a mouse scurrying beneath the pews.

Again he called. "I welcome all comers to God's house. This is s safe harbor, no matter your allegiance."

He hesitated at the threshold. Evidently his imagination was playing tricks. He waited a few moment, then shrugged and turned to go. "So be it. But in case someone is hungry, there is a hearty pot of stew on the fire. I will be happy to share with all who make themselves known."

"Wait," came a whisper.

Turning toward the voice, he saw a figure rise from a far corner. Then another. A moment later, one more stood up. He knew at once that they were the Yankee soldiers being pursued by his kinsmen, the Confederates.

Moving deeper into the sanctuary, he stretched out his hand. "God does not take sides. Neither do I. Please be my guests."

Over nourishing bowls of stew, the three Union officers described their ambush by J. E. B. Stuart's cavalry along the Warrenton Turnpike two days earlier. During the skirmish, their horses were shot from under them. The rest of their company scattered, leaving them no alternative but to flee into the woods.

When they had their fill, the minister indicated the festering shoulder wound of one officer and spoke frankly. "You are safe here for the moment, but that needs attention. If you are willing, I can hide you in my wagon and transport you tonight to a nearby plantation. The family is very compassionate. I know they will protect you until the Confederate troops leave the area. Then you will be free to rejoin your company." Smiling, he added, "You will be in good hands. My fiancée, the daughter of the owner, knows a bit about nursing."

CHAPTER FOURTEEN

Amanda revved the engine several times, but the car merely rocked in position. Goaded by fear and a large serving of anger, she stomped on the accelerator. The tires responded, spiraling deep into the gravel. In seconds, the undercarriage lifted off, propelling the car forward at what felt like jet speed. It ricocheted from side to side for several yards until, just short of the drainage ditch, it settled onto a smoother stretch. At the next crossroad, a faded signpost identified the path she was traveling as Ketoctin Road. She had indeed strayed from her planned route.

In all directions, the trees were bending and bobbing. Lightening zigzagged from cloud to ground behind Short Hill Mountain. The crack of thunder followed each strike momentarily. Although the prospect of rain hung heavy overhead, it had not yet begun, and Amanda knew that she must turn back to escape the storm and meet Burke.

But all her good intentions dissolved at the next clearing. She was transported back two centuries, so quaint was the low building hidden behind a stand of willows amid a tangle of boxwood and ivy. Its simple masonry and the inscription—*Short Hill Meetinghouse*—carved on a weathered stone post confirmed that this was the church founded by the Davis family.

Beyond the gravel trace circling the building, the road ambled northward alongside a fallow field. Mindful of the approaching rain, Amanda drew near the building, cut the engine, and got out to assess her options and survey the building. The windows set behind deep stone sills were thickly veiled with spider webs. Unable to peer into the sanctuary, she gathered her nerve and approached the wooden door. An open padlock dangled against the handle, a signal that someone recently crossed the threshold.

The moment she shoved open the door, Amanda was taken aback by a mournful cry. She paused, riveted, while her eyes became accustomed to the dim light within. Mindful of the continuing wail, she edged inside for a better view of the interior. Flagstones, rudely set, led into an austere chamber that was bare save for several rows of rustic benches. A man sat at the end of one, his back to her. As the eerie moan developed into discernible notes, she realized that he was creating the curious sound on a violin.

Unaware of Amanda's presence, the man studied an instrumental score propped before him on a wire music stand. A clip-on lamp provided the sole illumination. The man was intent on perfecting a spooky set of triplets, repeating the measures time and again with such chilling inflection that Amanda half expected a squadron of ghosts to float down from the rafters. Some minutes passed before he laid his bow across the bench and expelled a sigh.

Amanda cleared her throat. "Excuse me …"

The stranger leaped up and whirled about to face her. She caught the trace of an unfamiliar accent as he demanded, "What do you want?"

"I'm sorry to bother you, but I'm studying Early American architecture. I saw the unlocked door, so I decided to peek inside." The lie slipped through her lips as easily as if it were programmed by invisible caretakers.

Middle-aged, of average stature, swarthy complexion, and unremarkable features that would blur in a crowd, the man struggled with civility as he pondered her remark. "Architecture, is it?"

"The building's simplicity caught my eye. It must be very historic."

"Caught your eye? It's a long way from the main road to catch someone's eye. Are you sure you weren't sent?"

Using all the caution she could muster, Amanda said, "Actually, I'm a real estate agent and I've lost my way trying to find a house near here that I sold recently to a Mr. Elmont. It fascinated me when I went through it with the buyer, but at the time I was concentrating on making the sale instead of its historical features."

The man peered over his reading glasses, appraising her silently before nodding in understanding. "Then you've taken the wrong turn."

Amanda threw up her hands in mock desperation. "I found that out in a hurry. These unpaved back roads are really confusing. Treacherous, too."

That seemed to satisfy him. "I may know the house you mean. Take the road that cuts behind this building. At the next crossroad, turn left." He described the route with his hands. "About a half mile farther, you'll see the house you're looking for. It sits back from the road."

"I'm so grateful. But before I go, maybe you can tell me a little bit about the history of this meetinghouse."

He studied her closely, more annoyed than suspicious. "I don't know anything about it."

Amanda persisted, determined to learn why he was there. "Then how is it being used today?"

"It's not."

"But you're here …"

"Look lady, I'm practicing for a concert. Nobody uses this building. It gives me the privacy I need and stops people from bothering me. Now I'd like to get back to work."

"Of course. Forgive me for being such a pest. I thank you again for the directions and wish you luck with your … your music."

He snorted, turned his back on her, and began to sit down.

Determined to stall until she could sort out the situation, Amanda continued babbling, "I know a little bit about music, but I don't recognize the piece you were playing."

His head swiveled back in her direction. "Don't you?"

"Truthfully, I haven't a clue. I'm usually good at identifying composers, but this is out of my repertoire."

One corner of his mouth tried a brief smile before slinking back into a sneer. "That's not surprising. This music is from an obscure German opera."

"How fascinating. Who's the composer?"

He flicked back to the cover sheet and adjusted his glasses to read the small print. "Name of Heinrich Marschner."

"It's rather a weird piece, don't you agree?"

"It's also very difficult. Now I must get back to work. I've a concert coming up."

Amanda latched onto that revelation. "Then you're a professional musician?"

Hurriedly, he said, "Oh no. I just play for my own enjoyment, mostly in small community orchestras."

She pressed on. "Really? Which ones?"

He thought a moment. "Uh … Fairfax, Arlington, Loudoun …"

"That's very commendable. You're absolutely wonderful to keep at your hobby faithfully. So many amateur musicians nowadays aren't as dedicated as the older generation is to improving technique. Please forgive me for bothering you. You're very kind."

Relieved that she could walk away from a potentially ugly situation, Amanda turned toward the door, expecting to exit unscathed. But nature had intervened. As she drew open the heavy oak door, she was dismayed to discover that the anticipated storm was already underway. The thick stone construction had dulled the sound of the downpour. Sheets of water separated her from her car.

Already the man had returned to his task, and as he sawed away at a score that conjured up tales of the macabre, Amanda settled herself on a rear bench. Before the rain subsided, she traveled on wings of devilish sounds and discordant passages devoid of melody and rife with hints of death and destruction.

The final droplets of water squeezed from the clouds were cascading down the roof gutter as she crept away from the meetinghouse that now seemed as uninviting as a crypt. Before climbing into her car, she walked to the end of the driveway to make certain the lane ahead was navigable. As far as she could see, it appeared to be in decent condition despite abundant rain puddles that mirrored the trees lining its banks, the glints of sun filtering through their branches, and the fleeting clouds.

A more immediate problem was the car partially blocking the far end of the driveway. In order to make the sharp turn onto the road, she would need to maneuver around it. Still, its out-of-state license bearing the insignia of a rental agency solved one mystery; she now understood the means whereby the violinist reached the meetinghouse. His purpose in coming to this obscure location was another matter. Did he find his own way, or had someone given him directions?

If so, who? And why?

Retracing her path, she sidestepped the tall grasses gorged with water, determined to avoid soaking her feet. She landed instead in squishy red clay. As it oozed up and over the rim of her shoes, she glanced around angrily to determine its origin.

What she saw took her breath away. Several yards to her right was an excavation. The soil piled alongside was dissolving into the thick, muddy river now flowing around her feet. Beyond the hole was evidence of a very old cemetery, its weathered tombstones cracked and fallen.

Was this a freshly dug grave awaiting a casket? That seemed unlikely in an abandoned churchyard.

Was it an older grave occupied by someone who had expired years ago?

Or did it harbor a treasure that someone wished to disinter?

Amanda glanced about long enough to assure herself that she was alone except for the resolute musician indoors whose dreary music had drummed thoughts of terror into her brain. If his purpose was to prepare her for the fright of stumbling onto an open grave, then he succeeded. She wasted no time seeking refuge in her car.

Bent on escaping from a nasty situation, she accelerated toward Tom Grigsby's former house. Although the road was straight, it was too narrow for her to skirt the ruts now transformed into miniature lakes. A dingy signpost up ahead identified the crossroad she was approaching as Short Hill Mountain Road, exactly where she should have been had she not chosen unwisely. Relieved, she executed the turn without incident, but she had proceeded no more than a hundred yards when the engine coughed abruptly, choked once, twice, then seized up with finality.

Amanda clutched her throat. How could she keep her appointment with Burke?

Thoughts of what might befall her if she tried to hike back to Leesburg were almost as frightening as the scene she had just left. She grabbed the cell phone, but the sheet of office contact numbers was missing. She had left it in the Cameron car. Dumber yet, she had not taken time to store them in the new phone. She reasoned that she could knock on the door of a nearby house and ask to look at a phone book. But as far as she could see, there were no nearby houses. If all else failed, she felt certain that Burke would contact her. Torn between waiting for help and the dubious prospect of meeting either Elmont or the musician, she gathered her purse and a canvas tote bag, locked the car, and began trudging down the muddy lane.

The first farm field she passed was planted neatly with corn that would soon burst into succulent glory. Alongside, separated by a whitewashed fence, cattle lolled near a water hole amid clumps of Queen Anne's lace. The scent of rain-washed timothy and red clover vied with the sweet aroma of a honeysuckle vine, its tendrils gripping fence rails for support as they inched forward to curl around adjacent tree trunks and branches.

Despite being placed at the mercy of nature by the minor flooding, Amanda could not help admiring the sparkling countryside emerging in the wake of the storm. Rounding one more bend in the road, she came upon the house that she suspected held the clues to the crumpled paper in her pocket.

As she hurried up the driveway, she marked that the windows were closed tightly despite the pleasant temperature, further supporting her belief that the house was still unoccupied. All the better to try her luck.

She drew the paper from her pocket and studied the first line: *Drop the plumb line of truth to the all-seeing eye.*

From where she stood, she had a clear view of the entire structure. A simple rectangle, it was divided by the doorway into two symmetrical sections. Mentally, she drew a vertical line straight down the center of the house starting from the topmost level of the roof. It bisected the length of the front door and came to rest on the threshold.

She raced forward. The moment she reached the threshold, she recognized the carving on the stone for what it really was: an eye.

A God's eye. The very same one found on the dollar bill.

Now she knew exactly who carved it there. No matter his name, he was on the side of the colonists, if not as a soldier, certainly as a supporter.

Next, she scanned the second line of verse: *Find the key to the secret wedged halfway between.*

Halfway between what? Amanda backed off and regarded the geometric puzzle before her until the veil lifted. The point halfway between the top of her mental plumb line and the threshold stone was exactly where the keystone sat above the doorway.

She hurried forward. Standing on tip-toe before the door, she stretched to her full height. That was not enough by several feet. She searched around for a booster.

Not even a log presented itself, but there was a shed some distance from the house. Perhaps Tom Grigsby had left behind a ladder. She ran toward the shed, avoiding the mud puddles where possible. No matter, the tall wet grass did a nifty job of soaking her shoes clear through to her stocking feet.

The late afternoon sun barely illuminated the shed's interior. Thick cobwebs shielding the interior corners denied her quest for a ladder in their depths, but a stack of UPS boxes, still sealed, offered the perfect alternative. She chose one sufficiently light and manageable and carried it back to the threshold through the saturated grass. Although it supported her weight, she still lacked several inches. Back she went for another.

This time, by stacking them, she could touch the keystone. If her suspicions were correct, this was a false front. Her initial rap elicited a faintly hollow timbre that boosted her hopes. Unlike true keystones, this one was not pressured into a solid, stationary seal against the adjoining stones. A faint indentation around its perimeter invited her to pry further. She jumped down from her perch and retrieved a nail file from her purse. Tool in hand, she climbed back up and struggled to loosen the mortar around the rim. When several bits flaked off, she plunged the file deeper. Within a few minutes, she had chipped a border around the keystone.

Now it was time to flex some muscle. Back to her purse, this time for a lever of sorts. Using the best substitute she could find, she jimmied a ballpoint pen into the cracks. Soon she dislodged sizable chunks of mortar, but the stone held firm. Determined, she exerted even more pressure under its base until she felt a definite give, something not allowed by a builder who installs a keystone to support the doorway for the lifetime of the house. The third try was the charm.

She heard the stone emit a faint sucking sound. Another nudge and it pulled away from the building. Without warning, it fell straightway into Amanda's arms, far heavier than she had expected. Startled into a crouching position on the boxes, not daring to let the stone slam to the ground and crack, she cradled it against her body. When she had managed to catch her breath, she stepped down and laid it gently on the threshold.

Now, on to the anticipated revelation.

Mounting the boxes once again, she reached warily into the cavity. At first, she felt nothing. Had her theory been too wild?

But there it was. A wad of cloth. Grabbing hold, she pulled it into the light. It was much too heavy for a mere roll of material. She dismounted to inspect it closely.

The cloth was made of natural fibers yellowed and frayed from age and gnawing insects, its true nature evident the moment Amanda opened it out flat. The main segment, a nearly perfect square, was topped by a triangular bib. When tied together, the single strings on either side would encircle a waist, confirming its identity as an apron. Several words on the lower portion of the triangle were too faded to read, but the owner's name, *John Davis*, and the date, *1774*, were as clear as the day they were inscribed.

Amanda recognized it immediately as a Masonic apron. Almost identical to the one in a box of personal belongings she inherited from her father, this relic of the Revolutionary period was far more mysterious, for it contained a secret pocket. Even before locating the hidden seam, she knew its contents by running her fingers across the telltale bulge: a large iron key.

Broad Run Chapel, November 1905

The frail woman in widow's weeds clung to her son's arm. The two hung back from others assembled at the gravesite. Beneath their feet, the fallen leaves had turned brown and brittle. Overhead, the bare branches clawed grotesquely, manipulated by the stiff wind.

More than half a lifetime had passed since Lisette broke her engagement to the minister about to be interred. She had relived daily the moment she explained her decision to him and watched the color drain from his face. Bravely, he maintained his composure and assured her that he understood and bore her no ill will for falling in love with the Union officer he delivered to her care.

Now she was paying her respects to the man who loved her so dearly that he gave her freedom to follow her heart instead of her duty. Nobody present, not even her son, knew what the minister had sacrificed for her sake. She always explained him away as an old friend, but as the coffin was lowered into the ground, she had a flash of what might have been ... and what the next life might hold in store.

CHAPTER FIFTEEN

Amanda extracted the key with a mixture of awe and urgency and tried to decipher the symbols embossed on its shaft. A trowel, a compass, and a triangle superimposed upon each other were surrounded by ribbons and leaves. The business end, similar to that of a skeleton key, was forged to fit into a giant lock.

She plunged the apron and key into her canvas tote bag and climbed once more onto the boxes to replace the keystone quickly, for time was bearing down. One by one, she lugged the boxes back to the shed, minding their weight far more than before. It was urgent that she leave promptly and return to her stalled car.

But just as she gathered her belongings and the Masonic treasures, she detected the hum of an approaching motor. Remembering Sybil's revelations, her optimistic self wanted to believe it meant rescue by the all-seeing "company" and a ride back to Leesburg. Her suspicious self radioed a warning to hide.

The house was her nearest refuge. Although she expected the front door to be locked, a twist of the knob, a creak of the hinges, and it fell open to reveal a hodge-podge of furniture and cartons. A pair of soiled boots sat on the staircase three steps above the landing, as if their owner wanted them handy for easy access. In the adjacent parlor, a section of *The Washington Post* was tossed absently across a chair facing a television set. None of the few furniture pieces resembled those she had seen when Tom Grigsby lived there. This was ominous proof that someone had moved in already.

The oncoming motor grew louder, then ceased altogether. A car door slammed and gravel crunched beneath heavy footsteps. Panicked, Amanda fled into the library. On her first visit, Tom's extensive collection had filled the bookcase, but now the shelves were empty. Had the new owner already discovered the secret staircase?

Blindly, she ran her fingers up and down the woodwork trying to locate the magical spot that had responded to Tom. At last, her fingers felt the wooden peg and coaxed it from the indentation where it nested. With one light tug, she eased the entire wall of shelves forward. As she squeezed into the empty space, she examined the stairs that rose straight up, narrow and steep, like a ship's ladder. Standing on the first step, she was able to grab a rope dangling from the back side of the bookcase and pull it toward her until the section was flush with the adjacent wall. Plunged into darkness, she was forced to rely on her sense of touch to locate the hook on the inner wall. That accomplished, she secured the loop at the end of the rope to its welcome tentacle.

Once the rope and hook were connected and the safety of her hideaway ensured, Amanda groped her way up the stairs to the attic floor and waited for her eyes to adjust to the faint light seeping through cracks along the eaves. Down below, the front door swung open. Boards creaked and footsteps resounded, tracing the intruder's progression from the hall, across the parlor, and into the kitchen. The clink of utensils against pottery suggested that food was first on his agenda. Several minutes of silence were shattered by the sharp peal of a telephone. Terrified she would be found out, Amanda stuffed her cell phone under her jacket to muffle the sound.

The click of the receiver taken off the hook and a man's voice barking into the mouthpiece were as distinct as if next to her ear. The loud ring she had heard was not that of her own phone, but of one in the room below.

"Yeah? Erdmann speaking."

"Stoker here." The voice at the other end was equally clear.

"Where's Ellen?" This with an urgency.

"Dropped me at the station, then drove away. The sight of the rabbit turned her off."

"That wasn't supposed to happen."

"Too bad. We'll work around it."

Erdmann? Stoker? Ellen? The names eluded Amanda, but the voices were familiar.

"Got the shipment," Erdmann, the voice below, said.

"Just in time. One more day and we'd be looking at another game plan."

"We're in good shape. Once we face the music and eliminate the Falcon, we can concentrate on the antique shop. As soon as I left the rabbit, I picked up two team members and a metal detector."

"And ...?"

Erdmann's laugh was evil. "It didn't take long before we found a rabbit hole that looks promising. We didn't need her help after all."

"Is it the right one?"

"You never can be sure until you find out what the equipment's detecting. It could be any number of things, like minerals in the soil or the latch on a casket. Lots of people are buried with wedding rings, watches, maybe even weapons they used. Soldiers might have camped here during the Civil War and dropped a gun or a knife by accident that worked its way into the ground."

"Then you're saying you didn't get to the bottom?"

"Not by a long shot. The guys got tired and started balking. Then the Sandpiper called to say the weather report wasn't good. He ordered us to put the job on hold until things dry out. Tire tracks could trip us up. A few more feet, though, and we might hit the antique shop."

Amanda's heart pounded. The curious puzzle pieces that had whirled senselessly through her mind only a few hours earlier were sliding into place as if pulled by a magnet. Now she must arrange them logically.

The voices were easy. Erdmann, the man down below, was Ewing, aka Elmont. Stoker, his accomplice on the phone, was Ali. Wealthy horse breeder? Not a chance.

Ellen? All the clues pointed to herself. She had dropped him off after ... of course. The rabbit was Bunny. Her injury had not been planned, wasn't supposed to happen, Ewing had said. He was no up-and-coming businessman, legitimate or otherwise, but a crafty opportunist who coveted a fortune. If it entailed aligning himself with other unsavory characters, the more the merrier.

The rabbit hole? The open grave. And the antique shop? Its valuable contents, the treasure. Assuming that Ewing attacked Bunny, Amanda had to believe that she was now a target and possibly in line to become his next victim. She reached out and patted her canvas bag, its contents now coveted for even more reasons than were first evident.

The voices sounded so near she could almost feel the breath of the speakers. Why did they seem to be broadcasting over a radio with the volume turned too high?

Radio? Now that her eyes had mastered the gloom, she could make out the box balanced atop sturdy rafters. Protruding wires gave her ample reason to conclude it was a recording device. Now she understood why Tom mentioned the spooky feeling the secret room gave him. He was signaling her that it contained a secret electronics station. But why? How was he involved?

The terse exchanges continued while Amanda's thoughts tumbled between the sensible left side of her brain and the risk-taking right. For the present she was alone and safe, but she knew she had to escape without divulging either her presence or that of the secret room. Clearly, she was dealing with criminals. Perhaps murderers.

"Does Ellen suspect anything?" Ewing sounded tough, primed to get her out of the picture by the same treatment he gave Bunny if Ali—Stoker—gave the word.

"We're in good shape with this one. She's only interested in her job."

"Just make sure she doesn't start to think."

"She's so determined to find me a horse farm that she can't see past the manure."

Both men guffawed. Amanda's blood rose.

Ali pressed on. "Then you never found a map?"

"Nah. I searched the place over after I saw her go out. I didn't expect her back so soon. She must have forgotten something. When she caught me trying to crack her safe, she came at me from behind."

"You didn't get it open?"

"There wasn't time. She'd changed the lock. Threatened to turn me in. Even stuck a crazy poem in my face. Said it was exactly what I wanted."

Amanda heard Ali suck in his breath. "Poem?"

"Yeah. Real crazy. She was always writing nutty stuff, bragging that she could be a writer, or a prosecuting attorney, or who knows what."

"Did you read the poem?"

"Sure. Pure nonsense about plums, eyes, and hickory trees. Like I told you, it was gibberish."

"Maybe not," Ali cautioned.

"What d'you mean?"

"Maybe the poem really *was* what you wanted. I should have kept it."

"You had it?"

"I found it in the rabbit's paw. I think Ellen has it now."

"Ellen? How the …?" Ewing's voice rose so many decibels Amanda's ears hurt.

"She caught me reading it, so I had to show it to her. It didn't make sense to her, but she walked off with it before I could get it back."

"Get it." Ewing's bark carried authority.

"How?"

"Any way you can. And I mean *any* way."

"What if I don't see her before we face the music?"

"Make sure you do. Once the Falcon's blown away, we'll go directly to the antique store. If it turns out to be a dud, we might need that poem to steer us in the right direction so we can pick up the goods without delay and meet the Sandpiper. He has to decide pretty soon which farm is the best base for our operation. Our team's too scattered. We can't go on this way much longer."

Antique store. Sandpiper. Face the music. Falcon. Operation. Amanda struggled to put those terms into logical niches. The antique store? The grave, or perhaps the meetinghouse cemetery in general if the first excavation proved wrong.

Sandpipers run along the shore, so perhaps the answer lay in the sand or the sea. This corner of Virginia was a long way from the seashore. Since the term made no sense in the present context, Amanda put it aside for the moment.

Face the music immediately brought to mind the violinist and snippets of his strange, haunting music. Surely, she thought, there was a strong connection.

Falcon? Nothing other than a bird of prey came to mind. But the Operation scheduled to take place behind the innocuous front of a horse farm was bound to be nothing short of treachery concocted by twisted individuals.

As if reading Amanda's mind, Ewing said, "I met Tony last evening in in Fairfax. He'd just driven down from New Jersey. Like you suggested, I brought him back here for the night and this morning showed him where he could practice while the rest of the team worked outside. I warned him he'd better get those notes down perfectly."

"If he wants a cut, he will."

"Are you sure about him?"

"Listen, he's played all over the world and can keep up with the best of 'em."

"But how trustworthy is he?"

"The best, I guarantee. He's helped out in plenty of other situations like this: Yemen, Pakistan, Thailand, to name a few. It didn't take him long to learn that the Sandpiper's a busy guy." Their laughs were knowing and nasty.

Ali was impatient. "Look, I've got to get off the phone and contact Ellen so I can see her either tonight or first thing tomorrow. Suppose she doesn't respond to my plea for a romantic evening?"

"If you can't dispose of her properly, maybe in a runaway car, call in one of the team to break into her place and offer her a few choices. If nothing appeals to her, she can always lose her balance and fall off the balcony."

"Done." Ali spoke with finality. There was a click as the connection uncoupled.

Amanda shuddered knowing that Ewing was in the room below and Ali was trying to reach her. She was in a worse fix than she originally imagined.

For perhaps a half hour, she sat hunched against the wall before a ringing phone triggered her hope that it was Burke at the other end of the cell phone buried in her purse. Her heart sank as Ewing snapped, "Yeah?"

"Stoker again. Can't find her. Went to her office. They said she took the afternoon off. I used all my charms to coax the girl at the desk to tell me where she lives."

"I'm sure you were successful," Ewing said, a sneer in his voice.

"Naturally, she gave in, but when I stopped by there, the doorman said Ellen's never come back."

Exasperated, Ewing muttered an oath. "Don't waste any more time on her. Get out here. There's plenty to talk about. Eliminating the Falcon takes priority. This time tomorrow, we'll be concentrating on the music. If necessary, we'll take care of Ellen and the antique shop when that's over."

"It's rush hour," Ali reminded him. "Traffic's heavy."

"Move it." Ewing slammed down the phone.

Ali was coming here, Amanda realized, maybe with murder in mind. All the more reason for her to leave. The late-setting sun was a temporary problem that could be solved with patience, but what were her odds for eluding both Ewing and Ali later on? There was nothing to do but sit it out and stay alert for an opportunity to escape.

She began plotting her moves. Once out of the house, what should she do? Her car blocking the road was not a safe place to hide. Perhaps she could return to the church. The violinist should be gone by nightfall, leaving only the local ghosts to trouble her mind. But what if he came back to Ewing's house for the night? Then there would be three men to outsmart. Amanda remembered Sybil's assurance that someone was watching her at all times, but that was when they knew her itinerary. This time she was on her own.

The other option was to walk back to the main road, find a store or a telephone booth in Purcellville, and call Burke. As Amanda turned this possibility over in her mind, clearly the best of the three, it occurred to her that the Cameron Office would be closed by now. True, there was an answering machine, but suppose nobody listened to her message until morning? Would that be too late? She envisioned Burke monitoring the machine, hoping to hear from her. By now, he should realize that circumstances prevented her from calling. Why, oh why didn't he call?

Over and over, she pondered her situation until the headlights of an oncoming vehicle swept along the openings under the eaves. Ali? No. The engine hum peaked, then began to fade as the vehicle followed the road curving past the house and continued toward the base of the mountain. Probably a late commuter from Washington returning to his restful country dwelling.

Minutes later, a second pair of headlights pricked out from the dark. Their intensity increased until the car swung into the driveway. The engine cut off, and the door slammed. Even before Ewing answered the series of three short knocks and Amanda heard the two men exchange greetings, she knew that Ali had arrived.

Their footfalls traveled the length of the downstairs. Chair legs scraped on the kitchen floor as they sat down at the table to confer. Then someone switched on a rock station. Here was her out. The persistent percussion beat paired with the disc jockey's intrusive announcements would be her cover.

Adjusting the purse straps over her shoulder, the canvas bag of treasures on her arm, she crawled to the top of the stairs. The drone of voices and music from below never varied. She felt certain they could not hear her over the din.

Sitting on the floor, she swung first one leg, then the other, onto the top step. Once she managed a foothold, she reversed herself and began a slow descent backward, aware that each rung she mastered carried her inches closer to detection. Upon reaching the solid floor below, she paused to listen. Lulled by the steady hum of their voices and the background music, she reached high for the rope and was about to unhook it when her shoulder bag thumped against the wall.

Like a shot, the men jumped to their feet and Ali cried, "What's that?"

"Were you followed?"

"Of course not."

"We'll look around, anyway," Ewing said.

Their footsteps neared and Amanda heard a click as someone flicked on an overhead light. Their voices, a few inches from her on the other side of the bookcase, bespoke murderous anger.

Several heart-stopping moments passed before they moved away. After searching both floors, they paused in the front hall. "Must be squirrels or raccoons in the rafters," Ewing said. "They're pesky."

That explanation seemed to calm both men. Ali had already started toward the kitchen when Ewing circled back in Amanda's direction to turn off the light.

Moments later, he cried out, "Wait a minute! Muddy footprints. Looks like a woman's been here."

He was standing so close she could have reached out and touched him had the bookcase not separated them.

Ali stormed back. "Where?"

"See? They start in the hall and lead into this room."

Flattened against the inner wall, Amanda berated herself for failing to remove her shoes before entering the house. The mud they picked up from the graveyard, the road, and those trips to the shed had left evidence that could seal her doom.

"It doesn't make sense," Ewing said. "If somebody came recently, their prints would be wet, but these are completely dry. Could have been here some time."

"That doesn't tell us who was here."

Ewing thought for a moment. "Maybe it was an agent who doesn't know the house is off the market. Those footprints could have been here a couple of days, maybe more. I haven't been in this room and didn't notice them."

A long pause before Ali conceded, "That's possible."

From Amanda's precarious vantage point, it seemed forever before they left. After several more minutes, she sensed that they had tabled concern about the noise and footsteps and were once more seated in the kitchen discussing their strategies.

It was now or never. Mustering every ounce of bravery possible, she unhooked the rope. The bookcase slid forward and she stepped into the darkened room. The voices and music coming from the kitchen droned on. Shakily, she inched the bookcase back into place. As it merged with the wall and the wooden peg clicked into its slot, she expelled the breath she had been holding. Clutching her bag and purse, heart pounding, she crept toward the hallway. The true test came when she left the dark library and passed beneath the hall light, not daring to glance into the room beyond. Now she was in no better position than an escaped prisoner caught in a searchlight.

Just as she touched the doorknob, Ali shouted, "Look, there she is!"

His chair clattered on the floor as he leaped up and bounded toward her through the parlor. The knob was so much jelly in her hands.

He was about to lunge at Amanda when her final frantic twist hit home. Flinging the door wide, she sprinted into the night and headed mindlessly around the side toward the shed. She heard the two men storm out of the house, then pause to reconnoiter.

Ewing shouted, "Which way did she go?"

"I don't see her."

"You go that way. I'll go this."

Amanda kept moving, the purse and bag bobbing rhythmically at her side. The shed, she quickly realized, could be a disastrous choice. Not wishing the fate of a chicken pursued by the fox, she opted instead to stoop low behind the cover of overgrown shrubbery.

As the men's voices rose and fell, Amanda knew she had chosen wisely. Occasionally she could see their forms move like shadow puppets outlined by the light streaming from the hallway. Each time their angry shouts faded to the far side of the house, she moved stealthily backward, one step at a time. Finally, she reached the dense grove of trees. She stopped there to catch her breath, waiting for the optimum moment to make a break for it. But before she could move, someone grabbed her from behind.

Crestmont, 1918

The young Army corporal leaped from the horse-drawn wagon that had carried him from the Warrenton train station. His commanding officer had been sympathetic, but several days elapsed before his leave could be arranged. The journey from Georgia was painfully slow. Now the tears streaming down his mother's face confirmed that he was too late. His father had succumbed to the Influenza. He was not surprised. Many men in his barracks were ill and he knew several who had died in the holding room for the most severe cases. The daily newspapers were filled with statistics about the epidemic that had felled much of the civilized world. Still he had not expected tragedy to strike at home ... so quickly.

The funeral was swift and scantily attended. Friends and relatives were either ill themselves or afraid of contracting the deadly strain from others. There was no time to grieve; the corporal had barely enough time to catch a southbound train back to his base.

As he was preparing to depart, his mother handed him an envelope. "This has come down to the oldest child in each generation," she told him.

"Yes?" He was impatient to leave, but she blocked his way.

"I inherited it from my mother and it will go to you at my death."

His laugh was hollow. "There's plenty of time for that, Mother."

"Don't be so sure. We can't know that for certain. Ordinarily, you would receive this at the reading of the will, but I'm the only one who knows about it. So many things happen that are beyond our imagination. It could

be lost and nobody would be the wiser. That's why I want you to have it now."

He spread his arms in despair. "I can't take it now. There's no place to stow it with my military gear." Catching a glimpse of desperation in her eyes, he softened. "Look, if you're so concerned, why don't you put it in the secret compartment in my desk? That way, we'll both know where it is. When I get back—if I get back—we can discuss it then."

His mother wiped a tear from the corner of her eye. "You're probably right. There will be plenty of time when you come home for good."

Clutching the envelope in her hand, she watched her son go out the door. She had a premonition that this would be their last hour together; she did not know that he would return from the war and forget about the envelope. One day, his own son would inherit the desk and discover it wedged in the secret drawer.

CHAPTER SIXTEEN

Amanda fought to free herself, but her assailant's grip tightened. "Quiet," he hissed. His mouth pressed against her ear. A gun holster bruised her ribs.

"Burke?" She barely managed a whisper. His face was so close to hers she could have kissed him for joy.

His forefinger silenced her lips. The questions would wait. He reached for her free hand and drew her after him through the underbrush. They moved stealthily, hugging the woods. Just before the trees gave way to a farm field, he stopped and whispered, "I hope I didn't hurt you back there."

"I'm fine," Amanda lied.

"Good girl." He dropped her hand and drew a two-way radio from his pocket. "Live wire to phone company. Over."

"Roger. Line laid. Over," came the immediate reply.

"Roger. Collect call required. Over."

"Roger. Service granted. Over."

Burke returned the radio to his pocket and placed a protective arm around Amanda's shoulder. "We'll be out of here soon."

"What was that all about?"

"You'll see, darling."

"What did you say?"

"I said you'll see."

"No, after that."

His face was inches from hers. "You heard me, Amanda."

The blood rose to her cheeks. At the very moment she admitted to herself that she wanted nothing more than to melt into Burke's arms, the headlights of a large vehicle loomed into view. As it drew alongside and stopped, she was astounded to see that it was a telephone company truck.

Burke boosted her through the tailgate and directed her to crouch in the narrow space between equipment racks. "For just a few minutes," he promised, as he closed the rear doors.

Moments later, he swung into the passenger seat and the truck began to move. They bounced along the rugged track for only a short distance when the driver slowed. "There they are. They're waving us down."

"You handle it." Both men clapped on hard hats to convey the illusion of authentic telephone repairmen.

The driver leaned from his window and called, "Howdy. Anything wrong?"

"Yeah. We're looking for a lost girl. Have you seen her?" It was Ewing.

"Afraid not. Been working on a break in the line."

"If you see her, bring her back here, will you? She's confused."

"Glad to help, but it's hard seeing people at night. Morning will be better."

Amanda heard Ewing snort as the driver put the truck in gear and it rumbled past the house, emergency beacon rotating as if on a legitimate service call.

A short distance up the lane, Burke turned and called to Amanda, "Come on up, now. Hold on tight so you don't fall."

She rose and edged past the racks of equipment to Burke's outstretched hand. He pulled her onto the seat next to him.

"Good job, Amanda," said the driver.

Her head jerked toward the familiar voice. "Martin? So this is what you do when you're not working on my car."

The two men looked at each other and burst out laughing. A few more rotations of the tires and the main highway loomed into view. Burke's arm stole around Amanda's shoulder as the truck slowed to make the turn. Once it was on the straight-away, he hugged her warmly. "There's a lot you have to learn, Ms. Prescott."

Vividly aware of his muscular body next to hers, she shot back, "Such as what, Mr. Burke Cameron?"

"Such as the fact that you're consorting with people who don't exist."

The driver grinned. "Just for the record, Amanda, my name's not Martin, but I'll answer to it and to a couple of other names, depending upon the situation. When I'm with good friends, though, I answer to Joe. Joe Draver."

"I'm glad to meet you, Joe Draver," Amanda said. "You've saved me twice already, a very handy guy to know, even if your name changes with the territory." She looked up at Burke. "And whom might *you* be in your real life?"

"Hank. Hank Connors. Please forget everything else you've heard about me."

"Does that include your shouting match with the hapless Cameron employee?"

"I plead guilty, but it was all part of the plot. I'm glad my audience couldn't wait to fill you in on my evil ways. The hapless employee is an aspiring actress. Sheila gave her the script, paid her well, and told her she was auditioning for an upcoming show at Signature Theatre."

"She must have given a convincing performance. Janel said she left in tears. I fully expected the same kind of treatment from the evil Burke at our first meeting. If it hadn't been for your alter ego, Reverend Henry Conyers, I would have quit on the spot."

Burke/Hank hugged her again. "So you trusted the saintly clergyman?"

"Implicitly. His goodness came through in all he said and did, especially during our long chats on the phone."

"Hmmm. Would you have thought less of him if you knew that our nightly trysts were the high point of his day?" Even in the dark, Amanda knew Burke was grinning.

"They were mine, too, so the playing field was level. I didn't even mind about his bride-to-be once I realized that she didn't exist. But why did you give him a name so similar to yours?"

"A very strange coincidence. There actually *was* a clergyman at Pohick Church named Henry Conyers, the one Sheila and Sybil are convinced comes back as a ghost. When we began choreographing this plot, they latched onto the similarity of our last names and insisted that I play his role, not knowing that Henry actually is the name on my birth certificate and I've slipped through enemy barriers all over the world in clerical garb."

"That truly is an amazing coincidence. Do you suppose that the original Henry Conyers is a phantom psychics can see?"

He drew her closer. "That's one case I don't intend to investigate, Amanda. It's time to put that good shepherd out to pasture. Until you came along, men of the cloth have been my most reliable disguise, probably because I identify with their commitment to making the world a better place, no matter the God they worship. When did you figure out that Henry and I are one and the same?"

"Early in the game. You of all people should know that voice recognition is the ultimate security check. Besides, Meg tipped me off."

"Meg?"

"My friend in Palm Beach. You interviewed her for my security clearance."

An apologetic laugh. "Uh-oh. What did she tell you?"

"That your voice reminded her of Robert Goulet, the very thing that impressed me about the Pohick priest. And when that unique timbre cut through the next day in your office, it was all over."

"You never once hinted that you were on to me."

"I wanted to see where the plot went."

"Fair enough, but right now we need to know why you took it upon yourself to stalk some of the world's most notorious terrorists today."

Amanda sat up straight. "You're serious, aren't you? This is the second time today that word's come up."

Over her head the two men exchanged glances. Joe cleared his throat. "Hank has the authority to fill in the details, but you know a lot already, what with the tapped telephone conversations you overheard."

"They were helpful to me, but they would have been more effective if they went to someone in authority."

"Believe me, they did. The conversations were piped directly to our department at Langley."

"Then why could I hear them?"

"Tom sat it up that way to cover all bases. An agent secluded in that room could hear exactly what they were hearing at headquarters and prepare for whatever was about to transpire on his watch. You managed to arrive before any of our men took up that position. Fortunately, our team was able to let us know what the Scorpion has in mind for you."

If Hank had not been holding her close, she might have bolted through the windshield. Slowly, her voice husky, she said, "Scorpion is the code term for the terrorist Senator Shellenberger has been tracking. But who …?"

"Your handsome client. The romantic one."

That registered like the deadly bombs that earned the elusive Scorpion his international reputation. "You mean …?"

"Sure do. Ali, the lover boy. We knew he had a yen for good looking dames, and since you have all the qualities that matter to him, along with the common sense we require, you were the ideal lure. Our big concern was that you didn't end up the way a lot of his conquests do—in small, unrecognizable pieces."

Amanda looked Hank straight in the eye and demanded, "Dame?"

He grinned. "The Scorpion's term, not mine. I wanted to choke him when he got fresh this morning."

"You know everything, don't you?"

"Thanks to the wonderful world of electronics."

"Hank's your guardian angel," Joe said. "If he hadn't thought you'd be perfectly safe in the house tonight, he'd have added another character to his repertoire, a knight who rescues damsels in distress from secret rooms."

"I'm beginning to think that I work for Superman," Amanda said. "Do you often fly, or was the helicopter trip to Broad Run Church an exception?"

Joe laughed out loud. "You're right, Hank. She doesn't miss a trick."

"That was an emergency run," Hank said. "Before you pulled away from The Depot, Ali jammed something into your rear tire. We knew you couldn't get far before it gave out. At that point, it wasn't clear if he had romance or something more sinister in mind, so I hailed our surveillance copter and hopped on to keep you in sight."

"With your cassock in tow?"

Hank laughed. "It's an indispensable item in my briefcase."

"Then you never had a chance to finish your dinner."

"Thanks for caring, Amanda. Interruptions go with the territory, I'm afraid. Joe followed by car and helped Ali switch tires."

"Well of course. The good Samaritan. You two amaze me."

"You're a bit amazing yourself," Martin said. "It hasn't been easy keeping several steps ahead of you"

Amanda nudged the revolver strapped under Hank's arm. "It this also part of Reverend Conyer's wardrobe?"

"Men of the cloth plan for every contingency."

"That's what Tom Grigsby must have been doing when he told me about that secret room."

"Glad you understood. Had you already figured out that he's one of us?"

"When I saw the equipment and heard the voices from the kitchen clear as day, everything began to make sense. Where does Grigsby fit into your organization?"

"He actually does have a background in architecture, and he's into history when he's not inventing ways to survive," Hank said. "The underground house is a prototype of some he'll build when he takes his retirement pay and runs, but right now its primary purpose is as his communications center."

"Tom monitors the airwaves," Joe said. "Some of the world's most dangerous guys have infiltrated the Northern Virginia countryside because the location is ideal for their plans—near enough to Washington so it will be easy to strike the places they have in their sights, but far enough so nosy neighbors don't interfere."

"When we learned these guys were looking for places to store an arsenal, a real estate agency was the logical hub for our operations," Hank said. "After all, how many people driving past a horse farm ever stop to see if the residents are planning to overthrow the nation?"

Amanda would have trembled had she been in less dependable company. "So that's their goal?"

"In a nutshell," Joe said. "We'll stop them before they get lucky, but we're holding off to get enough goods on everyone involved to keep them behind bars for multiple lifetime sentences."

"Tell me about the leads, the houses where I took Ewing and Ali. Were they planned?"

"Did you think the computer pulled them up willy-nilly?"

"Originally, yes. But what about the old woman in the attic? Surely she was an innocent party."

Joe chuckled and began drawling in his best rocking-chair rendition, "Mercy me, I don't know where the time flies while I'm listening to the creak of the floorboards."

Amanda's mouth flew open. "Why were you dressed that way?"

My job was to wire the place to pick up the Scorpion's conversation and peg his voice. Like you said, voice recognition is key to positive identification. I'd barely finished when you pulled into the driveway. In case you two tried to inspect the entire house, I had to account for my presence. Mrs. Wardle—yep, she's an operative—and I went crazy rummaging through the closets. Finally came up with Grandma Goofy."

For the first time that day, Amanda laughed out loud. "We thought we'd run into a case of senior citizen abuse."

"That confirmed our wisdom in keeping you in the dark," Hank said. "Since your reaction was completely natural, you weren't likely to arouse the suspicion of either Ali or Ellis."

"Ellis? Who is that?"

"Jake Ellis is the real name of the guy you know as Elmont."

Gleefully, Amanda clapped her hands. "So I *was* right. The initials of his aliases are the very same as his real initials. He's Justin Elmont, Jerry Ewing, and Jake Ellis rolled into one. But who is he really? What's his game? Is he an international terrorist, too?"

"By default. He has a long police record as a small time swindler. Recently, he widened his scope to antiques and historic homes."

"How do you suppose a crook like that convinced someone with Bunny's background to marry him?"

"Either he has a good line or he's a great actor," Joe said.

"More likely both," Hank said. "By whatever means, he wanted access to the Davis treasure and talked Bunny into marrying him with that his only objective. None of that meant anything to us until our friends began tossing money at him hoping he'd become their front man, do all the dirty work, and let them stay under cover. It didn't take much to convince him to compromise his allegiance to this country because he's the kind of person who'd murder his own mother for her insurance. When we assigned you to him, his job was to locate a secluded headquarters for the entire team. You were directed to the underground house so the hidden cameras could photograph him and pick up voice samples. It was pure coincidence that someone working for the 'company' owned the house Bunny's ancestors built and Ellis coveted its treasure. Unexpectedly, Tom provided the lure."

"So Ellis bought the house thinking he'd find the treasure there."

"No doubt, but that's not exactly how it plays out, Amanda. Let me assure you that the commission is yours to keep—an advance on your salary—but the 'sale' was strictly phony, just a means of tightening the screws on him."

"Then Tom still owns the house?"

"Absolutely. However, he was happy to vacate it temporarily for patriotic reasons. Before Ellis took possession, Tom and Joe wired it from top to bottom."

"If Ellis purchased that place with the idea of bringing the others there, why did Ali show up at the agency?"

"The Davis house may be historic, but it isn't the kind of facility the Scorpion had in mind. He wanted a large, secluded spread with many rooms to accommodate all their nasty associates and enough adjacent buildings to store their arms. The kind of places you've been showing him. He realized immediately that Ellis had pulled a fast one. Instead of using the funds given him for the large hideout the Scorpion wanted, Ellis plowed a large chunk into Tom's house. He'd had the treasure in the back of his mind all along. By pulling that trick, Ellis lost his usefulness as a pawn. The Scorpion had no choice but to become personally involved. His expertise as a villain and ladies' man, combined with a good command of the language and customs, suited the role."

"Do you suppose Ellis would have betrayed him if Tom hadn't presented the opportunity?"

"That's hard to tell, but luck was on our side," Hank said. "Once it became clear to Tom that Ellis's interest in other matters allowed him to be swayed, it offered the perfect way to monitor his connection with the terrorists. He threw out those hints about ghostly sounds to alert you to the situation. In addition to owning a house with a secret room that could be fitted out with useful electronics, his intuition makes him a valuable member of our team."

"I didn't get it at first, didn't even see Ali's—the Scorpion's—connection with Ellis," Amanda said. "They're complete opposites in appearance and behavior. I'd never in the world connect them."

"Every terrorist group needs a variety of personalities in their organization to cover every potential situation," Joe said. "At this point, Ellis has spent a lot of their money and time's running out. They need a place that can house the large number of men they plan to recruit. Tom's house doesn't begin to meet their needs. They also wanted a very secluded location to avoid outside monitoring. When Ellis screwed them up, they had to start from scratch."

"The Scorpion and the others in his group must be furious with Ellis."

"Probably are, but they need him for the time being because of his knowledge of the area," Hank said. "Besides, if he comes up with that treasure, I suspect they intend to take a cut—probably all of it—before eliminating him when he ceases to be useful. Another reason Tom gladly turned over his house to Ellis is to give him plenty of latitude for locating the treasure. Obviously he hasn't found it because he's still looking."

"And now I have it."

"Have what?" The men shouted in unison.

"The first part of the treasure." Amanda patted the canvas bag. "Right here. And I know where the main cache is hidden."

Warrenton, Virginia, 1995

Bunny fidgeted in her chair. She disliked funerals. Even more, she despised the formal reading of wills. As the sole recipient of her father's estate after creditors and taxes, she resented waiting in the law office when she could be riding her favorite mount. She paid little heed as the lawyer droned through the document. It was only when he drew a tattered envelope from the sheaf of papers on his desk that she perked up and paid attention to the close of his narration, "... and this is the clue to the family treasure. Whoever deciphers the puzzle may claim it for his own."

Bunny fairly flew out of her seat. "Puzzle? What are you talking about?"

The lawyer shoved the paper across his desk toward her. "Your father wanted you to have this, along with the information that your Davis ancestors left a treasure for any descendant who solves the puzzle inside. Except for making certain that you understand what is entailed, my involvement ends. Now it's up to you ... or your descendants."

Bunny felt a sudden release. She loved challenges. Grateful that the lawyer had said all he planned to say and was about to dismiss her, she swept the envelope from his desk and bounded out the door. Not until she reached home did she understand the gravity of its contents. Until she could sort things out, she decided to store it in her private safe. Being the Crestmont heiress was burden enough. It was not easy meeting men more interested in her than in her assets. All the more reason why this family secret must remain just that.

CHAPTER SEVENTEEN

Hank's grip around Amanda's shoulder tightened. "Let's start again. What exactly do you have, and how did you get it?"

She began by describing the cryptic note Ali found in Bunny's hand. "I planned to tell you about it when we met in Leesburg, Hank, but when I left Sybil, I thought I'd have enough time to follow my intuition."

"Right into the hornet's nest," Hank said, in mock exasperation.

Joe perked up. "You were with Sybil, the psychic? That's treading on muddy waters."

"What do you mean?"

"When push comes to shove, Amanda, I prefer to get my facts from someone in the hard sciences. The company thinks it's necessary to study a problem from every conceivable angle, even if it's half-cocked. That's why we utilize people like her, but you can count on one hand the actual times she struck pay dirt."

Hank laughed. "More like one finger."

Amanda's eyebrows flew up. "She seems to know a lot about you, Hank."

"She's Sheila's friend, Amanda," Hank said. "Friends talk. Neither of them are on our payroll, but Sheila's connection through her husband gave us a means of tackling this infiltration. I went along with their ghostly priest scheme because it seemed like a non-controversial way of gaining your confidence, not because I'm sold on mind readers and their esoteric adventures."

"Then neither of you believe in clairvoyance?"

"I'm a born skeptic, but I'm willing to be shown," Joe said.

"Double that," Hank said. "Especially when psychic visions are backed by pure research. I'm sure you know that we have an entire department working on teleportation just because there's the extremely remote possibility that they'll figure how to move a dairy cow from Vermont to Montana in the wink of an eye."

Amanda giggled. "But that's not possible."

Both men laughed.

"You know it, and we know it," Joe said. "The only reason the head of that department still draws a fat paycheck is the infinitesimal possibility that it can be done. Teleport that cow and you can teleport an army from one continent to the next. Crazy as it sounds, they don't dare give up investigating ESP and teleportation for fear another country succeeds where fools have been treading."

"In other words, we must never stop believing that anything is possible," Amanda said.

"Never, Amanda." Hank smiled down on her, and she knew they both were thinking of something other than teleportation. Then he grew serious. "What did you think you'd accomplish by going off on your own? After we talked today, you must have known you were in danger."

"It was mid-afternoon. What can go wrong that time of day? Everything would have worked out fine if it weren't for losing my way, and the violinist in the church, and then my car breaking down … oh m'gosh! I forgot all about my car."

Joe sighed, much as a parent reacts to a naughty child's antics. "It's a good thing somebody was keeping track of you. Your tail homed in on it and had it towed back to the Cameron Agency. The problem was that he didn't know at first what had happened to you."

"My tail? The road was deserted. How could someone have followed me?"

"That's what helicopters and private planes are for, along with radios and telescopic cameras," Joe said. "If you'd stayed put, we'd have gotten you out of there fast, but you were nowhere in sight. In the meantime, Hank was completely out of the loop, getting all spruced up for his date with you."

"If I'd guessed you'd spend the afternoon getting into trouble, I'd have handcuffed you to my wrist before you left the office," Hank said. "As it was, I went home and was in the shower when word came that you'd disappeared."

"How did you finally discover me?"

"Simple," Joe said. "Your footprints led right to the house."

"Of course. The rain was the culprit. My hunters and my saviors both found me because of a clue as basic as footprints."

"It also helped that the secret room had sensors confirming someone was up there, and that someone had to be you," Hank said.

"And all the while I was stuck there, I was sure you'd call me."

"For a casual chat?"

"Don't tease. You *did* caution me earlier to hang onto my cell phone."

"Believe me, I was tempted to phone, but I couldn't take the chance that they'd hear it ring. Just for the record, why didn't you call me?"

Sheepishly, Amanda said, "I forgot to store the number in the new phone."

"I suspected as much, Amanda, thanks to the ESP we seem to share." He hugged her emphatically and she felt his lips brush her hair. "But let's go back. A minute ago, you added a whole new element to the case. Where does a violinist pop into the picture?"

She tried to ignore her racing heart. "He was strange, and his music was stranger still. I found the meetinghouse by accident, and even before I entered, I heard eerie music, like something right out of a horror movie."

"Go on," Hank urged.

"He wasn't the least bit friendly. The more questions I asked, the testier he became. He said the music is from a German opera and he was practicing for a concert, but I knew that some of what he told me was a lie."

"Why so?"

"Well, for one thing, the community orchestras disband in late spring and the season is over. He told me he plays with several, but one he named, the Loudoun Symphony, doesn't even exist. And he was driving a rental car with a New Jersey license plate. Obviously, he's not from around here."

Hank frowned. "A stranger in town couldn't stumble on a place that deserted unless someone gave him explicit directions. What do you make of him?"

"I wish I could fit him into the picture. I can't. Not yet. But I was right about the note Bunny was clutching. It gave the clues Ellis must have been after because it led me right to John Davis's apron."

"Apron?" Joe shot Amanda a look that questioned her stability.

"A Masonic apron. And a key. A huge key." She could not disguise her triumph.

Hank tightened his hold on her. "A key to what?"

"The antique store."

"Huh?"

"The fortune buried in the grave. At least that's how I interpret that term. I first believed that Ellis intended the grave for Bunny, but after I found the key, I realized that he simply was after its contents. The rain and mud that got to it today apparently slowed the gravediggers."

"Gravediggers?" The men stared at her, stunned.

"The men Ellis rounded up to dig up the graveyard. I heard him say they got a metal detector to figure out which grave is the most likely."

Joe grunted. "Sounds like they're prepared for all possibilities. I see lots of amateurs out on weekends looking for coins and other relics of the past that are usually found a few inches beneath the under the surface. While it's true that people are buried with wedding rings, gold coins for luck in their next world, or small trinkets, the deeper things are buried, the harder they are to detect. Only a crook would plunder a graveyard."

"They would have accomplished more if it hadn't been for the storm," Amanda said.

"Another bit of luck for us," Joe said. "Metal detectors aren't very effective in the rain. Otherwise the fortune, if it really is there, could be long gone."

"Look, from what you've told us, Amanda, it appears that the clues were unnecessary, after all," Hank said. "Ellis may be homing in on the fortune without them. If the Davis descendants hadn't been conditioned to believing they had to solve the puzzle to access the prize, any one of them could have dug it up years ago if they'd thought about it logically and concluded that a grave is the perfect place to hide a secret."

"Coulda, woulda, shoulda, it doesn't matter," Amanda said. "The point is that everything came together for me when I met Okey Luckett."

"Okey Luckett?"

"The trainer at Maplelawn."

Hank gave a low whistle. "Back up. Our people didn't target Maplelawn. You picked that out yourself. I thought going there was a waste of time, but maybe meeting Luckett was a freak accident."

"That's how I regard it. He told us that Bunny's most recent husband has been traveling around the area acting suspiciously. The first day I met Ellis, alias Elmont, he brought up the subject of old churches. That's not something the average person would dwell on when they're house-hunting. It must have occurred to him already that the graves in the adjacent cemetery might be excellent hiding places. After meeting Bunny, it was obvious to me that he'd managed to pry enough information from her to learn that the Davis family built a meetinghouse near their first home."

"Tom alerted me to that angle," Hank said. "As soon as he told me churches were on Ellis's mind, I checked the current county map. I accounted for all that are in use today, but when I consulted a map published in 1870, I found several in the vicinity that no longer exist. Our aerial surveillance confirmed that two have disappeared, probably torn down by farmers who worked the land nearby, and three are in advanced states of ruin. The Short Hill Meetinghouse is the only abandoned church missing on the current map that's still standing."

"Ellis seemed to have no trouble finding it."

"He could have examined the old map in the Leesburg Library, or maybe he simply poked around the area," Hank said. "Since all private property in the vicinity of Tom's house is fenced off, that leaves very little open land to explore. After all, you managed to find it without even trying."

"That's true," Amanda said. "The area's pretty well deserted. Even though the meetinghouse is at the intersection of two unpaved roads, the trees and bushes around it are overgrown. A person driving by wouldn't necessarily notice it. When I came upon it, the wind was blowing rather fiercely. Each time the branches whipped around, space opened up giving a clear view of the building. On the other hand, anyone passing by on foot, such as joggers or hikers, couldn't miss it."

"We can be pretty certain that Ellis combed the house as soon as he took possession," Hank said. "When he came up with a blank there, he set off looking for the meetinghouse."

"He must be the one who broke the padlock," Amanda said. "His first impulse would have been to check inside. I'll bet he combed through it meticulously, but except for the benches, the building is bare. The graveyard is the only logical hiding place left."

"That's when he realized he'd need some help," Joe said. "Instead of digging up each burial one by one, he decided that a metal detector was the quickest and most accurate way to locate potential treasure. Apparently it wasn't difficult for him to enlist help. That's why we need to know exactly how many people are involved in this operation and where they're holed up."

"Obviously there are quite a few because the Sandpiper needs a large base to accommodate them," Hank said. "We still don't know how much financial backing the operation has, or if they expect to dip into Ellis's resources."

"Tom's place is much too small for a big operation and it doesn't have the privacy that's required," Joe said. "Now that Ellis has decided the treasure isn't there, it's probably of no more use to him."

Hank nodded in agreement. "From what we've seen, Ellis has a much different agenda than the Scorpion has, and once he gets all he needs in the way of manpower to disinter the treasure, I predict he'll cut loose. If so, the goal shifts.

Typically, the Scorpion's response to tricks is to eliminate the trickster. I suspect he's already arranged for something to happen."

"Maybe they'll do each other in," Amanda said.

"That would be the easy way out," Hank said.

"We still can't account for those references on the telephone," Joe said. "Headquarters reported that Ellis called himself Erdmann. Why? The Scorpion called himself Stoker. Why? He called you Ellen. Why? Who's Tony?"

"The more I think about it, I'm pretty sure he's the musician," Amanda said. "Does that get you closer to a solution?"

Hank nodded. "Not yet. We'll have to sleep on that." He paused to grin at Amanda's expression. "Joe, if you'll drop us off at my car, you can take the truck on to the storage facility and I'll get Amanda settled in her new place ..."

Amanda perked up. "New place? Where?"

Hank smiled down at her. "You'll find out soon enough. For now, we all need to call it a day, take time to clear our brains."

"So you actually *are* working two jobs," Amanda marveled. "No wonder your eyes always look red and tired."

"Hear that, Joe, she noticed my eyes. That's the most encouraging thing you've said about me, Amanda."

"They're nice, but they take second prize to that resonant voice of yours. Meg was right. You *could* be mistaken for Robert Goulet."

"Vixen! I should point out that the resonance isn't so obvious in Farsi."

Amanda's stomach lurched. "Farsi? You speak Farsi?"

"Sure do. Since childhood. I picked it up from a neighborhood friend. His folks were natives of Iran. It became our secret clubhouse language. We drove our friends crazy. After I got into this business and my superiors discovered I was fluent in it, they tapped me to infiltrate behind the lines."

Amanda began to tremble. "I don't suppose you ever knew ..."

Hank took a deep breath. It seemed forever to Amanda before he spoke. "I've been waiting for the right time to tell you, Amanda. Yes, I know your father very well. Jim Prescott is the most honorable, intelligent man I've ever known. I last saw him in a small village just inside Afghanistan where he passed me some critical information."

"He was one of our top encoders," Joe said.

"Was?" Amanda searched his face.

Both men fell silent. Softly, Hank said, "Don't ever give up hope, Amanda. I know it's been tough for you financially and emotionally these past few years. Once an agent disappears, his salary is frozen. None of the benefits can be released until there's proof one way or the other. You're not the only relative of a missing agent left in limbo. Any number of things could have happened to him, but I personally know several agents who were missing for a long time before they resurfaced. Miracles do happen."

"How well did—do—you know him?"

"Extremely well," Hank said. "We worked together for several years. He often joked that I was like a son to him. After your mother died, he volunteered for dangerous assignments so the larger salary would cover your conservatory expenses. We both knew we were hanging by our fingernails, but he was determined to help you attain your dreams, and I hadn't yet come to grips with my own mortality. On that last day, I promised to watch over you ... if anything happened."

Tears stung Amanda's eyes. Shakily, she said, "Please don't feel obligated."

"Look at me, Amanda." Their eyes locked as Hank cupped her chin gently in his hand. "Obligation and duty flew out the window at Strathmore Hall. Do you understand?" She nodded, her heart pounding so loudly she knew he must hear it. He drew her close and planted a delicate kiss on her cheek. Amanda knew Joe was aware of everything passing between them, but he bowed to the discretion his business demands and kept his eyes on the road. At length Amanda collected herself. "It's a shock learning you knew him, even though the possibility has been in the back of my mind."

"It's probably no consolation for you to hear that you were encouraged to apply for a job on the Hill because the company supports relatives through roundabout means."

"I always suspected that's why I was recruited. The salary certainly helped, and the job was a blessing when everything else fell through. Nobody on the Hill ever mentioned my father. I never discussed him in case he was still alive and I would place him in danger by talking about him. The only word I ever received was that he was missing somewhere in the Middle East. Hope has kept me going. Since I grew up knowing the importance of keeping family secrets, I'm certain that my involvement in this project was no accident."

"Hardly," Hank said. "You had all the qualities I ... we needed."

"That explains why Senator Shellenberger fairly pushed me out of the office insisting that my clearance was delayed. It must have been confirmed even before you went to Florida to check that reference."

"Long before. With your credentials, top secret clearance was a snap." Hank drew a tissue from his pocket and dabbed at the tears trickling down her cheek.

She managed to return his smile. "As for you, Hank Connors, you might pass for just another spook in a dark suit or a cassock, but you blow your cover the minute you speak. When Meg told about her mysterious visitor, I knew I was in the same kind of convoluted CIA scheme I've been privy to on the Hill, but I didn't realize the extent of my role. At first I thought it involved international banking and loan frauds. It never entered my mind that I'd be a foil for terrorists."

"You had to be kept in the dark. So long as you weren't afraid, they couldn't pick up subconscious signals."

"What happens now that I know?"

"You and I bow out of the Cameron Agency at the earliest opportunity," Hank said. "Even though this is my real life, I've been showing up there daily to maintain appearances and give credence to my great dramatic role as the disagreeable, aloof son. While Sheila runs the company legitimately and delegates duties to the real employees, my assignment has been to project you at all costs."

"You're in capable hands, Amanda," Joe assured her, as they pulled into the Leesburg civic garage, now deserted except for a Honda Civic. He idled the truck while Hank jumped down and helped Amanda out.

"I believe you, Joe," she said. "You've been a wonderful help, too."

Even before the truck pulled away, Amanda's attention shifted to the unremarkable car. "This is yours, Hank? I expected something more appropriate for James Bond."

He grinned. "I work in Washington, not Hollywood. This car gets great mileage and turns the least heads. I don't care to be noticed in flamboyant wheels."

"I've seen it in the Cameron parking lot, always on the far side, where the custodians park. I thought it belonged to one of them."

Hank held the door while she climbed in. "That's exactly what casual observers are supposed to think."

They started down Leesburg's main street, but before they had driven three blocks, Hank pulled into a shopping center and cut the engine. "What would you like to eat?"

"Eat?"

Pointedly, he cleared his throat. "We did have a date, Amanda. I hope you don't plan to stand me up again."

"I thought it was a business engagement," she teased.

His eyes twinkled. "Not in my book. It's long past supper time and you must be starving after that ordeal. I know I am, so I thought we'd pick up something in the supermarket. In view of the events of the past few hours, I'd rather not put you on display in a restaurant."

"Now that you're directing my mind to food, I'm suddenly famished," she admitted.

"I knew I could tempt you. Stay here while I go shopping. You should be safe with the door locked, but if you need instant help, just push this button under the dash. It's an alarm like you wouldn't believe."

Amanda's wise protector flashed a smile as he stepped out of the car and locked the door with a flourish. In less that ten minutes, he reappeared bearing two large grocery bags.

"What did you get?" Amanda asked.

"Only the chef knows for sure," he said.

"Chef?"

"Let's lower his credentials to short-order cook. You'll have to bear with me," he said cheerfully, as he switched on the ignition and headed out of the parking lot.

Crestmont, 1998

Bunny did not know whether to lash out at the old man or play her favorite game of "Dumb Bunny." She chose the latter. This was not the first time a perfect stranger had boldly asked about the family secret.

Three years after her father's death, she sensed that everyone in Northern Virginia knew the story about a treasure left by her Davis ancestors. Despite the trust her father declared for his lawyer, she was certain that the leak had originated in that office, if not from the lawyer, then from his sociable secretary.

Donning the inscrutable expression that always served her well, she repeated the response she reserved for snoops. "There are lots of stories about hidden treasures. It's a romantic idea, but I doubt that many tales we've heard about pirates and grizzled old prospectors are true. Even if a treasure existed two hundred years ago, someone surely has found it by now. If so, I'm certain they'd keep it for themselves and not tell a soul."

The old man nodded. "You may be right, but it doesn't hurt to keep looking."

And so the rumor continued spreading throughout Loudoun County, eventually through all of Northern Virginia. A friend with school-age children in

Fairfax told Bunny that teachers were incorporating the story in their history lessons of the commonwealth.

In time, she became immune to the rumors, as if they pertained to another family, not hers. But she could not resist opening the envelope time and again to study the code.

No matter how she struggled to decipher the lines, they made no sense to her. She could only hope that one day, like a sharp slap on the side of the head, the solution would present itself.

CHAPTER EIGHTEEN

Hank motioned toward the grocery sacks on the back seat. "In case my culinary efforts bomb, I picked up a quart of rocky road ice cream."

"How did you know that's my favorite?"

Hank winked. "You and I are cut from the same mold, Amanda. I hope your fondness for Broadway baritones extends to the Big Bad Wolf."

"You've lost me."

"Not for long, I hope." He pulled out of the shopping center onto Leesburg Pike. Once they were tooling briskly eastward, he returned to the task of satisfying her burning curiosity. "Like you, I started out in music. At the suggestion of a buddy, after graduating from college I went to New York and auditioned for a new show. A few days later, they called me back and gave me the role of Prince Charming and the Wolf in *Into The Woods*."

Amanda burst into laughter. "I adore Sondheim, especially that dual role. You couldn't have picked a more appropriate one for a budding spy."

"Chortle if you must, Cinderella. It was my theatrical swan song."

"Why?"

"I told you we're cut from the same mold." He grew serious. "At the time, I was engaged to a girl I met in college. She and some friends were driving to New York for opening night. They never made it. A drunk driver crossed over the median strip, hit them head on, and they were killed."

Amanda reached over and touched his arm. "I'm so sorry."

His hand sought hers. "Everything happens for a reason, Amanda. That was my first encounter with death. It made me realize that I was unfit for the career that interested me the most."

"Performing?"

"No, that was my avocation, not really a long-term goal. For years, I had seriously considered studying for the ministry."

"I'm not surprised. My long conversations with Henry revealed that side of you. How did you end up on stage instead?"

"If you think about it, acting and sermonizing are closely related. I always liked the idea of helping people surmount their problems. Until the accident, I had the naive notion that most troubles can be overcome by singing an uplifting song or a magnificent anthem. I thought I could inspire mankind from behind a pulpit, backed by great organ pipes and a huge choir."

"You're right about the power of music to lift people from the depths. It kept me going when I thought I couldn't bear another tragedy."

"Your losses helped you find strength at a young age, but I was fresh out of college, happy as a lark, with no understanding of how the rest of the world gets by. At that moment, my primary goal was to make it big on Broadway. After amassing the fortune I believed was due me, I'd have the financial wherewithal to think about a real career in the ministry.

"The accident changed everything. My entire world came crashing down and shattered my foolish assumption that life is a musical comedy with a guaranteed happy ending. I couldn't handle the loss, so I dropped out of the cast and joined the Army. I suppose it was my way of doing penance for something that gave me a feeling of blame, even though it wasn't my fault. In typical Broadway tradition, my understudy went on to fame."

"No regrets?"

He tossed her a wry smile. "Over the years, I've learned that it's foolish to look back when you can look to the future. Like you, I found another career and circumstances changed. After being in Special Services for a few years, I was recruited by the CIA and discovered that time really does heal everything. In retrospect, I know that she wasn't the one for me. Too many of our interests and goals conflicted. She thought that the life of a minister's wife would be tiresome and unrewarding financially. Instead, she pressed me to go into business with her father once my infatuation with the theater ended. I would have been bored out of my skull without excitement and variety in my work. So you see, I understood exactly when Meg told me about your situation."

"I was afraid it made me sound selfish and ungrateful."

"Not a chance. It convinced me I'd made the right choice."

"That's a cryptic response."

He laughed. "Not as cryptic as that note, Amanda. You must have inherited decoding skills from your father."

As they drew near Tyson's Corner, Hank swung the car into an unfamiliar driveway. Amanda tensed. "Where are we?"

"This is what we call a 'safe house,' one of our many hideaways to accommodate defectors to our side, and anyone else in danger of attack by our adversaries. You'll stay here tonight."

"But my clothes, and …"

"All taken care of, my dear. Sheila arranged for your belongings to be moved over here so you won't wake up tomorrow morning protesting that you haven't a thing to wear." Hank broke into a grin as he turned off the engine and headlights. "We think of everything."

"I'm continually amazed. Every move is perfectly coordinated."

"We try hard. Truth is, the minute the Scorpion suggested tossing you off the balcony, priorities changed. Poisoned darts stored in ball-point pens are his specialty. I'll get you settled here tonight, then tomorrow morning I'll pick you up and take you to the office. To keep you out of the spotlight, I'll forewarn the staff that I've given you so much paperwork you won't be able to see clients."

"They'll believe that?"

"Do you question my acting ability?"

"Burke deserves an Oscar, but I much prefer Hank."

"Those words warm the cockles of Burke's cold, cold heart," he said as he took her arm and guided her into the "hideaway."

Amanda was impressed by the attractive townhouse in an upscale section of McLean. A Williamsburg replica in design, it was Twenty-first Century in security, with steel doors in triplicate opening into the entrance hall, heavy draperies swathing bullet-proof windows, and a surveillance camera in every room.

Amanda eyed them with alarm. "Where can I undress away from prying eyes?"

Hank affected a serious pose. "You may have a problem. Try the bathroom, or the bedroom closet. In fact, why don't you freshen up while I get our supper. If I can't see you through my magic mirror, we'll assume that Big Brother's wearing blinders."

"I'll take you up on that," she said. "After wallowing in the mud and being trapped in that stuffy loft all those hours, I can use a hot shower."

"While you whip yourself into shape, I'll whip up a quick meal," Hank promised. "Will thirty minutes be enough?"

"Just time me," she dared him.

Thirty minutes later, refreshed and refurbished in a soft blouse, billowy skirt, and sandals, Amanda swept into the kitchen where her master chef held forth amid the melodic strains of Stravinsky's "Firebird." Manipulating his utensils like a professional, Hank stood over a pan filled with a golden concoction guaranteed to whet the taste buds of the haughtiest gourmet.

Amanda clapped her hands in delight. "Omelets are perfect for a late evening meal."

As Hank's head swiveled in her direction, the spatula went rigid in his hand. At length, he found his voice. "*Omelettes au fromage* for the most sensational looking lady I've ever seen, and that's no cheese. When you blush, Amanda, your cheeks are prettier than those strawberries." He nodded toward the dining alcove where two cantaloupe halves were piled high with blueberries, sliced bananas, grapes, and opulent strawberries.

She tried to be blasé. "You have quite a line. Is that a company ploy to render your victims helpless?"

His gaze was steady. "A line? Hardly. Sometimes I play so many roles at work that my real self gets lost in the maze but every word meant for your ears comes from the heart."

She smiled up at him, afraid to speak for fear of saying the wrong thing. So much was tumbling through her mind. In the office, his tailored suits and austere reading glasses gave him the aristocratic, hands-off aura of the successful businessman; clad now in chinos and a polo shirt, he moved with the grace of a star quarterback, and yet his genuine smile came directly from the soul of a home-loving do-it-yourselfer.

Hank focused on his task, folding the omelets with all the expertise of a man who had learned to live alone well, if not contentedly. He ladled them onto the platters with a flourish, then studied Amanda expectantly. "You're not moving toward the table. Aren't you hungry?"

"Of course I am. I'm just amazed at how well you know this place, where everything is kept, right down to the pot holders. Have you been here often?"

"Quite a few times. This is one of our better local safe houses, so I've brought a couple of Soviet defectors here."

"Women?" she blurted.

His eyes danced with amusement. "Why do you ask?"

Amanda's cheeks flamed. "I didn't mean to say that. It just popped out. You seem so domesticated in this kind of situation, and ..."

"My, my, Amanda." He clucked his tongue. "I'm flattered that you're curious about my secret romantic life as an 007 clone, and I must confess that one person I escorted here was the most fascinating I've ever met." As her eyes widened, Hank smiled wickedly, assessing her reaction before adding his punch line, "It was a balding, paunchy Soviet ex-general. Now are you going to eat your supper like a good little girl, or must I confess more of my sins before you show me the courtesy of sampling my wares?"

She did not resist when he took her arm gently and steered her toward the table. "If this meal tastes as marvelous as it looks, I absolve you of all your sins," she said, slipping into the chair he held in an exaggerated act of chivalry.

"For my sake, I hope you're not disappointed. Now, may I join you?"

She returned his broad smile. "That's a given."

Exactly as they had done by telephone for so many happy evenings, they chatted easily about music, food, and politics. Their conversation was enhanced by the pleasure of devouring the savory omelets, a ham steak, the voluptuous fruit, flaky cinnamon rolls, and coffee so divinely rich that Amanda was filled with contentment of a gourmet kind. When their plates were clean, she cleared the table while Hank filled two bowls with heaping scoops of ice cream.

Amanda had not realized how hungry she was until she stared down at her empty bowl, dribbles of rocky road ice cream barely evident. "Everything was absolutely delicious," she said. "Thank you, Hank."

Hank laid his napkin aside. "Feel better now?"

"Much, much better. About everything."

He grinned. "Me too. I'm glad we're playing from the same score."

Reaching for Amanda's hand, he pulled her to her feet and drew her into the living room, where they settled themselves close together on the sofa, well out of the prying camera's range.

She smiled up at him. "I'm so comfortable with you, it seems we've known each other forever."

"Maybe we have." He let that hang for a moment. "This afternoon you'd reached the point where you needed to know the whole story and I couldn't chance being overheard in the office. I thought we'd go for a drive and find a quiet place in the country where we could have dinner, relax, and talk without the threat of being bugged."

"I was so looking forward to that," she said. "It was such a relief to receive confirmation that we were allies, true friends. Even though I instinctively felt our connection from the very beginning, I have to admit that I walked into your office that first day believing what Joe, alias Martin, told me about the incorrigible Burke."

"And now you know that his evil reputation was written into the devious script to get you on board and that Burke wasn't the real me. Both of us knew a great deal about you, however."

"That I'm frequently gullible and trusting and actually would believe that Sheila was hiring me to work for the Cameron Agency out of the goodness of her heart?"

"Enough to know that you were perfect for this tough job, thanks to Senator Shellenberger's detailed profile and your background." Hank was suddenly quiet. His eyes searched hers. "And perfect for me."

He enfolded her trembling hand in both of his. "Amanda, we were destined for each other. Right after I got back from Afghanistan, I heard an announcer on the good music station mention your upcoming concert at Strathmore Hall. During my last conversations with your dad, I still envisioned you as the gangling teen-age daughter he had talked about when we first worked together. But when I picked up a concert flyer and saw your photograph—wow! The woman of my dreams had been out there all along and I never suspected. Your program was even more uncanny. Every piece listed was a favorite of mine, as if you had planned it for me alone.

"I was determined to meet you for your father's sake, but even more for my own. So you wouldn't think I was just another single guy on the prowl, I invited a date. Big mistake. She was musically illiterate. Didn't know the difference between Papa Haydn and Puff Daddy."

Amanda giggled. "There goes my competition."

"It's funny in retrospect, but my mistake prolonged our meeting by several years. After the concert, we got in line at the reception. We were at the very end, and he ..."

"Craig," she supplied.

"... Yes, Craig. He was directly in front of us. Even though he must have known that others wanted to meet you, he kept talking. I thought surely he'd move away after giving you his card, but he continued to monopolize the conversation. I became annoyed and dug in, planning to wait as long as necessary to meet you. The longer we waited, the more my ill-advised date whined about eating. I'd picked her up right after work and she hadn't had time for supper, so she let me know she was expecting to be fed, pronto. At first I ignored her, but she kept getting louder and tugging on my arm. I was afraid you'd overhear and remember my selfish, thoughtless behavior, so I gave in and left with her."

"It comes back so clearly. I was upset to see you walk away and wondered if I had said something to Craig or done something that made you lose interest."

Hank sighed. "I can't tell you how many times that evening has played over and over in my mind. I should have sent her home in a cab and stayed in line, all night, if necessary. The next morning, I called your management to request your phone number. They wouldn't give it out, even though I explained that I'd attended your concert and wanted to phone my appreciation. They told me to send an email to your web site and mentioned your concert scheduled in London a month later."

"That's their job," Amanda said. "They act as a buffer for potential stalkers. Since Craig gave me his card, I told them to pass along my number if he called. Which he did. I never looked at my web site, so I didn't see your email. And that's where my side of the story begins.

"The minute I walked on stage that night, I felt electricity all around and somehow I sensed that the most important person in my life was in the audience. Each note I played was for him, and when I looked out into the audience and our eyes met, I was a goner. It was no accident that I added a second encore, a medley of romantic Broadway numbers." Hank smiled. "One of them, 'A Foggy Day,' was almost prophetic. It so happened that I was reassigned overseas soon afterward and landed in London the week you made your debut at Wigmore Hall. I had to leave the night before your concert, so that last day I walked along the Thames hoping against hope that suddenly I'd see you there, just as the lyrics say."

"If only I'd known. The Thames River was within sight of my hotel room and that song kept replaying in my mind. I remember shivers going up my spine and sensing that someone was waiting there for me, but I was too cautious to investigate. By then, Craig was pursuing me at every turn and the evening of the Strathmore concert had become a blur in my mind. Every time I tried to remember exactly what I shared with the stranger in the audience, Craig didn't seem to fit into the mold as a soul mate. I was all the more puzzled about him because I never experienced the electricity in his presence that had overwhelmed me that night. Still, I fought to believe that he was the one who had made my heart stand still for a brief moment."

Hank smiled. "That's exactly how I'd put it. My heart stood still the moment we made eye contact. You really had doubts about him?"

"Oh so many, even before we became engaged, but it would have been cruel to break off after his illness was identified. That was a terrible year, wondering what happened to my father, watching Craig die, and remaining loyal to him without ever betraying my true feelings."

"You did the right thing to stay by him, Amanda," Hank said. "That was a tough year for me, too. When I got back to the States and read your engagement announcement in the paper, I felt like I'd been kicked in the stomach. Instead of trying to locate you through our office, as I should have done, I reacted as rashly as I did after that fatal accident. I signed on to help the Kurds."

Amanda gasped. "What if something had happened to you?"

"Don't even think about it. It was touch and go, but there was a silver lining. By pulling it off better than I expected, I was rewarded with a big promotion to our Langley office and the challenge to squelch the Scorpion and his terrorists.

"I hadn't been home a month before I came across Craig's obituary on line. There was no mention of a surviving wife, so my hope was renewed. I tracked you to the Hill through the 'company' computer files, but before I could contact you and share your father's message, the Scorpion made his move. Right away, I consulted with Senator Shellenberger and proposed your name as a decoy."

"The morning I set out for Florida, my spirits were lower than they'd been for months," Amanda said. "Everything seemed to be going wrong, but there was no reason to suspect that I was in the midst of a devious plot."

"Two plots," Hank said, his eyes twinkling. "Kathy Owens and I became co-conspirators. She picked up on my interest in you even before I confided in her, and she encouraged my underhanded pursuit through our mutual love of music. I couldn't imagine why you stopped performing, given your talent, and I was determined to turn that situation around."

Amanda smiled broadly. "I might have known Kathy was somewhere in the background. She's the last of the true romantics. She urged me to continue performing, but Craig's health plan didn't cover the expensive treatments he needed at NIH and neither of us had family who could help. Selling my piano was the only way to raise enough. I knew that I was sacrificing my future, but giving it up helped me face the truth that I didn't want a career on stage."

"After all those years of training, it must have been wrenching to realize that you'd been chasing the wrong dream," Hank said.

"In the back of my mind, I knew it all along. Ever since childhood, I've loved music. Playing the piano has been my way of connecting with the ether, the mystical sounds far out in space, but shortly after my management put me on a busy schedule, the joy I'd known all my life began evaporating. I hated the hours spent sitting in airports and hotel rooms. The actual time devoted to sharing my music with others was only a fraction of the travel time."

"It must have been a lonely life."

"It was far too lonely for me. On top of everything, I couldn't take criticism. Reviewers don't mean to hurt feelings, I'm sure, but so many of them take glee in showing off their expertise by comparing the way a newcomer plays a particular passage with artists like Emanuel Ax or Jean-Yves Thibaudet who have been out there for years. It simply stopped being fun."

"Those experiences didn't alter your love of music, did they?"

"Heavens, no. I'll always enjoy playing, but for pleasure, not financial gain."

"Does playing for me figure into your idea of pleasure?" The corners of Hank's eyes crinkled into a loving smile.

"You must know it does. That's why I've been practicing faithfully … on Henry's fiancée's piano."

Hank looked her squarely in the eye. "Surely you're figured out by now that I bought the piano and house for you, my dearest, and that that my mysterious bride-to-be is sitting by my side at this very moment."

Amanda smiled back. "I have to confess that's what I've been hoping, with all my heart."

"In case you need further confirmation, this should make my intentions perfectly clear, Amanda." With that, Hank enfolded her in his arms, and kissed her emphatically.

Their first official kiss was as natural to Amanda as if they had been lovers for years. They kissed and hugged over and over again, their hearts beating wildly. Amanda even shed a few tears of joy. She was still catching her breath when he whispered into her ear, "Exactly what I wanted to do when you walked into my Cameron office."

"I might have beaten you off at first, but not for long," she said, wrapping her arms tightly around his neck and savoring his nearness. "From the moment you stood and asked me to stay, I've been in over my head, Hank. Despite what I'd been told about Burke, he didn't seem real, but you, whoever you were, were very real. If it hadn't been for the glasses you wear in the office, I would have connected you immediately with the face and those deep, deep eyes that haunted me at the concert. Each time we met, I felt closer to you, and today when you played my recording, I knew exactly who you were even though I didn't know anything else about you."

"You'll have a lifetime to learn everything you need to know," he said.

Just before melting into the strong curve of his body, Amanda paused. "By the way, darling, are you sure we're out of camera range?"

"Heck, who cares?" he murmured.

The remains of the omelets had congealed in the pan by the time they began restoring the kitchen to its former pristine state. They worked slowly, reluctant to part until the late hour and the prospect of rising early made the decision for them.

As he was about to leave, Hank cautioned, "One warning, sweetheart. At the office tomorrow, bad boy Burke must be kept at a very respectable arm's length. Can you manage?"

"If I try very hard, what's my reward?"

He drew her close. "A ring on your finger and one in my nose ... for the rest of our lives ... but only if you give an award-winning performance and neither of us becomes a target for the next few days."

Amanda gulped, back to stark reality. "That's a fair deal."

After bestowing a parting kiss, Hank left. She turned out the lights, glowing like a school girl, and retired to the bedroom where she very soon fell asleep and dreamed of her dearest love who now had a name she never would forget.

Crestmont, 2006

Bunny was swimming between two worlds. The one behind was dark and painful. It forced her forward, contorting her neck with excruciating pressure. The one ahead was eons distant, accessible solely through a narrow tunnel. Deafening sound swirled about her head, as if someone were beating her about the ears with a heavy plank. Through the din, a faint voice emerged from the past.

"Drop the plumb line of truth to the all-seeing eye ..."

Her arms reached out, trying to grab something, anything. Helpless, she began to fall, spiraling round and round, caught in a downward vortex.

The last thing she remembered was a cacophony of voices, a swirl of lights, and hands lifting her up.

CHAPTER NINETEEN

Amanda had just finished clearing away breakfast dishes when the buzzer rang.

"Burke here." Hank's voice over the intercom was all business, as promised.

She opened the door to an entryway flooded with sunlight.

"Ready?" he asked.

"For whatever comes," she assured him.

Before securing the door, he took charge of the Davis key, as they had arranged the evening before. After dropping Amanda off at the Cameron Agency, he would deliver it to the CIA's Langley headquarters down the road where a team of sleuths were about to be transformed into gravediggers. Happily relieved of that responsibility, Amanda basked in his presence during the short drive to the office.

Robin greeted her with word of Ali's visit the previous day. "I know it's against company policy, but he begged for your phone number and home address. He was so persistent and adorable about it that I was sure you wouldn't object to having a gorgeous specimen like that show up at the front door. Did he come around?"

Amanda donned a cloak of nonchalance. "If he did, I have no way of knowing because I was out for the evening—with a friend," this to Robin's upraised eyebrows. "If he calls this morning, tell him I haven't yet arrived and that you'll be glad to leave a message for me. To be truthful, Robin, I have lots of catching up to do and would rather not be disturbed."

Before Robin could probe further and question her excuse, Amanda scurried off to her office to await further instruction from Hank. When anyone passed by the open door, she feigned industry, shuffling meaningless papers across the desk to appear occupied. Beneath them were crossword puzzles and cryptograms to ease her boredom. After an hour, she could stand it no longer and decided a break to stretch her legs and mind was in order. She walked into the reception area just as Janel entered from outside.

"Amanda, great to see you."

"Same here, Janel. It's been a while. You must be very busy."

"The pace has been exhausting, exactly the way I like it. How about you?"

"It's exciting, a real education."

"Robin tells me you're working with a tall, dark, and handsome dreamboat."

"If you like that type." Amanda hoped her smile veiled her fear.

"I do, I do. If you tire of tending to his needs, feel free to toss him my way."

"Gladly," Amanda said, at the very moment Hank made his entrance as Burke, the aloof.

"Morning," he said, barely acknowledging their greetings.

Janel rolled her eyes in Amanda's direction, as if to convey her distaste for the "boss."

"A couple of messages on your desk, Mr. Cameron," Robin said.

"Thanks," said that man of minimal words.

Raising her voice for his ears, Janel said, "Listen, I've got tons to do. Not a minute to relax. That reminds me, Amanda. I have two tickets for Wolf Trap tonight, but I can't make it. Can you use them?"

"Only if I get caught up with everything," Amanda said, trying to act swamped. "What's playing?"

"Actually, it's a hoot," Janel said. "The National Symphony Orchestra is accompanying a spooky silent movie, 'Nosferatu,' the original Dracula story. The audience is invited to come dressed in vampire costumes. If you're into gore and ghouls, it should be fun."

Hank froze in his steps midway across the office. Everything clicked.

Amanda could not get the words out fast enough. "Absolutely, Janel. I'll take those tickets."

Hank's eyes met hers over Janel's shoulder and he began to croon, "B-I-N-G-O, BI-N-G-O, B-I-N-G-O, and Bingo was his name, sir!"

Janet whispered, "Is he crazy, or what?" She rummaged through her Kate Spade handbag to locate the tickets and handed over the prize while Hank, alias Burke, hurried down the hall to compose a note for Amanda's eyes only.

At his suggestion, they slipped out a side door shortly after noon to prepare for the evening. He dropped her at the safe house with a parting kiss and the promise to return after running several errands.

Late that afternoon, she opened the door of her hideaway to an imposing figure in a long, black cape and a slouch hat. "If I weren't expecting you, I'd be scared out of my wits," she said.

Hank bent to kiss her, then produced a box of long-stemmed roses.

"Oh, Hank, they're gorgeous, just like your voice."

He followed her to the kitchen and helped her locate a crystal bowl. After she arranged the flowers, he offered a second package. "Something to fit the occasion."

Inside the wrappings Amanda discovered a cape, a twin of the one he wore. "It's perfect. My favorite shade of black to flatter this pants suit. You did say to come prepared to sit on the ground, didn't you?"

"Just while we devour our picnic," he said.

"Picnic?"

"Part of the fun at Wolf Trap is having a picnic supper on the lawn before the show begins, so I picked up a basket of chicken, a tossed salad, sour dough bread, carrot cake …"

"You have a way with food. Let's go," she said, tucking her arm into his.

Two hours before the main attraction, cars were already snaking into the parking lots. "Spaces disappear quickly," Hank explained. "It'll be especially tough finding one tonight with the President and his family coming."

"The President?"

"The Falcon," he corrected, pausing until that registered with Amanda. "Wherever he attends a public performance, everyone has to pass through security gates. That eliminates handguns, but lots of other deadly weapons might very well go undetected. That's why the Secret Service and several other key organizations will be well represented tonight."

As they strolled across the spacious lawn sharing the handle of the picnic basket, Amanda noticed that many around them were deadly serious about entering into the spirit of the evening. Along with the usual casual summertime attire, black capes, long ghoulish gowns, and false fangs were in abundance.

"About a tenth of them actually are spooks," Hank said, using the slang term for his colleagues. "Now that we can connect this performance with the musician you met yesterday, we need a large contingent."

Kneeling on the cool grass within sight of the amphitheater, they took turns dipping into the basket for the tempting dishes. When the entire contents were spread on the cloth before them, they filled their plates, tasting and munching in delectable silence until a barbershop quartet strolled by harmonizing songs in vogue during the 1920s and early 1930s.

"They remind me of Mad Romance," Hank said.

Amanda frowned. "Mad Romance? That sounds a bit risqué. Please explain, sir."

He patted her hand. "It's quite harmless, my love. Before I hit the big time, I belonged to a college vocal ensemble that performed at proms, weddings, birthday parties, you name it. Since we fancied ourselves as a sort of collegiate offshoot of Manhattan Transfer, we wanted a name to reminded people of the kind of music in their repertoire that made them famous. After voting on several possibilities, we picked Mad Romance."

Amanda was puzzled. "Where on earth did that come from?"

"Remember Jerome Kern's 'Yesterdays'?"

She began to hum the tune, then brightened. "Here's the line you mean: 'Olden days, golden days, Days of mad romance and love.'"

Hank grinned in admiration. "A musician after my heart. You not only know the music, but you're into lyrics, as well. We included that song in every program to make certain the audience saw the connection."

"Very clever. End of story?"

"Not quite. The others put me in charge of the publicity, so I had to call various music agencies and convince them that we deserved bookings. Our name intrigued them, so we did pretty well until I rang up one local organization hoping to promote our group as entertainment for their upcoming convention. When the lady answering the phone heard me say, 'I represent Mad Romance,' she asked for my phone number and location, then sent the local police around to my dorm to arrest me."

Hank's description of his silly predicament made Amanda laugh so hard tears ran down her cheeks. When she finally collected herself, she tugged at his arm. "Tell me, whatever happened? How did you talk yourself out of jail?"

He grinned. "Actually, it turned out well. After I explained the phrase to the officers who came prepared to haul me away, they thought it was pretty funny, and when the woman learned the whole story, she ended up hiring us for a couple of gigs. Now that you know I'm not perfect, I'll take it from the top and start filling you in on the thirty-four years you've missed."

For the next hour, Hank led Amanda through his childhood in Allentown, Pennsylvania, his college days, his stint in the army and subsequent duty in special forces before he was recruited by the CIA. Until the ten-minute gong sounded, she forgot that they were on a serious, possibly treacherous, mission.

After returning the empty picnic basket to Hank's car, they headed to the press office. An armed detail was stationed outside. Pulling aside his cape, Hank revealed a badge to the officer in charge. Without hesitation, the officer saluted and motioned them around the temporary security gates installed just beyond the ticket office. They continued along a path to the main gate where another guard examined Hank's badge and admitted them through the turnstile with a flourish.

"Have a good evening, sir," he said.

Once they were out of earshot, Amanda whispered, "How did you manage that?"

He grinned. "Stick with me, sweetheart. I'll get you into the very best places."

An usher led them to seats inside the Filene Center. Moments after they began perusing the program, Amanda clutched Hank's arm and whispered, "Yes. This is it."

"What have you found?"

She pointed to the program notes. "Exactly as the violinist said, the score by Hans Erdmann was based on music from an opera by Heinrich Marschner."

Hank sucked in his breath. "Bram Stoker wrote the original Dracula story. And here you are among the characters. Ellen, the heroine."

"What do you make of it?"

He sorted it out as he spoke. "Stoker, the brains behind it all. Erdmann the operator. Ellen, the unfortunate damsel. Everything's clear except the method of elimination."

""What are we looking for?"

"A violinist in the orchestra who answers to the description of the one you saw at the meetinghouse."

At precisely that moment, the orchestra struck up "Hail to the Chief." Audience members rose en masse, eagerly craning their necks to catch a glimpse of the President and his family waving from the third row.

Hank groaned.

Following his gaze, Amanda immediately understood the problem. The orchestra, seated on a movable platform, rose from the pit as they played. In keeping with the theme, each musician wore an outfit worthy of a vampire fashion show. The half-masks on every face suggested a convention of phantoms.

"I hope you can see the string section clearly," Hank said.

Amanda stared in dismay. "They all look alike."

Once the stage manager confirmed that the President, his party, and the rest of the audience had settled back into their seats, the lights dimmed and curtains at the rear of the stage parted to reveal an enormous screen. At the downbeat, the orchestra struck the first of the evening's icy chords. The inharmonious passages built quickly into a cacophony of sound to create the sinister aura suggested on screen by the grainy black-and-white film.

From every direction, audience members reacted in chorus to events on the screen, shrieking in horrified delight at times, hissing the villain at others. All the while, Hank's eyes darted from side to side, observing audience reaction, scrutinizing the musicians, alert for any slight motion or deviation that could signal an attack on the President. Meanwhile, Amanda struggled to identify Tony, the violinist. Occasional streaks of light bounced off the screen, bombarding segments of the darkened stage. She leaned forward to examine the faces bent over the scores, but the masks and the shaded lamp bulbs on their music stands allowed no light to be cast on their identities. Suddenly she dug her nails into Hank's arm and hissed, "Watch the violin bows. One's out of sync. That's him."

"Which one?"

"Last row, sixth from the front."

Hank lowered his head and spoke urgently into his pager. Within seconds, Amanda saw two dark figures emerge from the wings and spirit the uncoordinated violinist behind the curtain. At the same time, a squadron of spooks at the front of the theater materialized around the President and his family. It all proceeded with such precision that folks mesmerized by events unfolding on the screen could not have noticed.

Ten minutes later, when the screen grew dark and the lights came up to announce intermission, audience members were detained briefly while the dignitaries were escorted to the V.I.P lounge. Bolting from his seat, Hank grabbed Amanda's hand and together they bulldozed through the aisle, issuing perfunctory apologies to everyone in their wake. With each flash of Hank's badge, guards cleared the way. Two steps at a time, he mounted the stage and pulled Amanda into the wings where his colleagues had the situation well in hand.

One of them swung a handcuffed prisoner around for Amanda to identify. "That's definitely Tony," she confirmed.

Tony snarled an epithet at her.

"You gave yourself away," she admonished him. "If you really were a member of the National Symphony Orchestra, you would have known the proper bowing because the string section always works that out well in advance."

Hank smiled broadly. "My fiancée, the musical detective, without whom we could be in the throes of a national emergency." After introducing Amanda all around he became sober and added, "If she weren't so clever, she could have ended up as his victim."

"You're both lucky," another agent said. "His M.O. was poisoned darts in the bow. They're ejected by pushing a button."

"The usual in an unusual context," Hank mused. "How did he get on stage without being noticed?"

"He eliminated the competition," the agent said, quickly adding, "But it's not so bad. No murder, just a nasty bang on the head that put one of the violinists out of commission."

"Where is he now?"

"Medics working on him below."

"Can we see him?" Hank asked.

Another agent beckoned. "Come this way, sir."

Amanda and Hank crossed the vast backstage area, dwarfed beneath the daunting display of ropes, flats, and hydraulic equipment that can transform the Filene Center stage into any manner of make-believe world a production dictates.

At the far side, the agent led them into an elevator. Two floors down, they entered a narrow hall to the dressing room area flanked by two stern officers.

"Here's where we found the victim," one said. He opened the door to a tiny cubicle monopolized by a harp case. "He'd just come to and was yelling his head off."

"What shape is he in now?" Hank asked.

"Fair. The ambulance just left for the hospital. As they were carrying him out, I overheard the medic say that a bad headache was the worst he could expect."

"Did the violinist know what happened?"

"He said he was walking down the hallway when someone opened a door behind him. Next thing, he felt like the walls came down on his head and that's all he remembered until he woke up in the dark. Thought he was in some kind of a coffin. Here's what hit him."

The officer indicated a metal music stand lying on the floor. "As soon as they finish taking the prints and photos, we'll be out of here."

"So Tony got on stage within close range of the President simply by slugging the violinist, stuffing him in the harp case, and taking his place," Amanda mused. "How did he get past the heavy security detail?"

"We figure he came through the stage entrance early in the day before the gates were manned," the officer said. "Once inside, he stayed low until he found a vulnerable violinist. The empty harp case was an ideal hiding place. With the body out of sight, nobody would suspect anything. That's just about the whole story, ma'am. The masks did the rest."

"One down, and at least two more to go," Hank said. While he was thanking the officer, another poked his head through the doorway to report that the President sent his regards and gratitude for the way the situation was handled.

Amanda gazed at Hank with awe. "You certainly do have friends in high places."

Back on the stage level, Hank conferred with his colleagues while she stood alongside. From their vantage point in the wings, they watched the orchestra tune up for the second half of the evening. The President's party returned to their seats momentarily and the final portion of the Dracula epic got underway. Except for a slightly long intermission and one less violinist, the entire incident was handled with such discretion the audience never suspected that the real drama was live, not on film.

But even Amanda was not prepared for the surprise that came over Hank's pager as they inched their way out of the parking lot.

His noncommittal expression blossomed into a huge grin. "All *right*. Sandpiper too? … No kidding? … It's unbelievable … What a piece of *luck* … You bet. We'll be out there tomorrow."

From the moment he uttered Sandpiper's name to the devilish wink he tossed her, Amanda suspected that the rest of the principals in the case were partaking of the same fate that had befallen Tony.

"They got Ali, the Scorpion, didn't they?"

He nodded. "It was perfect timing. Just as we'd hoped, he led us right to the Sandpiper."

"Who is …?"

"The brains behind multiple terrorist projects. We've been on his trail for a long time, but he's so slippery we knew our best chance to grab him would be when one of the others we're following made contact with him. It so happens that 'Sandpiper' is also the name of his boat. Pretty bold of him to broadcast his identity in that manner. We didn't know where he'd show up next, but we made a good guess. Found both the Scorpion and the Sandpiper on the boat heading down the Potomac with a small crew of tough customers. He'd been docked at a marina in Alexandria while the C4 was unloaded."

"C4? What's that?"

"A high-powered plastic explosive that could level the White House, the Capitol, the Pentagon, or an entire military installation. There's no limit to its incendiary power when a blasting cap's in place. It's hard for the casual observer to identify because each stick looks like child's clay or something equally safe, but a slight bump wreaks havoc. Terrorists consider it a favorite tool of destruction. Our source says it was packaged in UPS boxes."

"UPS boxes? Really? That's what I stood on yesterday."

Hank's head snapped around. "What are you talking about?"

"The boxes I found in the shed. I didn't have a ladder, so I just piled up a couple and climbed on top to reach the keystone above the front door."

"Are you telling me that you lugged boxes of C4 back and forth willy-nilly?"

In a very small voice, Amanda said, "Uh-huh, but I had no idea ..."

Hank expelled a long, deep breath. She was unable to read his face as he steered the car onto the shoulder of the road and cut the engine, but when he took her in his arms, there was no mistaking his purpose. "Amanda, I'm firing you this minute from the Cameron Agency and ordering you to marry me at once. I need to keep you under constant surveillance."

"Well for goodness sake, why didn't you say so sooner?" She would have added more, but his kiss eliminated the need.

The Short Hill, Loudoun County

Bunny stirred in the hospital bed. The headache was gone, but she could not shake the voices. They came to her in song, of that she was certain, a chorus of voices singing a familiar melody from her childhood. Now they drew closer. In a moment, she sensed them just beyond the window. It was a joyous sound, one that coaxed a smile to her lips.

"The land of my fathers, the land of my choice,

The land in which poets and minstrels rejoice.

The land whose stern warriors were true to the core

While bleeding for freedom of yore.

Wales! Wales! Favorite land of Wales.

While sea her wall, may naught befall

To mar the old language of Wales."

CHAPTER TWENTY

When Amanda called the office the next morning to say she would not be in, Robin fairly squealed, "Did you hear the news?"

"What news?"

"About Burke Cameron."

"Burke? Not a word. What about him?"

"Flown the coop. Gone for good. The prodigal son revisited. He told Sheila he's had enough of the business world. He's heading for the sunset with a new love. What kind of woman would fall for that grouch?"

"You can't account for some tastes." Amanda played it straight while Hank made faces at her from the doorway.

Freed from the Cameron Agency, they were on their way to several surprises Hank refused to divulge. Already the fates of the Scorpion, Tony, the Sandpiper, and a half-dozen of his thugs were in the proper hands. Even before Hank turned onto Short Hill Mountain Road, Amanda anticipated another coup in the capture of Ellis. The mechanism for his demise, however, was beyond her wildest imagination.

The historic stone house was cordoned off by police tape. Government vehicles and military personnel blocked the driveway and a portion of the adjacent road. A guard approached their car, nodding in Amanda's direction.

"Sorry, sir," he said. "Property's off limits to guests."

"We're not staying," Hank said. "I just want to show her the power she wields."

"So *she's* the one. Good shot, ma'am.

Amanda nudged Hank. "What's he talking about?"

"The keystone."

Amanda stared at the gaping hole above the doorway. "I'm *positive* I put it back."

"And so you did. Very cleverly, too," Hank said.

"I don't understand."

"Neither did Ellis when it hit him."

Her mouth flew open. "Was he hurt?"

"In the worst possible way. Cracked his skull and ended his various careers in one fell swoop. What I can't figure out is how you hoisted that heavy stone back into place."

"It wasn't easy," Amanda admitted. "Now please explain what brought this about."

"Apparently Ellis got wind that the Sandpiper advised the Scorpion it was in their best interest to skip town while Tony was doing away with the President, maybe let the trail cool down before their next move. That would leave Ellis to carry out the planned bombings of several facilities they'd targeted. They failed to grasp the fact that, from the beginning, his only interest was financial gain. He had no intention of becoming the main man.

"When you walked off with the code and the Scorpion began to suspect that you were up to something, his plans fell apart. At the same time, Ellis was stuck with a shed full of illegal explosives. He could either finish what the others had started, or pay them back for trapping him in a no-win situation.

"Based on the fire power he was packing, we theorize that Ellis was going after the Scorpion. When he slammed the front door, the force jolted the stone out of place. You put it back, Amanda, but not very professionally."

"They told me it was sitting at a precarious angle waiting for the perfect moment," the guard said.

Hank smiled. "Thanks to one persistent woman. By solving the cryptic message, Amanda, you tipped the scales—in this case the keystone—just far enough so that the secrets hidden for two centuries are about to be revealed."

Amanda grabbed his arm. "Is that the other surprise?"

"The lady's very impatient," he told the guard, who dismissed them with a grin and wave of his hand.

Returning the wave, Hank fired the engine and steered around the vehicles in their path.

The fresh morning fields along the country road offered no evidence of recent sinister events. At the next fork, Hank turned onto the lane leading to the Short

Hill Meetinghouse. Moments later, Amanda was viewing a scene far removed from what she remembered of her previous visit. In contrast to the gloom that had enveloped the churchyard during the storm, a brilliant sun beamed down on vehicles lining the circular driveway.

Hank's eyes danced with laughter as he parked the car and produced the iron key wrapped in the Masonic apron. "For your information, my adorable history buff, we've just traveled ten degrees west and fifty perches south."

"So the verse *was* right on the mark. And the hickory tree?"

"It's probably not the original, more likely an offshoot, but it stood guard over the grave of treasures until Bunny Phelps became guardian of the secret."

"Poor Bunny," Amanda said. "I hope she's recuperating from that terrible blow."

"Not only is she on the mend, but she's right inside."

Amanda's eyes widened. "Are you sure? How do you know?"

"Our team contacted her in the hospital yesterday, just before she was discharged. Obviously, we couldn't proceed without her approval. She was happy to give it because she's always wanted the treasure to fall into the proper hands. Since she's financially secure, she suggested that it go to a museum."

"How very kind of Bunny. Did she give any idea about which one she thinks would be most suitable?"

"She had only one choice, and when we contacted them, they were overjoyed."

"You love to keep me in suspense, don't you? Where is the treasure going?"

Hank maintained an enigmatic smile until they walked past a limousine with a familiar name painted on the door. "Behold, my love," he said. "A team from the Smithsonian Institution has already arrived."

Amanda smiled up at him. "You saved the best news for the last. The Smithsonian's American History Museum is the perfect resting place for an Early American treasure."

"Agreed. When they heard the entire story and discovered that you are responsible for bringing it to light, they insisted that you have the honor of opening the casket."

"That's very kind of them, but they're trained curators," Amanda whispered as they entered the meetinghouse. "I prefer yielding to their expertise."

"As you wish." Hank gave her a warm hug.

Inside, a casket propped on a gantry blocked the center aisle. It was surrounded by scholarly looking individuals talking animatedly among themselves.

Bunny sat on an adjacent bench. Except for a bandage taped to her forehead, she looked none the worse for her ordeal.

She turned and smiled as Amanda and Hank approached. "I wouldn't have missed this for anything," she said.

"Nor I," said Amanda, as the two women hugged. "It's a pity your Davis ancestors aren't here to share the joy."

"Oh, but they are," Bunny said. "While I was in the hospital, I felt the strangest urge to visit Wales. The idea never crossed my mind before this, so there's no other way to explain it except to believe that their spirits are hovering nearby."

Solemnly, Amanda nodded. "I know what you mean. Sometimes we have no control over our lives. It's almost as if we're in the grip of unseen forces."

Hank smiled down at her. "Right now, you're in the grip of a man eager to get this event underway, so if Bunny will excuse us, we'll let these folks get down to business."

After brief introductions all around, Hank passed the key to Dr. Richard Morris, an expert on the Masonic movement during the Revolution. He was flanked by eight specialists in Eighteenth Century artifacts.

As Amanda watched him turn the heavy key in the lock and raise the lid, she tensed, rather expecting the dust of a corpse to billow forth, but his triumphant smile banished her fears. One by one, he drew forth substantial wooden boxes and passed them to his colleagues until all were dispensed. The scholars began by loosening nails holding the lids shut. That accomplished, they withdrew parcels wrapped in leather cases and secured with leather thongs. Amanda watched them cast off so many layers of leather and cloth it seemed the spirits were playing a game with them.

Then came the first gleam of silver. A chalice. Next a paten and alms plates.

"These were taken—stolen, to be precise—from local churches by the dissenters," Dr. Morris explained. "Before the Revolution, most of the churches in the colony were offshoots of the Church of England. Because King George had a tight rein on them, the Freemasons didn't trust that organization at the time they were going underground to fight for independence. As the war progressed, the churches sympathetic to the King shut down one by one and the clergy fled the colony, some to Canada. They often left behind valuables such as this, so the dissenters ransacked the churches and took what was worth saving."

The experts continued unwrapping the casings. One by one, they extracted brass snuffboxes, dram glasses, a silver trowel, and badges, all engraved with Masonic emblems. Each revelation prompted appreciative murmurs. Tucked into the bottom of the coffin were assorted pieces of silver and gold jewelry fashioned in Wales. As the final item was exhibited everyone broke into applause.

"This is incredible," Bunny said. "I've always believed the treasure existed, even though most people regarded it as simply another legend. If the Davis family had thought there was no truth to the story, I feel certain they would have stopped passing the clues from one generation to another. When I inherited the code, I was so convinced the story had merit that I hid it in my private safe and never told another soul.

"One problem was that John Davis never considered what would happen to the treasure if nobody solved the code. It could have remained in the ground through eternity. I thought about the clues many times, but I, like everyone else, missed the point that the first few lines of the code referred to the home place, the original Davis house, and the last two to the meetinghouse. Nobody made any sense of the code until Ms. Prescott came along."

"Thanks to her, the Smithsonian has acquired a unique treasure," Dr. Morris said.

Bunny touched his sleeve. "I don't imagine you've had time to think about what the Smithsonian is going to do with all these valuable pieces."

"Not as yet, but once everything is catalogued, we definitely will build a display around it so the public can better understand the people who helped found this nation and the problems they had to overcome. I find it mind-boggling to be looking at ecclesiastical silver, Masonic treasures, and family heirlooms that were last seen more than two hundred years ago. They've bided time throughout the nation's birth, the Westward expansion, major wars, the thrust toward outer space, and the arrival of a new millennium."

Hank's arm slipped around Amanda's waist. "Closing the book on spies, terrorists, and stolen treasures is small potatoes compared with mastering the obstacle course to a romance like ours," he whispered.

Without glancing behind, they headed outdoors into the sunlight.

EPILOGUE

Sometimes we are forced to eat our words and laugh heartily in retrospect. This happened to Amanda the day she and Hank were married in Pohick Church.

Meg had come from Florida to be Maid of Honor, and Joe Draver was Hank's best man. Although she had intended to fly directly home after the wedding, Meg unwittingly became one-half of the plot Joe's wife concocted to boost her brother's social life.

The desk-oriented owner of a Washington public relations firm, he devoted far more hours of the day and night to promoting his clients than himself. But when Joe and his wife choreographed the couple's accidental encounter at the rehearsal dinner, Amanda recognized a light she had never before seen in Meg's eyes.

"I think she's captivated," Amanda whispered to Hank.

He winked. "She's not the only one. I've never known a tongue-tied promoter. From his reaction, I'd say that he's a goner. Reminds me of myself the day you walked into the Cameron office. Your presence was so magnetic that I forgot the script I was supposed to follow. It took a few minutes to bone up on it."

"And all the while I thought you were studying papers connected with your business affairs."

"Romantic affairs, not business. I was dying to take you in my arms. Lucky for us, that problem has been nicely solved." He squeezed her hand under the table.

And so, on a luxuriant summer afternoon marked by a cloudless, azure sky, low humidity—a rarity in Washington—and the explosion of red, white, and pink crape myrtle clusters encircling the historic brick edifice, they were united in a small, beautiful ceremony attended by their close friends.

Hank slipped the wedding ring on Amanda's finger and kissed her long and tenderly at the altar. Shortly after a brief reception in the church hall, they changed into evening attire and joined the Dravers in a waiting limousine. They all were going to the White House for dinner.

The unexpected invitation arrived after the wedding plans were firmed, and since Hank was one of those being honored for his part in cracking a knotty case and protecting the President, they could not refuse, even though it meant postponing the honeymoon for a few hours.

Unlike so many of the stiff, formal White House dinners honoring heads of state, this proved to be a low-key affair that Amanda found enjoyable. Senator Shellenberger and his wife attended because of his leadership of the Senate Select Committee on Intelligence, along with Kathy Owens, various other Congressional staff members, and a contingent of Hank's colleagues and their wives. As Amanda looked around the table, she was struck by the unremarkable and neighborly gathering, hardly the dashing, steel-jawed, cloak-and-dagger operatives depicted in spy movies.

During the meal of representative American cuisine, she indulged in pleasant conversation with those seated nearby about the local schools, favorite hiking trails, and the Broadway musicals booked into the Kennedy Center for the upcoming season. Afterward, the guests were ushered from the State Dining Room into the East Room where the U.S. Air Force Airmen of Note Jazz Band opened the entertainment with a medley of show tunes.

Even before the first number was underway, Amanda recognized one of the trumpet players, a former Peabody classmate who belonged to a small jazz group she often accompanied. As the first set ended, she saw him signal the leader. Moments later, they coaxed her up to the piano to sit in on a spontaneous journey back to the music of the 1930s and '40s, the First Lady's favorites.

By the close of the evening, the President, the First Lady, and the guests who weren't swirling across the dance floor were lounging around the Steinway singing vintage Gershwin. Nobody was more surprised than Amanda when the First Lady—whose musical expertise enabled her to recognize a remarkable vocalist—signaled the others to drop out and let Hank solo on "Love Walked In."

Amanda smiled to herself, remembering Sybil's enigmatic walk-ins and the elusive Pohick Priest she once was tempted to equate with Hank. As she brandished a lush arpeggio across the keyboard, one of the bolder women in the White House press corps elbowed her way to Amanda's side and hissed, "Who's that good looking hunk of a baritone?"

Amanda responded in an unbecoming icy tone. "The hunk's name is Hank." She realized that she should have shut her mouth at that point, but a devil walked right in, blew her usual sensible judgment to kingdom come, and compelled her to add, "He represents Mad Romance."

The next thing she knew, the roar of Hank's laughter cut through the music and that good looking hunk was kissing her right in front of the President, the First Lady, and the Airmen of Note.

Thanks to him, she had stayed in Washington and performed at the White House, after all.

978-0-595-46808-9
0-595-46808-X